A most grisly art . . .

"But, Holmes, if Whitney were already dead, why wouldn't the monster have just left him on the floor while cutting him up?"

"An excellent question, Watson, and I fear that the answer is as disturbing as the crime itself. I believe our killer considers himself something of an artist—not literally, although that, too, is a possibility—but an artist where murder is concerned. The victim is his canvas, and the canvas had to be positioned just so in order for our man to properly bring his talents to bear."

"This is ghastly," I exclaimed.

"Indeed," Holmes replied. "Particularly when we consider that no artist stops after merely one painting. I am afraid, Watson, that we have not seen the last of this business."

The Monster
of
St. Marylebone

—◆◆◆—

Wayne Worcester

A SIGNET BOOK

SIGNET
Published by New American Library, a division of
Penguin Putnam Inc., 375 Hudson Street,
New York, New York 10014, U.S.A.
Penguin Books Ltd, 27 Wrights Lane,
London W8 5TZ, England
Penguin Books Australia Ltd, Ringwood,
Victoria, Australia
Penguin Books Canada Ltd, 10 Alcorn Avenue,
Toronto, Ontario, Canada M4V 3B2
Penguin Books (N.Z.) Ltd, 182–190 Wairau Road,
Auckland 10, New Zealand

Penguin Books Ltd, Registered Offices:
Harmondsworth, Middlesex, England

First published by Signet, an imprint of New American Library,
a division of Penguin Putnam Inc.

First Printing, November 1999
10   9   8   7   6   5   4   3   2   1

For Maureen Croteau,
Minnie Mae and Donald M. Murray,
Albert R. Johnson,
Norman L. Hope, and
Amanda, Amy, and Jonathan Worcester.

ACKNOWLEDGMENTS

I would like to sincerely thank Laura Osterweis, Garret Condon, and my wife, Maureen Croteau, for their reading of this novel's original manuscript and most particularly for their many candid, insightful, and truly useful suggestions; also Bill Reynolds for his unswerving moral support; my agent, Philip G. Spitzer, for the professionalism and persistence that are his hallmark; and especially my editor, Laura Anne Gilman, and her staff at New American Library, whose knowing and exacting handiwork is most gratefully present on every page.

Jan. 24, 1999

A cache of what has been tentatively identified as handwritten journals of the late Dr. John H. Watson, the well-known chronicler and compatriot of detective Sherlock Holmes, turned up yesterday in the dusty rubble of a suite of offices being renovated on the outskirts of Eastbourne in Hastings.

Authorities postulate that the manuscripts may be among those reported missing from Watson's estate in 1941. When Nazi Germany laid siege to London in World War II, many venerable buildings in some of the city's most solid commercial areas were demolished, among them a repository jointly maintained by banks and insurers in the Borough of St. Marylebone in the city's West End, where Watson and Holmes lived.

The manuscripts, still protected by the battered tin box in which they were found, have been turned over to antiquities experts at Oxford University for authentication.

A letter, purportedly from Dr. Watson, was found atop the manuscripts and handed over to police forensics experts for dating.

The letter reads:

To Whom It May Concern:
The cases I have set down here are among the most perilous and sensitive that my good friend and compatriot, Sherlock Holmes of 221B Baker St., London, encountered during his long and illustrious career as the world's first consulting detective.

Untimely disclosure of the facts brought to light by my stories about these cases would have had dire consequences throughout the Empire, which doubtless any modern reader with even a modest familiarity with history will appreciate. What's more, Holmes' reading public—and mine, of course—most assuredly would have been scandalized by the unavoidable luridness of some episodes contained in the stories.

It took some arguing on my part, but my agent, Mr. Conan Doyle, reluctantly agreed to mask Holmes' involvement in these heretofore undisclosed cases by filling the appropriate time period with other stories of which the reading public by now, I am sure, is familiar. Such is the nature of poetic license. Given the gravity of the issues at hand, however, I have no qualms about having undertaken such a minor deceit, and neither did Mr.

Conan Doyle, once he clearly understood the implications.

I rest easy now, knowing that, albeit in secrecy, once more I have done right by Holmes, my Queen and my country.

John H. Watson, M.D.
June 6, 1889

Police were not surprised that such a potentially important and valuable discovery might be made in the Hastings area, a once-renowned South Coast resort that has become a haven for those on society's fringes.

"That sort come out here because they can live cheaper than in the city," said Inspector William Barrows of New Scotland Yard, "and there are so many of them now they don't have s'much as a mite of trouble blending in. It wouldn't be unusual for some to bring along their ill-gotten gains.

"Dr. Watson's journals," Barrows said, "wouldn't be the first good swag we've turned up in these parts."

Barrows didn't exaggerate the nature of Hastings.

The probation service has a large team in the town because of the number of ex-offenders on parole and living on benefit. In fact, 40 percent of East Sussex's long-term unemployed live in the town of 185,000, and 36 percent of all households claim benefits. Drug abuse and gang violence is a problem.

The Eastborne neighborhood supports six registered bed-and-breakfast hotels and a private-care home for the mentally handicapped. Nine care-in-the-community hostels are scattered throughout parts of town.

The disused offices were among several flats being renovated in Dabney Shopping Centre, which is set in a large council estate that features a Tesco superstore.

The tin box toppled out of the rubble when Thomas Langley, crew foreman for J. Anthony Johnstone, Restorationists, and two of his assistants, caved in a deep partition between two offices.

"There was an old safe in that wall, but she was rotted out and wide open, so I thought she was empty or I'd not have brought her down like 'at," Langley said. "I'm thankful the writings were sealed up tight, is all.

"As best I can figure," Langley said, "the tin box must have slipped down inside the walls when the floor of the safe rotted through."

Chapter 1

I stood before the parlor window overlooking Baker Street and stared down into the gaslit night. Snow had been falling steadily since early morning, and it lay all over London like a deep blanket, damping all but the most momentous of sounds and masking the hoary gray and brown of the city. At first the snow had fallen in heavy, wet flakes as big as coins, but by early evening they had turned to tiny specks that fell in dense, all-encompassing waves. They whirled and danced madly, swept about by a hard and cold wind, making progress through the city exceedingly difficult and clarity of vision nearly impossible. I peered into the orange-yellow pockmarks of lamplight, hoping to spot a passerby whose peculiarity of movement or profile would offer the slightest suggestion, the merest intimation, that my good friend was safely home, affecting a disguise, as he had done so often in the past. So adept was he at changing not merely his countenance but his bearing and mannerisms that he might be a hostler or seaman one moment, and a church deacon or even a Chinaman the next. Were a simple charwoman to pass below me this instant, bowed by her years and bent determinedly against the elements, I would suspect her to be but another of my old friend's incarnations, though in such a blinding snow I doubt I could even distinguish a man from a woman.

In truth, any passing figure would have been a most welcome sight, even if only as an unprofitable diversion, for much time had passed since our adventure began, and my old friend's unexplained absence these past two days had left me gravely upset and increasingly disconsolate. In ways that I could not explain, I was certain that some ill turn had befallen Sherlock Holmes.

Admittedly, some of my misgiving was a product of the times, for these were deceptively violent and uncertain days. The upper order in this year of 1889 fairly reveled in its own comfort and prosperity, taking smug, though deserved pride, in the vitality of the British Empire. But if you looked underneath that surface tranquillity, its security was increasingly threatened by a deep and simultaneous undercurrent of violence and despair that worried me greatly.

London's lesser neighborhoods, especially those of the East End, were swollen to bursting with masses of poor people and immigrants. Jobs were sorely wanting, and disease, violence and deprivation were as much an epidemic as unemployment; it seemed impossible to know where one problem began and the other took its leave, or which problem was cause, and which effect. The number of prostitutes throughout the city in those years was said to be in the numerous tens of thousands, and it was no longer surprising that there were entire streets in Cheapside, Whitechapel and Spitalfields where the police would not tread except in goodly numbers.

Among the well-to-do and informed of the great city's West End, the fear of social upheaval, if not outright anarchy, was so commonplace as to be a set of dark threads woven tightly into the fabric of daily life. Distrust of strangers and foreigners, such as the impoverished hordes of Jews, Russians, Poles, Slovaks, Irish and Italians who crowded the East End, was especially endemic in the prosperous West End Borough of St. Marylebone, where Holmes and I were fortunate enough to have our living quarters. I say "fortunate" because all around us was a kind of comfortable security, a refuge from some of the more unpleasant truths we encountered in pursuit of Holmes' cases. However, our constant involvement in one adventure or another also prevented our falling victim to the cloying insularity that so afflicted our fellows.

To them, the steadily flowing stream of murders, robberies, assaults, cholera-death tolls and coroners' inquiries that filled the city's many newspapers seemed to flow from a realm that was at once comfortably far and frighteningly near. And so the studiously unwitting and complacent hovered like so many huge flocks of well-dressed birds, flitting between the rich fantasy of their own lives and the grim reality in which so much of the city was mired. It was unimaginable to them that these two worlds, these two planets soaring in contradictory orbits, might at some point peaceably and quietly merge. What they feared were periodic, glancing collisions. The result of those collisions was always violent, and the repercussions always long-lasting.

It was four years ago, in January of 1885, that bombs planted by the Fenians and the Irish Republican Brotherhood exploded simultaneously in Parliament, the Tower of London and Westminster Hall. Anarchists and socialist reformers called it "The Great Day of the Dynamitards," and though no deaths were linked to the explosions, the panic and fear that spread through the city was enormous.

Then, a year later, in February of 1886, nearly 20,000 marchers with the Social Democratic Federation, the Laborers League and the Free Trade League assembled in Trafalgar Square. The police came running; but rage, drink and inflammatory speeches overcame all reason, and a monstrous riot broke out. Police cordons were ruptured, and angry throngs ran through Piccadilly and its environs, breaking storefront windows and looting private clubs and businesses.

The following year, on November 13, 1887, the Metropolitan Federation of Radical Clubs rallied thousands of wretched, unemployed and dispossessed Irish demonstrators and descended on Trafalgar Square in the name of free speech and fair and just treatment for one of their imprisoned comrades. Sir Charles Warren was the head of our Metropolitan Police, and the embattled commissioner had had enough. His well-organized battalions, backed by squads of hardened soldiers in full-dress uniform, mercilessly bludgeoned the masses of demonstrators until their ranks were ragged and broken, and the protest had fallen into humiliating disarray.

The day is remembered as "Bloody Sunday," an appellation used with respect by the wealthy, but with ever more venom and hatred by the angry poor.

And then in the fall and winter of last year came the Ripper murders. The unrelenting viciousness of the killings terrified the hapless denizens of the tenement slums of Whitechapel and shocked all of London. So savage and complete was the butchery of those five wretched women, and so helplessly inept was the police's handling of the crimes, that the whole of the East End was very nearly incited to revolt.

Though the murders stopped abruptly and inexplicably two months ago, in November, the city's respite from mayhem has been short-lived. There have been more killings, equally heinous, but of a decidedly different nature.

Whereas the poor victims of Jack the Ripper were prostitutes, most of these new prey were respectable men—among them a tobacconist, a clothier, a shirtmaker, a chemist and a solicitor. All were slain in the same horrible manner: blinding knife slashes to both eyes and a stab wound to the heart. Then the fiend's calling card: an upended pyramid, a triangle, carved into the chest and belly, two diagonal lines extending from the top of each shoulder to the navel, linked together horizontally right across the chest with a single deep wound. "The Monster of St. Marylebone," the newspapers dubbed him, because his work appeared restricted to that well-heeled domain.

For reasons known only to Scotland Yard, Holmes' remarkable talents had not been called into action in the Ripper case, at least publicly; but the great detective was consulted immediately when the Marylebone Monster's handiwork became known.

"It's one thing for someone to go about disemboweling a few bedraggled ladies of the evening," as Holmes put it with his usual acerbity, "and entirely another to foully exterminate professional men. That, Watson, truly offends our sense of propriety." But the Marylebone case had turned out to be among the most frustrating—and menacing—of his career. The killings were occurring more rapidly than we could work, and Holmes had begun to assume some sort of perverse responsibility.

"You must not blame yourself," I had told him.

"But I do, Watson. Yes, at this point I do," he had said. "Do you think Scotland Yard on its own will put this to rest? Hah! The populace will be decimated before that happens. It remains for me to do. And by now, I should have found the key. The key, Watson. It pains me that I have not yet done so. Why businessmen? Why does he slash the eyes? Why does he sign his bloody work with an upended triangle, if, indeed, that is what it is?

"And is the murderer, for certain, a 'he'? Might it not even be a woman, though I hesitate to think it? I fear there is something frightfully obvious that I am overlooking, something, which if seen in its proper light, would explain all, or very nearly so. These deaths, Watson . . . these deaths make no sense to me."

I tried to ease his anxiety, but no amount of solicitude or reasoning had any effect. I had begun to worry that if the puzzle were to remain insoluble for much longer, the pressure Holmes would continue to put on himself might cause him to become careless or reckless. Then, two days past, as if to validate my misgivings, he vanished.

On the street below, gaslights flickered in the wind, and the snow blew in fine biting flakes almost parallel to the roadway. The storm seemed to be increasing in its intensity, but a few intrepid souls had ventured out. They walked at a sharp angle to the wind, and I watched as one person, unable to withstand the constant, stinging cold in his face, turned around and walked backward, so as to protect himself.

"Doctor, come away from the window now. I've made a fresh pot of tea and some biscuits."

"Wha . . . Oh, yes," I said, surprised to hear our landlady's voice. "Thank you, Mrs. Hudson. Very good of you. I didn't hear your knock. I'm afraid I'm so preoccupied that . . ."

"I know. I know. Come and sit, Doctor. It'll do no good to worry yourself sick over Mr. Holmes. I worry, too, mind, but I'll not be making myself ill for it, and you won't, either. You never know what that man's about, do you now? Him with his taste for dramatics and all. Why, he could be anywhere, Doctor, and all got up as somebody else, besides. You did right asking Scotland Yard to help find Mr. Holmes. And then when you called on those ragamuffin boys to look for him, well, you know I've never cared much for their likes, but I said to myself, 'Dr. Watson has shared many of Mr. Holmes' adventures, and he knows better than you what to do at such a time.' So I've been satisfying myself that we'll have an explanation soon enough, and if meanwhile we are not reasonable, we'll both feel the fool for having worried so."

"I hope you're right, Mrs. Hudson," I said. I pulled the drapes closed across the window and walked to the hearth, trying in vain to find cheer in the flames that flickered there. I jabbed the poker into the coals, shaking a layer of ash from them and sending a small shower of dust and sparks into the flue. Wind howling across the top of the chimney made a deep hollow echo. Flames danced from the glowing coals. I squatted briefly, warming my hands in the rising firelight, and then, though my mood was black and my demeanor uninviting, joined Mrs. Hudson at our table.

The tea was steaming and hearty, and when its scent mingled with the rich aroma of the hot biscuits, the effect was calming and oddly reassuring, as was Mrs. Hudson herself. She was a short woman, buxom and rather heavyset, much older than Holmes and I— about sixty, I would say—but lively and energetic, qualities that her green eyes made obvious even when she was seated and immobile. Her eyes fairly sparkled with an alertness and independence, a quickness of mind and tendency to mirth that were obvious to even the most casual observer. She was pleasant and forbearing, and in her generally unobtrusive way she looked after us the way a mother cat must look after her kittens, with affection and resignation.

Mrs. Hudson was better suited to the management of a household such as ours than any person I could imagine. She never questioned the odd hours that Holmes and I so often kept, or our comings and goings, for she was well aware that our business commonly strayed from the ordinary. Nor did she ever express real annoyance at the odd parade of clients and characters, from knave to nobility, who frequented our rooms on the floor above her at 221B. On the contrary, it has always seemed to me that despite an occasional mild protest, she was somewhat amused by it all, or at least by the unpredictability and excitement that her lodgers represented. I suspect that after all of these years, more staid tenants would not have been as well received.

The farther Mrs. Hudson's welcome intrusion drew me from my self-absorption, the more I realized that for my sake, and I daresay her own, too, the good woman was merely putting up a steely front against Holmes' sudden absence. I understood the fundamen-

tal wisdom in that, and I could not help but be
touched by her implicit concern for me.

"Perhaps I am worrying too much, Mrs. Hudson.
Most likely you are right; but it is not like Holmes to
absent himself for so prolonged a time without notice,
at least not when he is as deeply involved in a case
as important as these murders. That is why I am so
convinced that something has gone terribly wrong. Did
he say nothing at all to you before he left?"

"Doctor, you have asked me . . ."

"I know, Mrs. Hudson, I know, but please humor
me once again. Did you notice anything different
about him? The way he was dressed? The way he
spoke? Anything at all?"

"No, Doctor. As I have told you: That boy, Dickie
Quinn, brought him the message and left, and then
early the next morning Mr. Holmes put on his usual
attire and a gray woolen scarf, which he wrapped
about his chin and neck, for the wind was as sharp as
a knife, and left the house. It does seem to me now
that he was in very good spirits, almost cheerful. He
smiled at me on his way out the door."

"You know his ways, Mrs. Hudson. Whenever
Holmes is noticeably cheerful, it is because he is on
the scent. There must have been some development
in this Marylebone business. In this damnable weather
nothing else would have sent him out in good humor."

The fire glowed, and the wind howled unabated. We
sat in silence for a moment. I was so engrossed in the
problem that the sudden pounding on our front door
seemed like gunshots. I sprang from my chair, upset-
ting our cups, threw open the door and raced down
the stairs. I could hear Mrs. Hudson stammering her
surprise behind me, and as I reached the door, which
was fairly shaking from the repeated blows upon it, I
could hear voices.

"Doctor! Dr. Watson! Open up! Dr. Watson!"

I threw back the bolt and opened the door. I wasn't
braced for the blast of cold and snow that assaulted

me. Nor was I prepared for the two bent, snow-covered figures who rushed inside as I had cracked open the door. They nearly bowled me over. One was shorter than the other. He swiped snow from his reddened face and unwrapped a scarf from his chin.

"Billy," I said, recognizing the boy instantly. Before he could reply, I turned to the taller figure. I knew from the voice which had called my name that it was Inspector Lestrade of Scotland Yard, the hatchet-faced policeman who had so often benefited from our inquiries. Holmes believed that when it came to investigations, Lestrade usually was out of his depth, but he was tenacious. To Holmes' way of thinking, that alone set Lestrade apart from the great majority of his colleagues. The inspector put down the high collar of his long coat and removed his bowler. "Sorry to barge in on you, Dr. Watson, but we've found . . ."

Billy pushed directly in front of Lestrade and, with no deference to the inspector's authority whatsoever, cut his words short.

"See 'ere, Cap'n. Doc Watson 'ired me and the boys to find Mr. 'Omes, and we did, and we did it whilst you coppers were prolly sittin' on your bleedin' arses keepin' warm. I'm 'ere to report and earn me money. Ya wouldn't be takin' bread outta me mouth now, would ya? Let me say me piece 'ere. 'Sides Cap'n, Dickie's me mate. Least ya can do."

Lestrade's face flushed with anger. He was staring intently at the boy, and I could see the knot of muscles in his jaw move as he clenched and unclenched his teeth while the boy spoke. Billy was the leader, as it were, of the street Arabs that Holmes and I sometimes employed to watch a suspect, help track one down or discreetly deliver messages. They were a ragged lot, but they knew the back streets and byways of London better than a legion of alley cats, and they were decidedly more loyal.

"All right, then," said Lestrade. "Only because of Dickie. You say your piece and be done with it."

I was growing impatient. "Billy," I said. "Please! What has happened? Quickly now!"

"I 'ate to tell ya, Doc. It's Mr. 'Omes. Someone done him, but good. Cor, 'e's 'urt bad. 'E's been beaten near to death." The words hit me like a fist, their effect physical. I jerked my head backward and was aware of a roaring in my ears that made the rest of Billy's words seem as though they had been uttered from far away, or in a whisper, though I could hear them plainly enough.

"And Dickie . . ." The boy's eyes teared up, but he manfully choked back his emotions. "Dickie's been kilt, kilt 'orrible, Doc. I dunno why anyone'd do a bloke like that. It's got to be like the papers say, this Marylebone Monster, 'e's some fiend wi'out a heart or soul, kill a boy like 'at. Thirteen Dickie was; 'at's all, thirteen.

"We found 'em in a stable over in the Marylebone Mews just a few hours ago. Albert and Duffy and me. We'd all been out this mornin', searchin' about and askin' folks did they see anybody looked differenter 'an usual, or actin' differenter, and Albert and Duffy and me, we got tired and liked to a' froze cold, and we had to break from it. But Dickie, he said he wanted to go on; 'e wanted to check the stables and a couple other places. Y'know, Dickie was partial to Mr. 'Omes, more'n even me or any of the other boys. We couldn't talk him out of it. So 'e went ahead, and we warmed up in back of me uncle's tap.

"Was about three hours later, we went back to where we'd left off wi' Dickie, but there's no sign of 'im, and the storm's gettin' worse. Cor, we'd like to a' froze, all of us, when that wind kept comin' up and up and drivin' the snow into ya so's ya can't see a hand in front o' your face or even lift your noggin up to look straight ahead. We was near one of the stables, and we just pushed on the side door till the latch broke, and we fell inside. There was a tin lantern Duffy almost fell on. It was right hot, so's we knew it'd been used recent. I lighted 'er up and 'eld 'er 'igh so's we could see, and that was when we found 'em. Mr. 'Omes tied up to a post and all beat, 'is 'ead 'anging down on 'is chest, blood drippin' from 'im. And Dickie layin' at his feet in blood all dark all over the floor in a pool and so fresh steam was comin' up out of it."

I heard a heavy thud behind me and turned quickly. Mrs. Hudson had fainted. She lay crumpled against the banisters at the foot of the stairwell, and though I have known my share of gore, in hospital and out, for just an instant I feared I might join her. These were not enemies, strangers or patients who had been so foully treated. I knew Dickie Quinn to be a good lad, and Holmes was the finest man it has ever been my privilege to call friend. The understanding that they had been so savagely mauled and left for dead in the bitter cold struck me to the core. But there was no time for weakness or reverie.

"Billy," I said sharply, "fetch some water in a basin and see to Mrs. Hudson, please. Lestrade, where is Holmes?"

"Charing Cross Hospital." Lestrade stood holding his bowler to his chest, turning the brim with his fingers, his head slightly lowered. He seemed ill at ease and somehow apologetic, as though Holmes' plight were of his making. I suspected at first that Lestrade's upset owed mostly to his having to deliver bad news to me, but the more I studied Lestrade, the more I realized that this hardened policeman was most upset by the condition in which he found the detective and the boy. I took a deep breath and implored him to continue.

"Speak plainly, Lestrade. Holmes is not dead?"

"No, Dr. Watson. The physician is doing everything that can be done. It's Dr. Charles Peacham. He's one of the finest medical men in the city. He said Mr. Holmes would live, but there's no telling what condition he will be in or how long it will take him to recuperate . . . if he ever does fully recuperate."

In a sense, this was the worst possible news. At times during my adventures with Holmes, circumstances had forced me to entertain the notion of his death and the immense loss that it would represent, but never had I dared contemplate the notion of his being alive but irreparably incapacitated. I knew with a sudden certainty that he could not bear it. Inaction produced boredom and a self-destructive lassitude in Holmes. He would be a powerful engine running without lubricant, destined to burn up. I had an urge to closet myself and weep like a softhearted fool, but the instant I said as much to myself, in precisely those words, I knew that I would never, indeed, could never, do so. My next inclination was to throw on my coat and rush to the hospital; but I did not do that, either. Lestrade had assured me Holmes was getting the best of care. In the detective's absence, I had a job to do. I found myself coldly and silently asking what actions Holmes would undertake first were he in my place.

I turned abruptly from Lestrade, walked over to the gasogene on the sideboard, and tapped some carbonated water with which to mix a drink. "Lestrade, I am going to make myself a bracer of whiskey. May I suggest that you join me? Then we are going to sit down and you, sir, if I may be so bold as to suggest it in Holmes' absence, are going to describe quickly but in detail how you found our mutual friend, and the boy, Dickie Quinn. Leave nothing out, mind you. Nothing."

I was not accustomed to giving orders to a policeman, and Lestrade was not accustomed to taking them, at least not from someone whose station in life had always seemed to be that of a biographer-companion or manservant; that much was clear from the startled look on his face.

I made my whiskey and soda and decided to press my advantage. "Well, Lestrade?" I raised my voice and glared at him, trying to goad him out of the stupor into which the situation had so obviously plunged him.

"My good man!" I said, irritated at his silence. "I am not asking you to compromise your case or your principles. Anything you can tell me now may help Holmes, and if fate should deal him badly and he proves to be beyond our service, then by all that's sacred, let it help us catch whoever has dared to do this!"

Lestrade blinked rapidly, then his eyes widened quickly, and a thin quick smile crossed his narrow face. For the briefest moment, he still said nothing. Then he threw his hat on the chair, draped his overcoat on the back of it and joined me at the sideboard. "Forgive me, Doctor. You are quite right, and I, uhm, I thank you for being bold enough to suggest it. Mr. Holmes has been such a help to the Yard these past years, and to my own career, at least, uhm, occasionally, that I think I have come to take his presence for granted. I don't mind telling you, Doctor, that when I found him and the boy, the heart went right out of me."

"I know, Lestrade. I know. Let's get on with it, now. Tell me how you found them."

I walked to the black marble fireplace and sat in one of the two armchairs that flanked the hearth. Lestrade followed me and sat in the other one.

"When you alerted me to Holmes' disappearance," Lestrade said, "I went to the commissioner and asked him if we could engage six of our men in a search. I asked for six knowing full well he never would consent to so many. In fact, he was somewhat put out. You know, it is a sore point with the commissioner that Mr. Holmes' methods have seemed to surpass our own sometimes. He prefers to think of Holmes as a meddler who has often been merely fortunate with his inquiries. If he were forced to acknowledge how many times Mr. Holmes actually has helped the Yard bring its cases to fruition, some heads would probably have to roll—my own included.

"That said, I *think* the commissioner knows Holmes'

true value, because without much fuss he consented
to releasing three men into my charge. Three was just
the number I wanted; any more than three, you can't
keep secret what you're about, and we didn't want any
headlines announcing that Mr. Holmes was missing. I
took Donaldson, Haverford and Watkins. Good men,
all. We set about it straightaway, and for the better
part of the week, we didn't get much sleep, any of us.
There's plenty out there who owe us a turn or two,
and we visited most of them. Mind, we were sharp
about it. I rapped a couple skulls to get their attention,
and twice I had to restrain Watkins. I don't approve
of such methods, but among your lower orders, sometimes a good knock is all they respect.

"Try as we might, we were comin' up empty until
yesterday. Donaldson questions a swag seller he
knows by the name of Coughlin, and he tells him
about a tosher who just that morning had tried to sell
him a ring he claims he'd raked out of the offal in
one of them sewers. Donaldson presses him, hard like,
but Coughlin doesn't know the bloke's right name.
Knows him only as Monkey Jack. Coughlin says Jack's
so bowlegged he bobs from side to side, like a monkey, when he walks. Not all that many of those mud
larks left now, but Monkey Jack's been around a long
time. Coughlin wanted the ring, all right, a man's fancy
gold signet ring with an ornate letter V, but Monkey
Jack wanted too much for it."

Such a ring had adorned Holmes' left hand for several years. The "V" stood for Victoria, her majesty's
token of appreciation to Holmes for one of his early,
and otherwise unheralded, services to the Crown. He
treasured the ring and would have parted with it no
sooner than he would have parted with his beloved
Stradivarius.

"I heard that description, Doctor, and I said to myself, 'That's Mr. Holmes' ring, sure as I'm standing.' I
had noticed it many a time, and I had hoped maybe
he'd left it to mark his trail.

"Some of the other toshers knew Monkey Jack had the ring. He showed it off as part of his haul. His band, the way all the toshers do, they all get together when they've called it quits for the day and divvy up the goodies that they've sifted and raked and panned out of the sewers. Jack and one of the others gets in a fight over who's to keep the ring, but Jack wins, so when we find him, he still has it on him.

" 'I ain't done nothin' illegal,' he says. 'That ring, it musta belonged to some right toff, but there's no tellin' who. I found it proper, I did. Ol' Monkey Jack ain't done nothin' illegal.'

" 'Maybe not where this here ring is concerned, Mr. Jack,' I says, 'but that's still to be seen, now, isn't it? If you didn't come by this the way you say, it'll go hard on you. If you're clean for it, and we find its rightful owner, you'll be compensated by the Crown, but right now, we're taking it as evidence in this here case we're workin' on. The important thing is for you to tell us just exactly where you found her.'

" 'I'll be tellin' you nothin', guv!' he says. 'I may spend my days pokin' around in other people's slime, but that don't give you call to take what's rightfully mine.'

"Well, Doctor, I didn't have time to spend wheedling what I needed to know out of him, and I was sure others had thumped him plenty of times before to no use, so I did something I've never done in all my years with the Yard. I gave him a guinea of my own, and then I ordered my boys to cough up some, too. Told 'em if the department didn't pay them back, why I'd do it myself. That's how strongly I felt—feel now, Doctor—about doing right by Mr. Holmes."

"Good of you, Lestrade, to be sure." I tented the tips of my fingers together and held them pensively to my lips. I realized in an instant I was unconsciously adopting Holmes' own mannerisms. I laughed to myself and said, "Pray, continue, sir."

"Well, that was more money than Mr. Jack would

be making in six months down in the sewers. That changed his tune. And then he says, 'That kid didn't offer me nothin' for the ring.' "

"What kid?" I asked.

" 'Kid. Some bloody kid, 's all. Said 'is name was Dickie. Dickie Quinn. Said he din't want the ring, just wanted t' know where it'd been found. Aye, and I'm Queen Vic's nephew, I am,' says Jack.

"See, he doesn't trust the boy, so he says he found the ring over behind the mews, and Dickie scampers off. But Jack tells us, 'Good riddance. Hah, that's a full two blocks from where I got 'er.'

"Well, Doctor, Monkey Jack took us right to the outfall where he'd raked out the ring. There were only two major sewers that drained into it; one at the south end of the street, the other a half block away. We split up; Donaldson and I took the buildings near the first of them two drains and started poking around. But the more I thought about it, the more I was interested in this Dickie Quinn. I thought that by the sounds, he might've been one of the bunch you and Mr. Holmes use sometimes. I know from having read a couple of your stories in *The Strand*, Doctor, that those boys have come up roses for you sometimes. So I played a hunch; Donaldson and I went up to the mews.

"It's all of one general area, anyway. The lay of the land is such that it's all downgrade from the mews, and if any other drains emptied into those two lines that Monkey Jack had been working, well, who's to say Mr. Holmes hadn't dropped the ring into one of the mews drains and over a couple of days, it just carried down to where Jack was working? I figured it was worth a try.

"We're in the mews, trying doors when we hears this long scream. Lor', it goes right through me. I'm shivering anyway, but if I'd been hot, that scream would've turned me stone-cold from skin to bone and then some. Donaldson hears it, too. We start running in that direction, and soon as we turn the corner we see a door wide open, half knocked off its hinges on the side of one of the stables.

"It's like that boy Billy said, Doctor. Him and his mates get there first, just a tick ahead of me and Donaldson, but first nonetheless. They're shock frozen, those three boys: and it's not hard to understand why. Makes me queasy just thinking about it, and Donaldson, he's seen more than his share of killings in fifteen-odd years with the Yard, but he goes off to the side and retches his insides out.

"There's Mr. Holmes lashed to this post with his hands high up over his head, and he's stripped naked. He's got a long gash on his chest starting from the top of his left shoulder going diagonally down his body to just above his navel. The wound is raw, and it looks like the skin over it has been pulled off in a strip. He's still bleeding, and he's already lost a lot of blood from the looks, because his face is near white as snow, at least where you can see any of it through the blood and the bruises. He's been beaten hard and long. All swollen up, he is. Both his eyes are closed up near shut from it. His jaw's slack and off to one side, broken like, and his lips are all swollen and cut from blows. I check for a pulse, and I can't believe it's there. It's pretty faint, but he's alive, all right. I holler at the boys and Donaldson, and order them to cut him down and get some clothes and his heavy coat on him 'fore he dies then and there. All his clothes are off to the side, all folded neat as a pin, mind, and stacked up careful like, which strikes me as odd, but just then I'm more concerned with getting Mr. Holmes out of this charnel house. Then I takes a good look at the boy.

"Bad as Mr. Holmes has been hurt, Doctor, it's gone much worse for poor Dickie Quinn. He's lying on his stomach in a big pool of blood. He's been done like the other victims we've found. It was all a grim sight, Doctor, but that wasn't the . . ."

I interrupted Lestrade. "Billy said the blood was steaming. Am I to understand that the attack took place just before the boys broke into the stable?"

"Aye, but I was getting to that, Doctor," Lestrade said. "It's freezing cold in that slaughterhouse, and there's steam rising all right, but it isn't coming from Holmes' wounds or from the cuts into Dickie Quinn."

"Where then, Lestrade?"

"It's coming from the boy's neck, sir. His head's been chopped off, completely severed from his body, and it's sitting a few feet away right in front of Mr. Holmes. The poor boy's mouth is open, stuffed with a rag so as to keep it open that way, and it looks like poor Dickie Quinn is screaming at Mr. Holmes."

I excused myself from Lestrade's presence, and in the privacy of my bedroom quietly wept.

Chapter 2

Holmes had been taken to Charing Cross Hospital for expediency's sake. It was not the most distinguished medical institution in the city; that honor was reserved for Bart's, or the Hospital of St. Bartholomew the Great, as it was properly known. Bart's also was where I had met Holmes in 1881 when he was a research student, and all things considered I would rather he had been taken there. However, given his need for immediate attention, I could make no complaint; quite to the contrary, really. I had often read Dr. Peacham's name in the pages of the *British Medical Journal*, usually in association with physiological research. It was clear that Holmes would be well served there, and by early morning of the next day, when Lestrade and I arrived, it was apparent that I had been correct.

The inspector had ordered that Holmes be set apart from the hospital population in a room of his own, so that his identity and whereabouts might remain secret. Lestrade's circumspection surprised me, but pleasantly. He was well aware that it would not do for the city's criminal element to know that Holmes was laid up and vulnerable. As an additional precaution, Lestrade posted a plainclothes police officer outside Holmes' door around the clock. But at no point did Lestrade utter Holmes' name. In fact, the true identity of the patient was known only to Dr. Peacham, as the physician in charge, and Lestrade had warned him that absolute silence in this regard was of the utmost importance.

The doctor was a stern-looking, bespectacled fellow of medium height with prematurely white hair. I judged him to be in his mid-forties, about the same age as me and Holmes. His face was ruddy and round, but made to seem angular by virtue of a rather full beard that he kept meticulously trimmed to a point. Dr. Peacham had cold blue eyes that seemed practiced at masking all traces of sentiment, but it was obvious from his demeanor that he resented Lestrade's instructions, and our intrusion into his personal domain.

He led us to Holmes' room, a small but scrupulously clean chamber in the north corner of the fourth floor. My old friend lay unmoving and unconscious in the bed. Much of his head was wrapped in bandages, and most of his face was reddish-purple with bruises. His lips were indeed swollen and stitched where they had been laid open. From the tight bandaging beneath Holmes' chin, I realized that his jaw had been broken, as Lestrade had suggested. Much of Holmes' upper torso was bandaged tightly as well, a fact that spoke plainly of broken ribs. It sickened me to see him in such condition.

"I have given him morphine for the pain," Dr. Peacham said without preamble. "He is badly bruised, but I believe all of his internal organs are intact and functioning. He is fortunate, at least in that regard. There is a single long cut that extends down his chest to his navel; actually two parallel cuts only several centimeters apart. The top layer of skin has been flayed off for the full length of the cut. The wound is garish, but relatively superficial, though painful even now, to be sure. I gather that in most respects the wound is similar to those found on the victims from St. Marylebone we have been reading about in the papers, but this one was not deep enough to be mortal. I suspect that was intentional. I do not believe Mr.

Holmes' assailant wanted to kill him, at least not the way he has killed the others. The attacker was more interested in causing him great pain. I believe he rubbed salt into the chest wound, gentlemen, literally, so as to inflict agony. The pain was probably excruciating. Under the circumstances, such a direct insult would have been enough of a shock to induce unconsciousness. Three of Mr. Holmes' ribs are broken; his jaw as well. It is fortunate that your friend has been in good health and enjoys a generally robust physique. Without exaggeration, sir, a lesser man would be a guest of the coroner right now.

"I am rather more bothered by the blows to his head, though I detect no fracture of the skull. He has suffered heavy blows, a series of concussions, I believe, and it is not possible to know what the effect of them has been, particularly regarding what seems to have been a blow to his right temple.

"I am certain that his internal magnetic field, which, as you know, always has great bearing on one's behavior, has been thoroughly upset, and perhaps severely damaged. I have no way of knowing whether it will repair itself or whether some form of external intervention will be necessary.

"He has not regained consciousness yet. Perhaps in a day, he will; perhaps in a month; or perhaps, gentlemen, much, much longer."

"It will have to be soon," said a gruff and commanding voice. I turned to see Holmes' brother, Mycroft. My gaze had been so riveted on Holmes throughout the interview with Dr. Peacham, that I had not seen Mycroft seated in the far corner of the hospital room. Given Mycroft's size, that would have seemed an impossibility.

He was a tall corpulent man, seven years Holmes' senior, and according to the detective, his unequivocal better in nearly all matters of deduction. The primary difference between them lay in Holmes' incessant need for stimuli and action and Mycroft's penchant for repose; he disdained virtually all forms of physical activity. Rarely did Mycroft venture beyond his offices at Whitehall, his rooms on Pall Mall or the studiously sedate recesses of the Diogenes Club. It simply was not necessary, he said. The truth was that quite on his own Mycroft possessed all of the faculties and resources that he needed to function as a special high-level consultant to the government. Indeed, as Holmes has noted, in many respects, Mycroft *was* the government.

"Dr. Peacham," Mycroft said, "my brother does not have a lot of time to waste in your hospital. It is imperative that you . . ."

"Excuse me, sir," Peacham said, bristling visibly at Mycroft and stepping in his direction. "With all due respect, in Whitehall your word and counsel may be sought after and heeded by all in your domain, but in this hospital, Mr. Mycroft Holmes, you will not tell me what I must do and what I must not do where the care of a patient is concerned.

"Your brother's life is in my hands, sir, quite literally in this case, and that is a responsibility which I will not negotiate with you or anyone else. His recovery will proceed at a pace that is commensurate with his own recuperative powers and his emotional wherewithal. There is no way to hasten the process, and if there were, I would not do so because such an act could well jeopardize his long-term health.

"If you are not willing to abide by my rules, Mr. Holmes, I suggest that you remove your brother from my charge without delay. But be forewarned, when it comes to handling injuries such as these and their cumulative physical and emotional effects on a patient, I have few peers in this city or, for that matter, any other. You would do well, sir, to choose my replacement carefully; that is, if you have any real concern for your brother's well-being. Is that understood?"

"Quite," said Mycroft Holmes. He turned awkwardly in his chair and, bracing himself on an arm of

it, pushed himself slowly upright. When he turned and
lumbered toward Dr. Peacham, he had a slight smile
on his broad face. Mycroft towered over the man and
was silent for a moment; then he extended a hand
in friendship.

"I would no more remove Sherlock from your care,
Dr. Peacham, than I would try to run a footrace in
Pall Mall. You are precisely the man I want. You have
determination, sir, and a measure of integrity, and I'd
have to say, courage, too, and I admire those qualities
in a man. Outside of my brother and," Mycroft said,
turning his head toward me, "the company he keeps,
they are too infrequently found these days."

Dr. Peacham nodded and smiled, though tightly. He
shook Mycroft's extended hand.

"I will not interfere with your ministrations in any
way, Doctor," Mycroft continued, "but I must be kept
apprised of my brother's progress. I have considerable
and varied resources at my disposal, and if they can be
of any help, you need only to ask. Here is my card."

Mycroft turned from Dr. Peacham and nodded to
me and the inspector.

"Watson, call on me when you can. Lestrade. Good
day, then."

Lestrade tilted his head toward Mycroft. I smiled
after the big man as he strode through the door,
touched by his kind description of me, and decidedly
moved by his clear and abiding concern for his brother's welfare. I had never witnessed any antagonism or
ill will between them, but neither had I ever seen
much warmth or affection. Their mental capacities
were so finely honed and their respective experiences
so far removed from that of the average person, that
they seemed to exist on a different plane altogether.

While I much admired their abilities, I must confess
that now and again I tired of them, too. I am, even
now, loath to admit having had such feelings, but hon-
esty compels me to acknowledge them. Not all of life,
despite the brothers' seeming insistence to the con-

trary, can be understood and appreciated with hard work and the cold reasoning of pure intellect and deductive faculty, and for that reason, I sometimes felt a bit of sadness for the two men. Something was missing in them both, though the deficiency seemed most profound in Mycroft. He had chosen to remove himself from most human contact beyond that which pertained exclusively to the functioning of his high office, and he had done so for so long that I suspected it would be foolish to think that anything, or anyone, might ever change him.

Such was not the case with Holmes, though he most definitely shared Mycroft's single-mindedness and devotion to occupation. Holmes' sphere of experience, by virtue of the great variety of his cases, was broader and more encompassing. He savored, it seemed to me, virtually all forms of life and human endeavor. His infinite curiosities; his love of music, especially the violin; his appreciation of drama and painting and of good food and wine; his lifelong interest in beekeeping and the vicissitudes of man and nature; his compassionate indignation in behalf of the victims of crime; his relentless pursuit of wrongdoers, and his passion for justice, even justice privately meted out—all of these attributes bespoke the potential completeness of the man. And yet, in more personal ways, Holmes' preferred position was very much that of the observer, that of the sentinel at life's banquet; only too rarely was he the willing participant.

Holmes approached everything and everyone with complete professional reserve, as though whatever true emotion might dwell deep inside the man was destined to remain forever locked away, released only in small, restrained measures that were appropriate to the demand of the moment. And all to what end, I wondered. To what end? Holmes' aloofness uniquely befit a gentleman of our times, to be sure, but there is much more to life than obeisance to its many proprieties.

All of these thoughts filled my mind as I stood by Holmes' bedside, looking at his pitiable state. In truth, I felt sorry for him, for the plight into which he had been so mercilessly plunged, and for the poignancy of what I had come to understand was the undeniable loneliness that lay at the very core of his existence.

I put my hand on his cool forearm and spoke aloud, knowing full well that he could not hear me, and caring not at all that Lestrade and Peacham could. "Well, my old and dear friend. I am here, as always. We will heal you as best we can, and then by all that is holy and much that is not, I swear to you that we will run this monster to ground. Together."

I cleared my throat and turned to the two other men in the hospital room. "Come, Lestrade," I said. "We have much work to do."

Chapter 3

In the weeks that Holmes lay immobile in his hospital bed, I had much with which to occupy myself; too much in some respects, and not enough in others, for with Holmes in the hospital, our empty rooms in Baker Street left me feeling forlorn. It struck me one morning that our common area had been given over entirely to Holmes' use. So thoroughly had I managed to subjugate my interests to his that the rooms in no way reflected my presence. It was almost as though Holmes lived there by himself.

The bookcase was packed tight with various maps, scrapbooks and monographs, commonplace books and journals, and a reference shelf which was bested only by those in a public library. A complete encyclopedia and a gazetteer could be found here; so, too, could texts on chemistry, anatomy, law, toxicology and soil analysis. There were, as well, books on swordsmanship and boxing and numerous volumes on the criminal element. The works of Flaubert and Tacitus and Horace were well represented, as were those of George Sand, Goethe, Carlyle and the American Henry David Thoreau. But all of those tomes belonged to the detective. My medical journals and military histories were in a bookcase beside my bed, for no other reason, I suppose, than that happened to be where I put them.

My small writing desk sat on the other side of my bed. Holmes' desk, which I noticed was locked, had a prominent spot in the main room. Beside it was a

stack of the city's newspapers. I noticed that he had
been reading editions of *The Irish Times*, too, which
struck me as odd. An article had been cut from the
front page of one edition, and I could not help but
wonder what goings-on in Ireland had piqued his
interest.

His unanswered correspondence, as always, was
pinned to the fireplace mantel by the blade of a common penknife. A Persian slipper, stuffed with his pipe
tobacco, hung nearby. He stored cigars in the coal
scuttle, handy to his fireplace easy chair, and his
amber-colored Stradivarius rested upright beside its
bow in a corner.

As if all of that were not enough, one entire corner
of the sitting room was given over to Holmes' chemistry experiments. The focus was a simple deal-topped
table, its surface heavily stained by acids and chemi-
cals. When the detective wasn't working at the table,
it was always littered with reagent bottles and beakers
and retorts and his much-used Bunsen burner.

The wall opposite the fireplace always drew the attention of visitors. A series of bullet holes perfectly
placed in the wall formed the outline of two script
letters, a "V" and an "R," for "Victoria Regina."
Atop the letters sat the Queen's crown, which had
been etched into the wall in the same manner. The
tableau was testament to Holmes' marksmanship, not
to mention his knack for putting Mrs. Hudson in a
bad mood.

Well, I suppose it was only logical, really, that our
living area mirrored Holmes' eccentricities and not my
own. It was his cases that defined our professional
lives, after all. And as far as our respective roles were
concerned, it was I, not Holmes, who insisted on en-
tertaining the world with stories about his investigative
successes and our exploits together. The role of reporter, biographer and publicist suited me quite well,
and although Holmes often decried my lack of scien-
tific detachment and objectivity, he clearly benefited

from the public interest and attention that my stories generated.

In that sense, I decided, I was every bit as important to Holmes' work as he was. Thus buoyed, I put my brief self-absorption aside and busied myself trying to rechart what knowledge we had gleaned of the slayings in St. Marylebone.

With Lestrade, I plotted the murder sites on a street map of London, and we tacked it over the bookshelves in the study. I cleared off the deal-topped table and used it to organize the police reports and coroner's findings for each murder. We reexamined all statements that the interviewing police officers had taken. We carefully reconstructed the scene in the stable, re-interviewed the three boys from the Baker Street Irregulars and even questioned Monkey Jack again.

Still, we seemed to be making no appreciable progress, though I did feel as though I knew the particulars of the entire bloody affair more completely than I had known any other.

In our reexamination of the murders that preceded the attack on Holmes, we discovered that the interval between each slaying was different from the one that preceded it. The length of time had noticeably shortened: about two weeks between the first and second murders, less than one week between the second and third, one day between the third and fourth, less than a day between the fourth murder and the fifth, which was simultaneous with the savage assault on Holmes and Dickie Quinn, whose murder was the sixth.

The attack in the stable seemed to be not only a frenzy of butchery, but a frantic culmination of the monster's work. Could that have been the end of it, as well? Would it all stop now, as abruptly as had the Ripper killings?

In fact, there had been no further evidence of the Marylebone Monster's handiwork. I thought it was at least possible that he was done for good, and Lestrade agreed. But how could we know for certain?

And if the murders did stop, might whatever started them not rekindle and burn with as horrible a flame at some unpredictable time in the future? Regrettably, both Lestrade and I lacked Holmes' inventiveness and insight. Neither did we possess the dispassionate creativity with which Holmes always has been able to examine facts for their causal relationships, one to the other, or to fit them into scenarios that seemed, to me at least, so far beyond predictability as to sometimes beggar belief.

The work on the Marylebone case, however frustrating, did, at least for a time, serve to divert me from my preoccupation with Holmes' condition. I was thus absorbed in Holmes' hospital room when my thoughts were interrupted.

"Excuse me, sir. Sir?"

"Oh," I said. "Hello."

"I must change the patient's bandages now."

I barely had time to rise to my feet, for the nurse had moved into the room with such effortless grace and quickness that she seemed to glide; the effect was almost as disarming as her features. She was beautiful, and I am embarrassed to report that my reaction was noticeable.

The woman was standing directly before me, not three feet distant. Her nurse's smock of starched white muslin could not disguise her pleasing figure; nor did it detract from her striking features. She was about five feet four inches tall, but with posture and bearing so elegantly and comfortably correct that it gave the impression of greater height. Her hair was auburn. It was rich with highlights and flecks of red, and the color made her delicate skin seem even pinker than it already was. Her lips were full, and her cheekbones high, but it was the woman's eyes that were so remarkable; they linger in my memory, even now, as a rich and clear green, almost the color of an emerald. I could not stop staring.

"Are you all right, sir?"

"Uh, yes," I said. "Of course. I am Dr. John H. Watson, the patient's friend and companion." I extended my hand, and she took it. Her hand was soft and warm, but her grip was firm and honest.

"It is a pleasure to meet you, sir," she said. "Abigail Masterson. Dr. Peacham has assigned me to Mr. Holmes."

"You are aware of his identity, then?"

"I am, but had I not been, the mention of your own good name would have been all the disclosure necessary."

I was flattered, but also a bit mortified by my obvious blunder.

"He . . . he seems to be improving physically," I said, "and from that I infer a good deal about the quality of his care."

"I am doing everything I can," she said, "but much of the credit should go to Mr. Holmes himself. He is a tough fellow and, I gather, a determined one."

"I only hope he is tough enough," I said, half to myself.

She touched her fingertips to my arm and rested them there for an instant as she spoke. "Give it some time, Doctor. And if you don't mind my saying so, sir, I think you need some rest. I will help you keep vigil. You have my word. Don't worry."

I didn't know what to say. Until that moment I had not realized just how overwrought I was. My visits always left me with the ghastly sensation that I was attending Holmes' wake; all that was needed was a coffin and flowers. Sometimes I imagined him to be one of Madame Tussaud's famed wax figures, in repose but so uncannily lifelike that you would swear that blood coursed through his veins. And then, shaking the dreamlike torpor from my mind, I realized that Holmes' blood truly did course, that he actually was alive and breathing, and he might yet rise and impatiently insist that we get on with the chase. I had seen patients in comatose conditions before; indeed, I had attended to them on numerous occasions, but my frustration was enormous, and my sadness profound. It had only taken the briefest display of tenderness from Mrs. Masterson to bring all of my emotion to the fore.

I knew that what she said was nothing more than the truth. I was becoming exhausted and without respite I soon would be of little use to myself, let alone to Holmes.

"I should leave now," I said to Mrs. Masterson, then mumbled a simple "Thank you."

She nodded twice, and I left the room.

Straightaway, I returned to Baker Street and told Mrs. Hudson that I did not want to be disturbed before noon of the next day. I poured myself a rather large tumbler of whiskey and drank it slowly while I soaked in a tub of water as hot as I could tolerate. By the time I dried myself off and donned my bedclothes, I felt as though my bones had turned to India rubber.

I climbed into bed and slept through the night and well into the following morning. I awoke with a ravenous appetite, and after a big lunch at Simpson's I returned to my lodgings to consider what course I might take, that would serve both Holmes and myself. I knew that I needed to remain on the case, and I wanted to be constructively involved. Writing was the answer, and not for the first time. I was practiced enough at my craft to know that honest and disciplined writing could be a way to discover threads of the rational order that hides amid life's chaos. It was a way for me to find the truth, and to give it a clarion voice.

I determined that so as to not intrude unnecessarily on my narrative or, worse yet, to lapse into supposition and conjecture, I would reconstruct several key interludes as though I actually had been present, as I have been wont to do while writing up those cases which we had solved. However, I vowed to do so only by relying on my notes of extensive interviews with

those who actually had been party to the scene, or by
scrupulously incorporating entries from key people's
diaries and journals, presuming that they agreed I
might judiciously use them. Thus able to vouch for
the continued accuracy of my report, I was content to
begin, as the saying goes, at the very beginning, with
the slaying of Nigel Whitney.

He was the sole proprietor of Whitney Limited, Tobacconist, at 12 Victoria Crossing. Holmes and I both
had patronized the shop on occasion, Holmes for
quantities of the noisome shag that he smoked incessantly when puzzling through a particularly onerous
case, and I for the Arcadia mixture that I enjoyed
after a meal or sometimes with a brandy.

Whitney was a pleasant enough fellow, nearing the
distant edge of middle age, fifty-three at the time of
his murder. He was a bachelor without living kin of
any sort and no associates close enough to be identified as friends. He lived alone in two small, undistin-
guished rooms above his shop. Yet, for all his monastic
existence, he seemed happy enough. He was an energetic little man, as thin as a pipe stem with bright blue
eyes, bushy salt-and-pepper eyebrows and a full shock
of white hair that he trimmed quite severely, but only
at the sides. The effect was to make his ears seem to
protrude at a sharp angle, and his hair appear to sit
atop his head rather like a vase full of drooping flowers, adding several inches to his height, which otherwise might have been considerably less substantial.
Whitney walked with a pronounced limp, from what
cause I did not know. He moved about his small but
prosperous shop in fits and starts as though he were
a cheerfully sputtering engine, tranquil one moment,
all abustle the next. And he had the annoying habit
of talking not so much to a customer as at him, asking
a question and answering it all in one breath.

"Right cold out there, i'n't it? Not as bad as yesterday, though. I suppose you'll be glad to get home and

get snug by the fire. Myself as well. Have me a nice smoke and read the papers, I will. That'll be five shillings four pence, sir." And he would launch into another brief monologue with his next customer even as he settled up with the first. Thus did he manage to be convivial without actually engaging his patrons in any conversation that might be taken as unnecessarily opinionated.

It was a police constable, Martin Dibble, who found old Whitney in the early morning hours. Martin had noticed that Whitney's customary "Closed" marker was not in the window, and though the store was darkened, the front door had been left slightly ajar. Dibble held his lantern over his head as he moved warily through the store. The sight that greeted him in the lamplight was gruesome.

The poor man lay sprawled lengthwise down his service counter, his hands bound together and outstretched above his head. His eyes had been slashed. His shirt had been removed, folded, and set in a neat square at the opposite end of the counter. A triangle-shaped wound was cut into the man's torso. It began as a line atop each shoulder, extended diagonally down his chest and ended in a precise point at his navel. The lines were joined by a third incision that was made several inches below the shoulders and directly across the chest, so as to touch the diagonal lines. But the mortal insult was a separate cut, a very deep knife wound directly into the heart.

Lestrade had been called at once. He summoned Holmes, and I accompanied the detective.

"Where is the officer who found him, Lestrade?" Holmes asked.

"Inside. I asked him to stay beyond his round. I know your methods, Mr. Holmes."

Holmes nodded politely, and we entered the shop.

"You are Dibble?"

"Martin Dibble. Yes, sir, Mr. Holmes."

"Has anyone entered here before us?"

"No, sir. Only the inspector and yourselves."

"And what have you moved since finding the body, Officer Dibble?"

"Nothin', sir. Not a hair or a dust mote, if y' please, sir. Beggin' your pardon, but I knows better than to go muckin' about in such as this."

"Splendid," Holmes said. "Splendid. You are unlike so many of your fellows. You will do well to maintain this approach, Officer. Tell me, Dibble: Given the nature of Whitney's wounds, don't you think there should be more blood on this counter? I should think he would be fairly awash in it, don't you?"

"Aye, sir. That he would."

"Yes. What time did you say you found him?"

"It was 'alf one, sir."

"One-thirty. It is now well after ten a.m.," said Holmes, holding his pocket watch in hand. "The body has lain here for very nearly nine hours, then?"

"Yes, sir."

Dibble was dismissed by Inspector Lestrade, and Holmes and I undertook our examination of the victim's body.

I was appalled by the condition of the corpse, but in truth, I had, in fact, seen much worse. It was perhaps the coziness of the location that so upset me. It did not support a corpse in its midst.

"What impresses you about this, Watson?" asked Holmes.

"As you have already noted, Holmes, the lack of blood, most certainly."

"And what else?"

I felt, as I sometimes did in these investigations, that I was a student in the presence of a teacher, and it annoyed me.

"Well, Holmes, I must say the ritualistic nature of the killing impresses me, though I dislike putting it in those terms. There is a cold-mindedness at work here that seems attuned to torture. Think of it: To be first bound and then blinded, and then to have your chest bared and carved upon in such a manner. Positively barbaric! The fiendishness of the deed is most unsettling."

"Perhaps, Watson. Grisly and brutal, to be sure, but especially cruel only if it were done in precisely the manner you describe . . . and I don't believe that was the case."

"You don't?"

"No, Watson. Observe. There is little to suggest that the victim put up a struggle. There is no bruising, except around the stab wound to the heart, which, I might add, is almost triangular. This is odd, though not as odd as the bruising that surrounds the wound, but I will come to that in a moment. The limbs are not cut or slashed in any way. Is it not reasonable to presume his assailant would have met with at least some resistance?"

"Yes, I suppose it is," I said, "but . . ."

"Similarly, the fingernails give no sign that he clawed or grasped at his attacker. The nails are clean, save for some strands of tobacco beneath the nails of his right thumb and forefinger. And see how the tips of those two fingers are darkened slightly."

With a pocketknife, Holmes carefully scraped the strands from Whitney's fingernails and held them close to his eye, then his nose. Taking the dead man's hand in his own, he held the darkened fingertips to his nose and inhaled deeply.

"As I suspected, Watson. Latakia, without a doubt," Holmes said. "The smell is singular and unmistakable. So is the taste, for that matter. It is Turkish in origin, and very strong and rich, as are many of the tobaccos from that part of the world.

"Lestrade, if we can determine who, among Whitney's customers yesterday, late yesterday, had a taste for Latakia—mind you, it would be part of a blend for it is too robust to be smoked wholly on its own— then we might be able to interview our murderer."

"But how," Lestrade asked, "can we know who

came into the shop? Whitney's was a popular establishment. Any number of people might have come in."

"True," Holmes said, "but Latakia is rather expensive. Might it not be reasonable to assume that such a person, having the means to indulge an expensive taste in tobacco might also be the sort to maintain an account with the proprietor? Surely, Whitney's books must be in order. He seems to have been a methodical sort of fellow, as you can tell from the neatness of his shop."

"Very good, Mr. Holmes."

"Elementary, Lestrade, but nothing that you, I am sure, would not have deduced yourself . . . in time. You did read the monograph I gave you on the subject of distinctive varieties of tobacco and their ashes?"

"Uh . . . yes," said Lestrade. "Of course. It was most interesting; most interesting."

"Quite," Holmes said with a quick, almost imperceptible pursing of his lips, as if to avoid betraying a knowing smirk.

"Now, Watson, if you have concluded your perusal of the body . . . I can see from the hint of discoloration that there is some livor mortis already. Help me turn this poor devil over so that we may examine his backside, will you?"

We did so, and Holmes stared intently at Nigel Whitney's back.

"There, Watson! Do you see it? The slight-seeming wound in his back, directly behind the heart?"

"Yes. What do you suppose caused that, Holmes?"

"That is the villain's blow to the heart. It was administered with such force that it actually penetrated the breast bone, internal organs and then exited, if you will, through the back, however slightly."

"The blow would have had to have been administered with nearly the force of a rifle shot."

"Hmm, Yesssss," said Holmes, somewhat distractedly drawing out the syllable. He was looking down at the floor.

"Hullo! What have we here?"

In an instant, Holmes was down on his hands and knees with his head bent low to the floor, twisting every which way.

"Lestrade, could I borrow a bull's-eye lantern from one of your stalwarts?"

The inspector nodded to a policeman standing in the corner of the room, and the man quickly unhooked a small tin box from his belt and gave it to Lestrade, who opened it and lighted the candle that was set inside. He positioned a round, built-in lens behind the flame, and it cast an intense narrowly focused beam directly in Holmes' eyes. The detective winced in annoyance, but said nothing.

Holmes took the lantern from Lestrade and set it on the oak floor. Blinking repeatedly so as to refocus his vision, Holmes reopened the blade of his pocketknife, held it beneath the lens of the large, round magnifying glass he usually carried, and gently stuck its tip in what appeared to be a gouge in the floor. He withdrew the blade and held it against his thumb for measurement.

"Watson, this floor is made of white oak, which is remarkably hard, and yet this gouge is very nearly as deep as my thumbnail is long!"

I must admit, I could not understand his fascination, or his excitement. "What are you saying, Holmes?"

"This gouge, unless I am mistaken—for it is a singular mark, indeed—was somehow made by Whitney's killer. It is nearly triangular, as is the fatal wound to our tobacconist. The sides of the gouge slope in an equidistant fashion toward a long and especially vicious point. And the mark is fresh; you can tell from the exposure of clean wood. There's been no time for it to collect the dirt of so much as an hour's worth of customers' muddy boots."

"But, Holmes," I protested, "anything might have made that mark. Perhaps old Whitney dropped something. Perhaps a customer stamped his cane on the floor in impatience."

"If so, Watson, it was a singular cane, indeed. More like a sword, I should say. A sword! Upon my word, Watson. Thank you. Thank you. Once again, you have not so much shed light on the subject, but reflected it in a most illuminating way."

"You're welcome, I am sure," I said, "but I have no idea what you are getting at, my good man. Are you saying Whitney was killed with a sword?"

"No, not precisely, for that would not explain the bruising around the wound unless the blade were run through him up to the hilt, and damnably hard at that. As you know, I have some skill as a swordsman, and I do not believe that I could create such a bruise as that."

"Well, what then, Holmes?"

"I cannot be certain, Watson, at least not yet. But it is clear that this case already possesses some interesting features. What, for example, do you make of the fact that Whitney's hands were bound?"

"With his hands tied, he could not resist his attacker, of course," I said.

"Very logical, Watson. Very good. Completely erroneous, but logical enough."

"Holmes, really! Are you saying that old Whitney was slain and then tied up? What possible reason would there be for tying up a dead man?"

"We'll get to that in a moment. Do you notice anything about his bonds?"

"Nothing in particular," I confessed, looking at the rough hemp rope that remained wound around the victim's wrists. "There is nothing telling about the knots. They are not sailor's knots. They seem to be simply a couple of square knots."

"Watson, you see, but you do not observe! Look here. The rope is coiled around the left wrist twice and knotted once, and then, in a separate action, coiled twice around the right wrist, and again knotted

only once. There is a space of approximately two
inches between the bound wrists. This is not very se-
cure, would you say? It would take only a minor bit of
struggling to loosen these. But there was no struggling,
because the man was already dead.

"Come, let us have a look around. Ah, the smell of
the shop is intoxicating. So many different tobaccos.
Sorting them out is an olfactory challenge, don't you
agree?"

"Quite," I said, but, in truth, I was becoming nause-
ated. I found the agglomeration of odors to be heavily
sweet and cloying. Nevertheless, we walked about the
shop proper for a number of minutes before Holmes,
upon entering what I took to be a storeroom at the
rear, called out to me.

"Watson! In here."

A broad pool of blood covered the middle of the
storeroom floor.

"This is obviously where the mutilation took place,"
Holmes said.

"Indeed," I said.

"Be careful not to disturb the blood, Watson. We
owe a small debt of gratitude to Officer Dibble. Had
he or any of the metropolitan constabulary tramped
about at will, they might well have happened upon
this, and in so doing caused us to lose a bit of information. There is no fresh air in this room, Watson. No
windows. No exterior doors. No drafts. The blood has
sat here undisturbed since the deed was perpetrated.
How fortunate! I must study it for a moment. Bear
with me, please."

Yet again, he withdrew his round magnifying glass
and pocketknife, and this time lay flat on the floor
with his head pressed tight against it so as to look
across the top of the dark pool. Without blinking his
eye, he slowly lowered the tip of the knife to the surface of the liquid and withdrew it even more slowly,
carefully watching the droplets of blood that fell back
into the pool. This examination was repeated innumer-

able times, and each experiment he punctuated with some indecipherable expression of interest. "Aah . . . Hhmm . . . Yes . . . Very good . . . No . . . Hmm."

I confess that had I not seen Holmes at work many times before, and therefore grown accustomed to his peculiar enthusiasms under such circumstances, I'd have thought him quite mad. At last he sprang to his feet.

"The body was discovered at one-thirty this morning, Watson, and if I am correct, judging from the extent to which the blood has begun to coagulate, the murder took place some four hours earlier, at roughly nine p.m. or nine-thirty p.m. I cannot be precise, of course, but I suspect that your consideration of the extent of livor mortis will verify the feasibility of that time frame?"

"Why, yes," I said. "That is reasonable, in fact." But the detective, again, was paying little attention. He had scored his point and moved quickly on. He was now staring up at the ceiling in silence.

Moments later he pointed to one of the exposed cross beams that rested about four feet over our heads.

"Whitney was strung up from that beam, hence the pool of blood beneath it," Holmes said. "Once he had been loosely trussed up, and a longer rope passed between his bound wrists and thrown up over the beam and secured, the weight of the man's body kept the rope tight and the killer was free to do his work as he saw fit. There can be no doubt of this. You can even see a slight mark where the hanging rope chafed the cross beam."

"But, Holmes, if Whitney were already dead, why wouldn't the monster have just left him on the floor while cutting him up?"

"An excellent question, Watson, and I fear that the answer is as disturbing as the crime itself. I believe that our killer considers himself something of an artist—not literally, although that, too, is a possibility—

but an artist where murder is concerned. The victim is his canvas, and the canvas had to be positioned just so in order for our man to properly bring his talents to bear."

"This is ghastly," I exclaimed.

"Indeed," Holmes replied. "Particularly when we consider that no artist stops after merely one painting. I am afraid, Watson, that we have not seen the last of this business."

Chapter 4

Holmes was always correct, or very nearly so, a trait that I admired but also sometimes found exasperating and occasionally a trifle frightening. This instance was to prove no exception. The Monster of St. Marylebone struck again three weeks later. This time his victim was a Bond Street merchant, Alexander Gibbons, the well-known proprietor of Gibbons' Gentleman's Apparel, a venerable establishment that was among the most popular and prosperous of any of the fine shops that lined the street.

Gibbons had earned a measure of notoriety as founding chairman of the Bond Street Civic Improvement Association, a ten-year-old union of shopkeepers whose primary function was to both enhance and safeguard Bond Street's status as one of the city's most fashionable shopping districts. The association accomplished this in a number of ways that, for good or ill, became as well known as the high-quality goods for which the street was so regarded.

Every store that belonged to the association had its own crossing sweepers and suited them up in royal blue waistcoats and top hats, the better to be seen industriously brooming the dirt, mud and manure that was so plentiful in the city's streets out of the paths of Bond Street patrons. The sweepers also served as doormen. They cheerily offered their arms to ladies alighting from their carriages, held open the doors to their employers' shops and, whenever requested, also would hail a hansom cab or have one waiting when a patron's shopping was completed. For these services, the sweepers accepted no gratuities; they were paid handsomely by the association.

The association also had its own staff of deliverymen, whose job it was to personally transport goods to buyers' homes for a nominal fee. These clerks, too, all wore the distinctive blue waistcoat and bowler that had, at least among London's gentry, quickly become associated with the expensive shops on Bond Street.

There was, however, at least one unsavory aspect to the civic group, and that was its use of a small but effective cadre of those blue-coated hirelings to keep Bond Street clear of the costermongers and newsboys who hawked their wares all over the city. More than one peddler found his cart suddenly upended in the street for merely trying to enter the exclusive area, whether from its terminus or any of the side streets that poured into it.

If such rough treatment were not quite enough of a deterrent, one of the association's agents would be quick to provide a thrashing to the offender, usually well out of sight of the throng of self-satisfied shoppers. Officially, the police condemned these occasional contretemps, but in practice did little to stop them, partly because they seemed to be relatively few in number and partly, I suspect, because regardless of the association's methods, it had managed in a short period of time to enhance commerce and prosperity in an area that was already generally prized for its refinement, if not always for its probity.

Alexander Gibbons himself was a tall, beefy man with an ivory complexion and a band of red wispy hair that made a semicircle around his otherwise bald head. He had thin bloodless lips and small round ears that stuck out from his head very much like two inadequate handles on a large pot. Gibbons wore gold wireframe spectacles with thick lenses that made his small, piercing black eyes seem considerably larger than they actually were; and for a big man, he had an unfortunate voice; it was reedy and as high-pitched as a penny whistle.

One could surmise that being possessed of such features, it might have been difficult for Gibbons to command much influence among his peers; but nothing could have been further from the truth. In fact, he was generally regarded as a bold, even visionary, businessman, shrewd but scrupulous, a gifted leader in commerce and something of a champion among them. His regular customers were devoted to him, and even his competitors were said to revere the man. It was not by accident that Gibbons' Gentleman's Apparel was the best name on Bond Street. The store set the standard that the rest of the shops followed.

Alexander Gibbons believed this commercial fealty was only his due. He did not hold himself to be merely a servant of highborn clientele; rather, he considered himself, if not quite their equal, then at least their natural friend and compatriot. As such it was, he believed, very nearly his birthright to share equally in their wealth and lofty station. What was merely slight pretension in him, he owned, would be outright and hopeless delusion among his lesser colleagues; so quite naturally, it was their station—their duty, really—to follow his lead.

Then, shortly before Christmas, Gibbons' shop burned. The blaze erupted well after the close of business, when all lamps had been long doused, leading the authorities to suspect immediately that an arson had taken place. So intense was the fire that it gutted the building inside of an hour. The firemen had all they could do to contain the conflagration, and had Gibbons' been made of anything but good Dorset quarry stone, one of several on Bond Street that were, the blaze most assuredly would have spread and engulfed the entire block. By dousing the adjoining wooden buildings with water from their pump trucks, the firemen were able to limit the damage to the clothiers' shop. An article in *The Times* two days later reported that the firemen's suspicions of arson had been borne out. The story reported that Marshal Chauncy Brothers of the Hyperion Fire Company had smelled the unmistakable odor of coal oil immediately upon entering the charred ruin of the building.

Alexander Gibbons was distraught over the fire, as well he might have been, for all that it left him was his reputation and a thirty-one-year history as a fixture on Bond Street. He had been a young man of twenty-four when his father, Aubrey Gibbons, welcomed him to the firm as a partner. When the founder died four years later, his son took over the store. Long hours, unflagging attention to his trade, and an insistent belief that service to his customers was even more important than the high quality of his goods, helped him to double his clientele, and hence his profits, in two years' time.

Gibbons was fifty-five at the time of the fire, and his announcement, via the press, that he would not rebuild shocked his compatriots. "I haven't the heart," he said. But when he was at his lowest point, Gibbons' customers and fellow merchants rallied about him, and that apparently made a difference. Six days after the blaze, he announced that the outpouring of support had buoyed his spirits sufficiently so that he would, in fact, undertake to rebuild the well-known store. The outpouring from his less able colleagues also had touched Gibbons personally, for it was said that at this juncture in his life he became less haughty and more affable than he had ever been.

It was merely two days later, a little more than a week after the fire, that Gibbons was murdered, not on Bond Street but in the study of his own home, a large brick town house on Upper Wimpole Street.

Lestrade called on us at once.

"This one's a lot like the first, Mr. Holmes, and there's not much doubt in my mind that both were done by the same hand—though not as neatly, if you would."

"Meaning?"

"Meaning, Mr. Holmes, that Alexander Gibbons was horribly mutilated. The gashes on his face are so numerous as to make his features unrecognizable."

I winced.

"Were there other cuts?" Holmes asked.

"Aye. Same as before. The triangle and a thrust to the heart."

"Really? Most interesting," Holmes said. "And where did this take place, Lestrade?"

"As I said, sir, in his study."

"I mean, Lestrade, was the victim hung up and then deposited elsewhere on the premises, as was so with our first murder?"

"I don't believe so, Mr. Holmes. There's enough blood on his billiard table and on the floor beside it so as to indicate he was done right there."

"I see. And who found Gibbons, Lestrade?"

"His wife, Mary. She had been out in the gardens quite some distance from the house for much of the morning, and she found the body upon returning."

"And were there maids or servants in the house at the time?"

"None."

"Who fetched you?"

"She did, Mr. Holmes. She came to the Yard to report the crime immediately, and I returned to the house with her directly."

"How much time, then, has elapsed since the murder, Lestrade?"

"Not much more than an hour, I'd say."

"Excellent. Excellent! Watson, are you game? We should get over there at once."

"Of course, Holmes. I'll get my coat."

"I locked the door, Mr. Holmes, so there'd be no disturbing the body," said Lestrade, holding up a key for us to see.

"Yes, of course. Good, Lestrade."

Holmes said it with a perfunctory and, I must admit, condescending air, as though Lestrade's locking of the room should have been so automatic a response as to not warrant mentioning. In anyone else an attitude such as Holmes' might have been exceedingly boorish or mean-spirited; in Holmes, however, it was merely a sign of impatience and his unwillingness to tolerate anything less than completely professional behavior. Lestrade, to his credit, had come to understand this about Holmes, and so he simply swallowed hard and let the remark pass.

"Let us proceed, gentlemen," Holmes said curtly. And we quickly left Baker Street.

Minutes later, we were admitted to the Gibbons home by a woman in a dress of black, gray and white, the recent widow herself. Mrs. Gibbons was a lean and striking woman of indeterminate age. I had not anticipated that she would be so attractive, though I knew not why; perhaps because her late husband had seemed so physically unappealing. Mrs. Gibbons had long, thick raven-black hair that fell below her shoulders. Her eyes were dark, and made to seem darker still by her milk-white skin. Her chin was slightly dimpled and well defined, and her lips were full and naturally red. She comported herself with an almost regal bearing, which seemed to add a foot to her height. She appeared to have been interrupted in the middle of chores, despite the pall that a murder of this magnitude would have had to have cast upon the household.

Lestrade addressed her. "Mrs. Gibbons, this is Mr. Sherlock Holmes and his assistant, Dr. Watson. They often consult for us in cases of great import."

Holmes nodded to the comely widow.

"May I extend my sympathies, Mrs. Gibbons," I said.

The woman looked inquiringly at Holmes and then at me, but did not so much as acknowledge my comment. Indeed, she seemed hostile, an impression that was soon to be verified.

"You took long enough," she said to Lestrade with great indignation. "I presume that you will get on with your business and be done with it."

The woman then looked at us and snuffed the air in an unmistakable gesture of disdain. "I find it less than reassuring that Scotland Yard would need the help of professional meddlers in such a matter."

"Madame," I said sharply. "Excuse me, but I do not . . ."

"Pay no mind, Watson," Holmes said quickly. "This is a trying day for madame. Let us investigate the circumstances and be out from under foot, shall we?"

It was Lestrade who directed us to the study, however, not Mrs. Gibbons.

"This way, gentlemen."

He inserted his key in the escutcheon of the door, but it opened before he could turn it.

"What's this?" he exclaimed. "Mrs. Gibbons, I gave precise instructions that no one be admitted to this room. You made no mention of there being another key to this room."

"Nor did you think to ask," she said, and for the first time I noted a distinct trace of Irish in her voice. "And who might you be to be giving me orders in my own house, Inspector? Just who do you think you are?"

"You well know who I am, madame," Lestrade shot back, "and I represent Scotland Yard in an official inquiry into the murder of your husband. If you have disturbed his body in some . . ."

Holmes rushed by the policeman so quickly as to give him a start.

"Blast!" exclaimed Holmes. "I do not believe it. Madame, where is your husband's body?"

The woman was as indignant as Holmes and Lestrade were angry. "Sure and it's rolled up in bed linens and waiting near the pantry door to be removed."

"Why have you done this?" Lestrade demanded. "Why have you done this? You even have gone so far as to cut the felt from the billiard table."

"This is my home, and it was a frightful mess. It is my duty as mistress of this house to keep it presentable, and keep it presentable I will."

Lestrade threw his arms into the air and turned away, muttering to himself in exasperation.

Holmes had been walking around the billiard table, bent almost in half studying the floor. When Lestrade's conversation ended, Holmes strode briskly to within three feet of the woman, glowered at her, and spoke rapidly but in an even and clear voice.

"Madame, in your misbegotten tidiness you may well have destroyed clues that would have aided us in our investigation of the crime. You do not seem to be hard of hearing, so I gather that you chose to deliberately ignore Inspector Lestrade's instructions. The fact that you moved the body, disposed of the table felt on which it lay, and then went so far as to scrub the area clean, calls into serious question your eagerness to have the murderer of your husband brought to justice."

The woman's face colored, but not in embarrassment. She stepped toward Holmes and glared at him, her face craned upward at his, for he towered over her by more than a foot.

"How dare you, sir! Neither you nor anyone else may enter this house and tell me, Mary McCormick Gibbons, what I may do or not do. And as for my eagerness to have this horrible crime solved, what good will that do, pray?

"My husband made a good many enemies, he did, though he was well liked by just as many. But whether you bring his killer down or whether you do not, which is more likely, my life from this point onward has changed. Fer sartin, it has."

She paused as if to regain some of her composure. When she spoke again, there was still fire in her voice,

but now it evinced firmness and control, and her Irish
lilt had lessened.

"Other aspects of my life have not changed, and
will not. I have always, sir, kept a fine clean house. I
will continue to do so. This room was a mess, so I
cleaned it. I do not give a tuppence whether you like
it or not. If you choose to make more of it than that,
sir, you'll deal with my solicitor. Do I make myself
clear?"

And with that the wretched woman moved a step
closer to Holmes. If the two of them had been men,
there would have been blows by now, I'm sure. As it
was, they were aimed nose to nose, hers straining upward into Holmes' face, over which, to my surprise, a
look of bemusement suddenly passed. The tension left
his posture, and he took a nearly imperceptible step
backward.

"Forgive me, madame," he said with a sheepish
smile. "Please. You are, of course, quite right. We'll
not bother you further, and I beg that you will excuse
our intrusion under what must be the most trying of
circumstances. Lestrade, I think I can be of no further
service here tonight. I bid you good evening, madame.
Come, Watson."

Holmes nodded, turned, and we were at the door
in two steps, at which point, he turned toward Mrs.
Gibbons and said, "I beg your pardon, but has it only
been you here, alone with the body of your late
husband?"

She seemed startled. "That is correct," she said.
"My youngest son lives here with us, but he is away."

"Away? I see," Holmes said. "He is married?"

Mrs. Gibbons seemed distracted. "Uh, no. He . . ."

"On his own, then?" Holmes persisted.

"He is simply an independent young man, and . . ."

"This would be Master Jamey?"

Mrs. Gibbons had only started to shake her head
when Holmes quickly interjected.

"Ah, then, Albert. And why is your eldest not here with his family?"

"He chooses to live alone," Mrs. Gibbons said, her jaw held tight.

"I see," Holmes said. "But Master Jamey is absent as well?"

"I said he is away."

"So you did, madame. So you did. Well, we will take our leave. Again, I thank you."

Lestrade followed us, but not before addressing the widow.

"Madame," he said, "I am going to attribute your behavior today to your being distraught over the tragedy that has been visited upon this house. But tomorrow is a new day, and you will see fit to cooperate with this investigation or 'pon my soul, you will be the first widow I have ever had the displeasure to see clapped in irons on a charge of obstruction.

"Now, do *I* make myself clear?"

"Why you little poppinjay, you . . ."

Lestrade spoke to Mrs. Gibbons so sharply and quickly that I took a step backward, and so did the unfortunate woman, though her milky complexion reddened noticeably.

"Do you understand!!!!??"

The widow said nothing. She just stared balefully at the policeman, her fists clenching and unclenching by her side, her chest rising and falling with deep, rapid breaths.

"Very good," said Lestrade. The inspector turned abruptly from the woman and inadvertently stepped on the tail of a fluffy black-and-white house cat. The animal let out a screech and ran off. I watched its heavy belly sway as it ran. It was obvious the cat was nursing a litter.

"Oh, Mildred," shouted Mrs. Gibbons. "Here, kitty. See what you've done now? Here, kitty. Here, Mildred."

The woman ran off after the cat, and the inspector

strode down the steps to the sidewalk. He hailed a black police wagon that was moving slowly along the street, as if uncertain of its destination, and it pulled up beside the curb.

"In here," he told the driver and his companion curtly. "First floor. And step lively!"

We called a hansom cab, and directed the driver to take us to Scotland Yard, because Holmes said he wanted to examine Gibbons' corpse as soon as it arrived there.

"Why, the cheek of that woman!" I said. "Holmes, I don't believe I have ever seen you give ground so abruptly."

"The more I stared at the woman, Watson, the more I realized that she was very near to breaking down. Her defiance, I think, was the only way she had to maintain a measure of control over her emotions. This is a strong and willful woman, Watson, but I think the day's events had brought her to the brink of hysteria.

"Her mental state does not jibe with the coldness it would take not only to murder a person, but to maim and disfigure him as well. True, she may have done our investigation some harm; the disposition of the body could mean everything or nothing. We do not know, thanks to her. But were she the killer, would she not have taken pains to do nothing that would antagonize the police? If she were the guilty one, I suspect she would have given much thought to whether she wanted to arouse suspicion with so flagrant and willful an action."

"I hadn't looked at it that way," I confessed. "I suppose you are right, Holmes."

"This is bad business, Watson. Very bad, indeed. We should know more after we see the body. And as for Mary McCormick Gibbons, unless I am gravely in error, we may wish to question her again. I need to have that door, if not open, then at least slightly ajar.

As it is, I suspect it may go easier for us in another meeting with her than it would for Lestrade.

"Meanwhile, I am intrigued as to why of the two sons, only Jamey lives at home. It is Albert who is associated with the store, but he has left the roost. One wonders if he flew willingly?"

"Do you mean to suggest that he may be at odds with his mother and brother? Or they with him?"

"It would seem to be a most interesting possibility, don't you think? And if that is the case, perhaps we could turn such sentiment to our advantage."

"I follow you," I said. "You think that Albert might be willing to inform on his mother and brother. Is that it?"

"I do not know that he would have anything to say about them worth our hearing, Watson. Besides, 'inform' seems so devious a term. Let's just say that should our little investigation proceed further in that rather odd and tragic household, it might prove useful to have one of the Gibbonses on our side."

We arrived at Scotland Yard as the two mortuary workers were carrying Gibbons' body inside.

The coroner's room was a brightly lighted, foul-smelling chamber in the basement of the building. It was a dank and stark place, with brick walls covered by so many layers of white paint that the bricks seemed rounded. The whiteness and the lights gave the room an eery harshness, and it always seemed to me that the effect of such surroundings was to turn every corpse within into a ghastly, unnatural specimen, regardless of the condition of the body. The effect was multiplied dramatically when the death was marked by savagery, as was the case with Alexander Gibbons.

The workmen laid the clothier on a long stained table and removed the blankets that enveloped him.

The sight of his face made me catch my breath, imperceptibly, I hoped.

"Lestrade did not exaggerate the extent of mutilation," said Holmes, his face betraying not a hint of emotion.

"Frightful," I said. "Totally unrecognizable."

"Yes," said Holmes distractedly. "Watson, what do you make of the hands? The right is clenched in a tight fist. And the fingers of the left are spread and extended to such an extent that the fingers are like talons. Ah! See here," Holmes said. He took Gibbons' lifeless hand in his own and held his pocket glass to the dead man's fingertips. "Once again, the fingernails hold some telling interest for us. These flecks of green?"

"Felt from the billiard table?" I asked.

"Without a doubt," Holmes said.

"A suggestion of agony, I would say, Holmes. He was in such horrible pain that he clawed up bits of the felt. That could mean he was not killed quickly and then set upon, as was Nigel Whitney."

"I agree with you on the first point, Watson; he died in horrible agony. But whether his death was relatively quick or prolonged, I cannot yet say. I am rather more concerned with other aspects of the case. It is similar to the first murder in certain key respects: the thrust to the heart, and the carving of the triangle into the poor devil's torso.

"But this murder is markedly different in other respects; there was no bruising around the stab wound to the heart, for one thing. And curiously, I found no gouge in the floor beside the billiard table. It was the first element I looked for.

"I find it interesting that the body has stiffened," he said, "and yet it is but three hours since the murder."

"Perhaps Lestrade was wrong in his estimate of the time that had elapsed between the murder and the reporting of the crime," I suggested.

"Perhaps," Holmes said, a puzzled expression on his face. "Perhaps." He walked silently around the body twice before speaking again.

"This is most interesting," he said finally. "I am

impressed, Watson, although that is hardly the proper word to use, by the extent of violence that surrounds Gibbons' murder.

"Certainly, the crime itself is even more violent than the murder of Nigel Whitney, but what is unique here, I think, is its completeness. Don't forget, this man's livelihood was destroyed only days before he was murdered. I do not believe in coincidence, Watson, as you well know.

"I am certain the arson and the murder are related. The arsonist's work was a measured cruelty. Our killer brought Gibbons to what surely must have been the lowest point in his long professional life, and only then did he slay him. This is not just murder; it is complete and utter destruction.

"And the blows that were struck against Gibbons were especially ferocious. I cannot help but wonder why. What's more, it was a decidedly brazen attack. Nigel Whitney was murdered after dark in his place of business, you'll remember. But Gibbons was slaughtered in the light of day, in the privacy of his own home, with his wife, though somewhat removed, right there on the grounds."

"Perhaps the madness that drives this monster is worsening, Holmes."

"Quite possibly, Watson. Yes, I fear that is a distinct possibility. Or perhaps there was a cooler, more objective reason that we cannot yet see. And one other option presents itself."

"A second killer?" I asked.

"Just so, Watson! A second killer. Very good."

"But one with a like purpose?"

"Coincidence is for fools to abide," he said.

"Yes, of course, Holmes. But the prospect of there being two fiends is rather daunting, wouldn't you say?"

"Yes, it is," the detective said. " 'Daunting' is a good choice of words. Well, we shall see. More information is needed. Yes, we shall see."

In the days that followed, the police investigation became complicated by the public's rising consternation over the presence of another murderer on the streets of London. Delegations of businessmen descended upon Scotland Yard with demands for increased protection. The blue-jacketed Bond Street crossing sweepers began carrying saps, and the association doubled the number of bruisers it hired to watch the area.

Elsewhere throughout London, even merchants and shopkeepers who had rarely encountered any trouble with the public took to carrying a firearm or keeping one close by. On Saville Row, a customer who was dissatisfied with the work of a well-known hatter found himself looking down the barrel of a shotgun after raising his voice in anger at the shop's manager.

Meanwhile, the newspapers mined every interview and police statement for clues to the slayings. Journalism can be a reliable rough draft of history, but future generations would be well advised to read carefully when they peer back at times of great public unrest. The noble and passionate desire to ferret out the truth, under the pressures of the moment, too often yields outlandish conjecture, wild inaccuracies and fantastical theorizing. That is precisely why Holmes as politely as possible declined all comment on our involvement, though we were at first dogged mercilessly by reporters from Fleet Street.

Eventually, however, his patience gave out. A rude young man braced us outside our quarters and declared, "Mr. Holmes, we're going to publish a story that has reliable police informants saying you believe that a prominent merchant is tied to the murders."

Holmes told him to print whatever he pleased because he never read the man's publication and never would, and if he persisted he would complain to his editor and then the authorities. The threat had the desired effect: The reporter left us alone, and eventually he and his fellows tired of the game. Holmes would never have made good on his threat, but the reporter had no way of knowing that. The detective believed in the worth of an unfettered press, despite its periodic excesses. And his comment about never reading the brazen fellow's newspaper was a bald lie; Holmes was a voracious reader of every newspaper in the city.

The papers continued to run numerous stories in which uninformed citizenry were quoted at will with novel explanations that were treated as though they had merit. One headline even boldly proclaimed, "Jack's Back!" Another painted the murderer as a Robin Hood set on avenging the bilking of the public by retailers. And one story even suggested that the garish murders in society's upper orders were meant to even the score for the police having allowed the Ripper to have his way among the lower elements.

Holmes read the accounts with some amusement and occasional guffaws of disbelief, as did I. Otherwise, we busied ourselves with the methodical and tedious legwork that always lay behind the solving of extraordinary puzzles.

The outcry Lestrade faced over the second murder made him more intent than ever to forge ahead with his inquiry into the slaying of Nigel Whitney. The inspector had taken Holmes' suggestion and scoured the tobacconist's ledger entries from the day of the murder. He discovered that one Quincy Morton of Leicester had purchased one quarter of a pound of Latakia and a one-pound mixture of burley near day's end, billed, just as Holmes had hoped, to his account.

Because Lestrade was in charge of the case for Scotland Yard, he had been able to arrange for Inspector Tobias Gregson to interview Morton. There had always been some competition between the two policemen, but on balance both maintained a professional attitude. Lestrade advised Gregson to pay particular attention not only to Morton himself, but to descriptions of any other customers Morton might have seen entering Whitney's near the close of business.

Inspector Gregson complied willingly, which was no surprise; Holmes had always considered him the most promising of the Scotland Yarders. "His deductive and analytical abilities show great promise," the detective had confided, "and he is a careful interviewer. A good choice on Lestrade's part, I must say."

Holmes wanted to hear Gregson's report himself, which was to say he did not want the accuracy of the accounting to depend on anyone's powers but his own. Not wishing to needlessly offend Lestrade, Holmes simply arranged for the four of us to meet over supper in a quiet corner of the Holborn Restaurant.

"Well, Mr. Holmes," Gregson began, "as I was telling Inspector Lestrade, Mr. Morton had been in the city on a day's business and as he oftentimes did, stopped by Whitney's Limited for some of the tobacco he favors. They exchanged pleasantries as Whitney measured it out and wrote out the bill, but Morton cut it short with an explanation that he had to catch an evening train out of Paddington.

"He was in such a hurry to be off that he rushed to the door and barged straight into a young man who was entering the shop. The collision caused Morton to drop his parcels of tobacco; the other person got quite a bump and staggered almost off his feet. Morton guessed the fellow was in his late twenties, early thirties, and was all dressed up dapper-like, as if he was going to Great Albert Hall or something.

"Morton was still apologizing while he was bent over picking up his parcels, but he swears that even as he did, the young man half raised his walking stick as if to strike him."

"Indeed?" said Holmes, his voice rising in inquiry.

"Morton just saw it out of the corner of his eye, and when he straightened up, still apologizing, the look the dandy gave him was enough to convince him he hadn't been imagining the movement.

" 'Positively venomous,' says Morton. The man had dark, piercing eyes and Morton swears that the man's face was, well, powdered, such as what a lady or an actor might wear."

"Most intriguing," Holmes said. "Did the young man say anything to Mr. Morton?

"Aye, he did. He spoke sharply to him in a low voice. He said, 'You don't know how fortunate you are, sir.'

"Morton said, 'Beggin' your pardon, sir, but I did apologize. And I do so again. Good day to you.' Then Morton bowed and hurried out the door."

"A good report, Gregson."

"Thank you, sir, but I have to say Morton's recollection was particularly clear. The incident had left him a bit rattled."

"Nevertheless," said Holmes, "it was you who managed the interview. This walking stick, Gregson. Did Mr. Morton remark on it further, by any chance?"

"Aye, when I kept pressing him for details he did."

Holmes smiled slightly and nodded his approval. "Go on, please, Inspector."

"He said the stick was black and had a fancy silver handle, a ball-shaped knob."

"Anything else?"

"If the stick was peculiar beyond that, Mr. Morgan gave no indication, sir."

"I see," said Holmes, the animation suddenly gone from his voice. I sensed his frustration and chose to fill the uncomfortable silence by finishing my drink, promptly ordering another and then, as our steak and kidney pie was delivered to the table, smacking the palms of my hands together over the feast.

"Well," I said, all full of cheer, "let us enjoy this marvelous meal, shall we? If you're going to work a horse, you've got to feed him, eh?"

"Aye," Gregson said. "I'll grant you that, Doctor." Lestrade muttered an assent. Holmes smiled politely.

"Aach! There was one other thing, Mr. Holmes," Gregson said.

The detective turned his head sharply to the speaker.

"There was someone else in the store at the time, off in the corner, but Morton says he took almost no notice, being in such a hurry and then bumping into that strange fellow as he did. The person, whoever it was, was dressed in dark clothing," Gregson said.

"Surely, there is nothing odd about that," I interjected.

"True, Dr. Watson," Gregson said. "But—and this is the part I found interesting, Mr. Holmes, probably the only reason I remembered to jot this down in my notes, in fact—Quincy Morton couldn't tell whether the person off in the corner was a man or a woman."

"Gregson," Holmes asked, "you did say that Quincy Morton didn't pay much attention to the person in the corner, did you not?"

"I did, sir, but that's not to say he didn't get a clear look."

"And?" Holmes seemed perturbed.

"And Morton still couldn't tell whether it was a man or a woman."

"What do you make of that, Holmes," I asked.

"Well, I must say that I have no idea what to make of it," he answered.

Holmes seemed unsettled. He blinked his gray eyes rapidly a couple of times, but said nothing else, and for the rest of the evening we did not speak of the murders, preferring, instead, to discuss matters of no more consequence than the weather.

Even so, he was relatively quiet and rather preoccupied. I knew that he was churning the new information over and over and weighing its importance, for Holmes did not so much undertake a case as he did offer himself to it so that he might be devoured body and soul. It was as if the biblical Jonah allowed himself to be swallowed whole by the whale only so that he might know his antagonist from the inside out and later emerge better able to vanquish it. Holmes always seemed to end up safe and on dry land eventually, but I could not help but wonder if someday he might get chewed up and eaten, instead—and me with him.

Chapter 5

As I sat by Holmes' bed in Charing Cross Hospital working on my narrative, it occurred to me just how fortunate we had been until now to have suffered only minor injuries during even our most harrowing adventures. I do not mind saying that we were blessed with a strong sense of duty and the nerve to carry it out, but Holmes always preferred to rely on his wits and superior powers of analysis and deduction to carry the day. He considered violence a failure of reason and a last recourse, as did I; but given the nature of our work and the uncertainties of the times, we always were prepared to use force if the situation absolutely demanded it, as, indeed, it sometimes did.

I often carried my trusty revolver, but Holmes, who was by far the better shot, carried his weapon only infrequently, largely because he brought other formidable skills to the contest. He had surprising strength and could bend an iron poker into the shape of a horse's shoe; he insisted that straightening the poker afterward was considerably more difficult, but he could do that as well. Holmes was also an expert boxer and a fan of the prizefights. What's more, he had studied the ancient Japanese martial skill of baritsu and became adept at it long before many Europeans became familiar with it. So I was troubled as I sat beside my incapacitated friend, writing pad upon my lap, that despite our confidence, defensive skills and considerable experience, I had become aware of a numbing fear of some magnitude.

In truth, the facts of the St. Marylebone case made my flesh crawl, and it did me little good to be immersed in them without benefit of my companion's keen instincts and incomparable insights. I had hoped with my writing to begin forcing the pieces of the puzzle into a coherent and soluble pattern, but the entire affair suddenly seemed most ominous.

I knew that I was weary to the bone and frustrated by Holmes' condition; despite my medical training, I did not know what to make of it. At times, he seemed to regain consciousness for a moment or two and then lapse back into insensibility. Two nights past, the policeman outside his room was startled to hear Holmes crying, "Nooooo. Nooooo. Nooooo," over and over. When the policeman rushed to his side, all Holmes could say was, "My rooms. Let me leave here. Let me leave. I must get back to my rooms." Dr. Peacham gave Holmes a sedative, and the rest of the night had passed uneventfully.

The next night, the incident repeated itself, but with a difference. Holmes screamed a cry so piercing and altogether horrible that the guard thought murder was being committed. He rushed into the room and found Holmes standing naked beside the bed, running the tips of his fingers up and down the edges of the long, livid scar on his chest, as if it were the most curious thing he had ever seen. He turned to the guard and said one word, and one word only: "Abba."

As luck would have it, Dr. Peacham and I were walking along the hospital corridor the next morning discussing the event, and our puzzlement must have been obvious on our faces, because when Dr. Peacham bade good day to an elderly Anglican clergyman of his acquaintance, the old fellow stopped short and peered up into the doctor's face.

"Why, Charles," the old ecclesiastic said with a kindly smile, " 'tis much too early in the day to seem so vexed."

"Oh, I am not 'vexed,' Edward," Peacham said.

" 'Puzzled' would be the correct description. . . . Forgive my bad manners. Vicar, this is my friend, Doctor John H. Watson. Doctor, this is Vicar Edward Richardson."

"My pleasure, sir," I said.

He smiled politely and nodded in greeting. "I do so love puzzles. May I be of some help?"

"Do you know the word 'Abba'?" Peacham asked.

"Of course," the vicar said.

My mouth fell open in surprise.

"Oh, anyone in my occupation might be expected to know 'Abba,' the clergyman said. "Father. 'Abba' means father. The word actually comes down to us from the Aramaic, and appears in Scripture with considerable frequency. It is the root of the word 'abbot,' the head, or patriarch if you would, of a monastery. I have always enjoyed etymology; rather a hobby you know."

"Fortunate for us," I declared.

"Indeed," Peacham said. "Thank you, Vicar."

The old man smiled politely and resumed his slow progress down the corridor. My jubilation over our solving even this tiny piece of the mystery quickly faded when I realized that I had absolutely no idea what an ancient word for "father" could possibly mean to our case. And that, too, I found frustrating.

I was thus lost in my thoughts and, in truth, was feeling a bit groggy when the door to Holmes' room opened and Dr. Peacham entered; I was grateful for sentient company.

"It has been a very long day, Dr. Watson, and if you won't be scandalized, I am going to have some brandy. Would you join me?"

"Willingly," I said, following him to his small office.

"Can we speak candidly, Doctor?"

"Of course," I said.

"It is my considered opinion that Mr. Holmes is almost ready to return to his quarters in Baker Street," Peacham said.

"You can't be serious."

"I am, Dr. Watson, quite."

He smiled, but cast his eyes downward for a moment. "He himself wants to go home. In some respects, it is, against my better judgment. He will have to be watched, and watched closely. But apart from that care, which may prove quite enough, ultimately, I think there is little else that we can do for him here. He is mending and . . ."

"Did I hear you correctly, Dr. Peacham?" I was stunned. "Did you say Holmes wants to leave? Are you basing your decision on what he has muttered in delirium?"

"In part, yes," Peacham said with a small, almost conspiratorial smile. "There was an urgency to his words, was there not? I surmise that he really does want to return to Baker Street, though I daresay he would be in no real condition to do anything once he is there.

"I do not want to belabor this or give you false hope. These waking moments of Holmes' could be a kind of emotional death throe. Such things do happen, you know. One final series of horrendous spasms of the mind before complete and unalterable relapse; and I must confess, that was what I feared at first.

"Had that been the case, I would have sought permission to apply electrical stimulation to the frontal lobes of the patient in hopes of reversing or at least nullifying the damage he has suffered.

"But when I realized that none of the physical signs that usually accompany such dramatic failure seemed to be present—pallor, emaciation, irregular, weakened pulse— and that, in fact, the patient's health seemed otherwise to be improving with every day, I became convinced that Mr. Holmes was starting to come out of his present state, though slowly and in an episodic manner. After last night, I am convinced of it."

"I had begun to fear that his dreadful attack had cost him his mind, Dr. Peacham."

"Mr. Holmes is not beyond repair, Dr. Watson, but in some respects he has, in fact, lost his mind. But I believe it is a temporary loss. As pitiful as it may seem the incidents we have been watching represent his piecemeal efforts to recover just such a loss, to repair the damage that has been wrought to his mind. It amounts to a complete breakdown of the faculties, compounded by extreme and prolonged physical trauma. From a medical perspective, it is a fascinating healing process to watch, though, I hasten to add, I take no joy in doing so, for it is so tortured. We know so relatively little about the workings of the human mind. I do believe, though, that Mr. Holmes is beginning to heal, uhm, mentally, as well as physically, at least in some measure, and I think we should all take heart in this.

"I foresee two related possibilities, Doctor. One, these moments of wakefulness will increase in duration and frequency, and gradually outweigh his periods of catatonia to become the continuum we know as complete and rational consciousness. Or two, there will be a prolonged period of this alternating between consciousness and unconsciousness, and then a sudden breakthrough. Envision a harbor seal trapped under ice on the Thames. He swims and swims and swims until he finally finds a fissure in the ice sheet, rams up into it from the river bottom and breaks his way through to freedom.

"I would prefer the former, slower eventuality to the latter, because it would almost certainly be less traumatic. But either way, Doctor, I am rather convinced that Mr. Holmes will recover fully."

"Thank God," I muttered, almost in a whisper. "Thank God." My voice quavered and, to my abject humiliation I began to weep.

"Don't be embarrassed, Dr. Watson," Peacham said. "Your vigil and your worry have left you exhausted; it is only natural."

I took a deep draught of my brandy and said nothing for what seemed like several minutes while I regained my composure.

"You are quite sure of this prognosis?" I asked Peacham.

"Everything in my experience points to it," he said.

"How long will it take?" I asked.

"There is no telling. A day? A month? A year? Even longer? I do not know. Much depends on the patient himself, on the extent of his resolve and his innate emotional stability. Those attributes are there, or they are not. They cannot be administered like a potion or taught like a lesson. They can only be observed, nurtured and supported. As you would expect, Dr. Watson, Mr. Holmes has these traits in far greater measure than most, but for the past few weeks he has not even been able to bathe or so much as relieve himself without someone in attendance to help. He needs a great deal of physical attention while his mind continues to reexamine and come to grips with the horror of what happened to him in that stable."

"Is that what he is doing mentally? Going through it all over again?"

"In a sense, yes. But I think not in an entirely rational or linear way."

" 'Entirely rational' is the only way Holmes functions."

"Ostensibly, yes; but in this instance, I think not. He is merely a human being whose strongest faculty, his reason, has been very nearly broken. Remember, Dr. Watson, man's first instinct is to survive. That is the one driving force. It transcends the physical, the spiritual, the magnetic and the mental.

"I believe that when the mind has been so severely traumatized that it is disabled, in the process of repair it deals only with what it is actually able to handle at any particular time. The mind may consider images and experiences and associated stimuli in the memory in what would seem to us to be a completely arbitrary and random fashion, but in actuality it is making defensive selections, choosing to examine only those pieces of memory that it can best deal with at that moment. Recovery begins to occur when the patient is able to reassemble all of those randomly handled images and memories into a coherent and acceptable recollection."

"But this is a long and uncertain process, Dr. Peacham. Are you sure it is wise that Holmes leave the hospital?"

"No, I am not, but I can say that if he does not leave here soon, it will be only a matter of time before we have to move him to an institution for the insane. I do not want that to happen, Doctor. Those places are little more than warehouses of anguish and impenetrable illness. Few who enter as patients ever leave. They gradually worsen, and eventually die. But after these incidents with Mr. Holmes, I do not know how long we can contain him.

"I also believe it may be helpful to Mr. Holmes to be in familiar surroundings. That is at least logical, is it not? What's more, his own insistence on leaving must be considered. I think the impulse must be directly associated with the resolution of this horrible murder case. There must be something that is pulling him, beyond all reasonable concern for his own health, to insist that he return to Baker Street."

"That would be very much in keeping with Holmes' methods," I said. "And yet, that part of me which is always a physician worries about how he is to be cared for during his convalescence. I believe Holmes needs the attention of an extraordinarily good nurse, someone with special experience."

"Precisely, Dr. Watson. Precisely. And I already have someone in mind. She will still have to meet with your approval, of course, but I recommend her without reservation. I have discussed this with Mr. Holmes' brother. In fact, it was Mycroft Holmes who suggested we use the woman, and I immediately concurred. He has offered to recompense her handsomely on a weekly or monthly basis. But again, Dr. Watson, this presumes that you are amenable, both to her and the arrangement."

I was taken aback by this development, but not in an entirely unpleasant way. There was wisdom and compassion in Mycroft's recommendation, and it had Peacham''s imprimatur besides. But the propriety of a woman's moving into the quarters of two single men seemed dubious at best, nurse or not.

"I will have to consult Mrs. Hudson," I said, "but I am sure she will agree, as will I, to anything that benefits Holmes."

"Splendid, Doctor. Splendid." Peacham pulled his watch from a vest pocket beneath his white hospital coat. "Ah, it is 5:45. I took the liberty of asking the nurse to come by so that you might meet her. She should be in the anteroom now. If you will excuse me, I will summon her."

"Of course," I said, though I was somewhat ruffled, I confess, by the awareness that Mycroft and Peacham were manipulating Holmes' situation without first so-liciting my opinion. Given my willingness to serve as Holmes' Boswell all of these years, I should not, I suppose, have been surprised to find myself readily taken for granted.

At heart, however, I knew that my peevishness ema-nated only from exhaustion and frustration, not jeal-ousy or genuine resentment. If I had thought for a moment that either man were not acting in Holmes' best interest, or that their decisions reflected the least amount of arbitrariness, I would have taken them to task at once and held my ground, for I realized in-stantly what they did not yet seem to fully compre-hend: that despite Holmes' horrible beating and agonizingly slow return from what must surely have been the awful specter of his own demise, he was, even now, manipulating and controlling the course of events as best he could. He wanted to return to Baker

Street, however prematurely, and that is precisely what he was accomplishing. I smiled to myself and shook my head in a pleasing and oddly reassuring kind of disbelief: Holmes was still on the case.

Chapter 6

Peacham returned to the room and jarred me from my reverie. With a slightly exaggerated backhand flourish toward the open doorway, he said, "Dr. Watson, may I present Mrs. Abigail Masterson."

As Holmes' nurse out of hospital I had envisioned an older, dowdy sort of person with the demeanor of a Prussian, not such an elegant creature as Mrs. Masterson. She moved as quickly and elegantly into the office as she had into Holmes' room when I had first met her. She spoke first and had the courteousness to not embarrass Peacham by noting that we had already met.

"I have truly enjoyed reading your adventures with Mr. Holmes," she said. "You are a marvelous storyteller, and I am sure that you are no less effective as a physician."

I fairly stammered with pleasure. "Why, thank you," I said. "Thank you very much. You are most kind. As for my medical skills, well, I have maintained my small practice, but I can't say it has been very demanding of late, unlike my work with Holmes. Won't you sit down?"

"Thank you," she said, seating herself in one of Peacham's straight-backed office chairs.

I suddenly had no idea how to proceed, and was relieved when Peacham began speaking.

"Doctor, I am recommending Mrs. Masterson for several reasons. She apprenticed as a nurse with Florence Nightingale, a hard and controversial master of the healing arts but a fine and compassionate one, regardless of the fact that much of our profession even now views her methods with so little approbation.

"Secondly, I know Mrs. Masterson very well. She has been under my tutelage at Charing Cross for two years, and she will make a fine doctor."

"I am certain she will, Dr. Peacham," I said. "Mrs. Masterson, let me be frank with you. I could care for Holmes quite adequately were he simply incapacitated indefinitely, but what is needed here is someone with specialized training. Do you have that?"

"I do," she said, "and let me tell you that many people in Mr. Holmes' condition have died, or, I believe, been mistakenly buried alive."

I had, of course, heard of such things, but shuddered to think of them, and my distaste must have been evident on my face.

"Yes," Abigail Masterson said, "it is true. Their near-catatonia has, on occasion, been taken for death and treated accordingly, a horrible consequence, but it is easy to understand how it happens. Fortunately, we know more all the time about such lapses of consciousness, so we are more inclined to look for it than ever before.

"Doctor, if I might add something in my own behalf . . ."

"Yes, of course," said I.

"I think you should know that in addition to my training with Sister Nightingale and Dr. Peacham, I undertook two years of the most grueling work with the insane at the Hospital of St. Mary of Bethlehem, or Bedlam, as most of England knows it, and I believe my peculiar insights into the dark world of these unfortunates will be of inestimable value to Mr. Holmes.

"I have spent most of my recent mornings with the patient, so I am intimately familiar with him. I have forcibly fed him and bathed and cleansed him, of course, but more importantly, I have studied him. It is of the utmost importance as he continues to break through this debility that has so completely enveloped him, that someone be constantly by his side prepared to accommodate and stabilize him."

"Have there been any, uh, incidents in your presence, Mrs. Masterson?" I asked.

"Not as you mean the word, Doctor, no. But there have been indications of change and even voluntary movement, though subtle and slight, and there also has been some limited vocalization. At first I thought he was merely repeating his name. But then I realized he was saying, Home. Home.' He had to get home."

"I think, Mrs. Masterson . . . It is, uh, 'Mrs.' is it not?"

"Yes, my late husband . . ."

"I see. I think that we should be most fortunate to have you with us. I do believe Holmes would approve. I know that I do, and for now, that seems to be what matters most."

She smiled and turned to Dr. Peacham.

"Though there are clear risks involved, I think we should move Mr. Holmes as soon as possible," she said, "within the week, if you are amenable."

"I will speak with Mrs. Hudson at once," I interjected. "Presuming her agreement, we will make Holmes' room ready, and that will be that. We will prepare a room for you as well, Mrs. Masterson. Will you require any special accommodations?"

"Yes," she said, leveling her gaze directly at me. "In addition to whatever household adjustments you kindly choose to make for me, I will require a cot or small bed for myself in Mr. Holmes' room."

This startled me. I did not like being on the defensive where this woman, or any other, was concerned, but I felt I had to object. "I, uhm, I do not wish to seem prudish or uncooperative, Mrs. Masterson, but isn't that rather out of the ordinary?"

"Yes," she said, "I would say it is rather extraordinary, but then so is Mr. Holmes' circumstance. At least for a time, it would be best that I be at his side constantly. You will recall that the patient's most prolonged conscious activity has come very late at night."

"That is true," I conceded

"Is it agreed, then?"

"Very well," I said, my displeasure and reluctance obvious, if not in my expression, then in the tone of resignation with which I gave my assent.

"Doctor, please understand. My opinions may sometimes be scandalous, but, at least in general, my personal behavior is not. I am a professional, I assure you. I only have Mr. Holmes' best interest in mind. But my devotion to what is commonly referred to as 'New Women' causes compels me to point out additionally that had Dr. Peacham made the very same proposal, not an eyebrow would have been raised. Think of me, if you must, merely as his representative."

"My dear," I said, "had Dr. Peacham made the same proposal, I would not have reacted similarly because propriety would not have been an issue. Your being a woman, and a noticeably attractive woman at that, if you don't mind my saying . . ."

"Not at all," Mrs. Masterson interjected, though I thought I detected a trace of disapproval, if not anger, in her tone.

"Well, that simply raises questions of appearances that would not otherwise be at issue. Certainly, you see that and must understand my reluctance."

"Understand, yes," she said. "Condone it, no. Dr. Watson, I really do not think you are ready for . . ."

"Ready?!" I blurted. "Do you mean to imply that on some evolutionary scale . . ."

"Enough, please." It was Peacham. "That is enough." He was smirking at us and scowling at the same time. "I will not sit here and listen to you two quarrel like children. I suggest that you put aside whatever nattering little differences you may have, real or imagined, and that you do so immediately. Holmes will leave here the day after tomorrow—but only if he is attended by Mrs. Masterson. Are we agreed?"

I nodded, chastened, but not embarrassed.

"Dr. Watson, you will have accommodations prepared for all concerned by then. Mrs. Masterson, you will have your bags and equipment packed and at the ready, and I suggest you put your opinions aside for a time. I will arrange for transport, first for Mr. Holmes, then for you. Are you still at the Langham Hotel?"

"Yes," she said softly.

I could not contain myself. "The Langham?" I blurted in disbelief. "You are staying at the Langham?" This was one of the most elegant and expensive hotels in London. Visiting dignitaries, the socially and culturally prominent, the famous and would-be famous, all stayed in one of the Langham's six hundred fine rooms when they were in the city.

"Dr. Watson, my late husband left me a woman of means. It has been necessary for me these past two weeks to . . ."

I was not certain that I had heard her correctly. "For the past two weeks, you have been staying at the Langham?"

"Why, Doctor," the woman said with a smug smile. "I do believe you are envious."

"Perhaps we should move Holmes into your quarters," I suggested.

"If I thought that it would help Mr. Holmes, I would do so in an instant, but I doubt you can understand that. I must see to my patient now. I believe this discussion is over."

"Quite," I said. She nodded abruptly to Dr. Peacham and left the room as quickly and gracefully as she had entered it.

"Well," Peacham said with an audible sigh, "she certainly does make a lasting impression, doesn't she?"

"Yes," I said. "She does, indeed."

Chapter 7

Mrs. Hudson was thrilled to have Holmes back in Baker Street, despite his woeful condition, and she readily accepted Abigail Masterson as a necessary, albeit somewhat awkward, presence. That awkwardness did not long persist, however. In fact, within a mere matter of days, Mrs. Masterson proved herself to be an unassuming and welcome addition. She ministered to her patient with an admirable single-mindedness, and in moments of respite chose to help Mrs. Hudson with the management of the household, from cooking to laundering and sewing and cleaning. Her amiability was as disarming as it was genuine. I had not for an instant anticipated that she would so easily move between the realm of her profession and the mundane chores necessitated by daily life at 221B. Rather, I had anticipated that Mrs. Masterson might have eschewed any such involvement in the household whatsoever. I have to say that this unexpected facet of her personality, especially in light of her professionalism where Holmes was concerned, lent a unique femininity to her very presence. Our quarters suddenly seemed more like a home than a household.

I felt mollified, and over tea one evening the following week, I took the opportunity to say so. As I poured a cup for her I said, "I misjudged you, Mrs. Masterson, and I am sorry for that. Please overlook our little set-to at the hospital."

She laughed politely. "Oh, it is already forgotten, Doctor. I think it is difficult to take a woman at face value; we're such a conniving lot. But the more truly independent we are, the more difficulties we pose, I think. Be assured that you may take me as you find me. I tend to speak my mind in the same manner in which I am most inclined to live my life: without a 'by your leave,' and without undue regard for the consequences. I confess this often gets me into trouble. I am glad that we seem to have surmounted it."

"More tea," I asked.

She shook her head and smiled.

"Of course not," I said. "I just filled your cup a moment ago, didn't I?"

She laughed, and so did I.

"Forgive me, Mrs. Masterson. When all's said and done, I believe we are getting on splendidly."

"I am relieved, Doctor. Thank you. It is so . . ."

Her words were interrupted by a crash in Holmes' room, followed by the sound of breaking glass and a cry of anguish so piercing that it seemed wrenched from the soul. We reached Holmes' door together. I flung it open and rushing inside found Holmes standing with his back to the shattered window. In his right hand he clutched a piece of window glass, which he was in the process of drawing sharply across the exposed underside of his left wrist, which bloodied immediately. His face was white and haggard, his expression frantic.

Mrs. Masterson screamed, "Mr. Holmes! Stop!"

Holmes looked up at the sound of Mrs. Masterson's voice. I rushed at him before he could rake the vicious edge of the broken glass across his wrist again. I threw him beneath me on the floor and pinned his left arm, a feat that, given Holmes' strength and agility, I knew I could never accomplish outside of these extraordinary circumstances. The piece of glass slipped from his fingers, and his body went limp beneath me. I heard fabric ripping behind me. Anticipating my move, Mrs. Masterson had torn a strip of cloth from Holmes' discarded nightshirt. She handed it to me to use as a tourniquet, for Holmes was exsanguinating rapidly.

As I covered him with the bed blanket, she laid out bandages beside a washbasin that she had already filled with water. I used the tourniquet to staunch the flow of blood, administered a sedative, bathed Holmes' ragged wound and sewed it shut. By the time I had finished applying the bandages, he had slipped into a drugged slumber.

I was exhausted, not so much from the extent of the work in which I had been feverishly engaged, but by the strain of the frenzy itself. I quite forgot myself. "Dear God, Abigail. What do we do now?" I collapsed into the nearest bedroom chair, and no sooner had I finished speaking than I could feel my cheeks color. Mrs. Masterson smiled. "I . . . I'm sorry, Mrs. Masterson. I did not mean to be overly familiar."

"Tut, tut, Doctor. Don't trouble yourself."

"I just did not expect this," I said. "No one ever could have convinced me Holmes would try to take his own life, under any circumstances."

"Don't be unduly alarmed," Mrs. Masterson said. "If he had truly wanted to kill himself, he most assuredly would have done so, and he could have done much more damage to himself than he did. Did you notice how shallow his wound is, and how faltering the single cut that he made? No, Dr. Watson, I think that this may be the worst of it. I judge that he could never bring himself to utter a simple plea for compassionate help and sympathy. Even if he were so inclined, he may not have those words at his command just now. But with this desperate action, he has rather dramatically achieved the same end. Don't you see?"

"You seem so certain of this," I said, half in question. "So we minister to his daily needs and wait. What more is there?"

"Acceptance," Mrs. Masterson said. "We, I, must show him acceptance and reassurance in the most basic of ways. I think that Mr. Holmes is scared, horribly scared, and in a way that perhaps he never has been."

"To be sure, Mrs. Masterson, this murderer is an evil fellow, but we have dealt with such before, and quite handily. Though the way poor Dickie Quinn died was bestial, I don't think Holmes . . ."

"Doctor, I am not talking about horrible crimes or physical danger. I believe that for the first time in his life, Mr. Holmes has come face-to-face with his own humanity and mortality, and therein, his own short-comings. He is, after all, only a human being, a remarkable one to be sure, but only a human being, as Dr. Peacham pointed out.

"Think about it for a moment, Doctor. For all of his life, Mr. Holmes has been a paragon of rational invincibility, a man of reason and reasoned action. But what has happened to him here? He has been taken by surprise, rendered helpless, and then made to suffer the worst physical beating of his life.

"When he is in his most weakened and pitiable state, he is slowly tortured. And at precisely that point at which his mind is screaming for sympathy, for some hint of kindness from his beloved torturer—and that, as perverse as it may seem—is much the way the tortured regard their torturers at some point in the horrible agony—at precisely that point, and only then, does the fiend commit his most gruesome crime, the decapitation of a thirteen-year-old boy.

"And Mr. Holmes is left, in effect, to participate in it all, to be the helpless tortured watcher of this most heinous of crimes. He has never met horror at such depth. He feels he has been reduced to a state of ignorance and uselessness and even—by his inability to act, because he was bound and helpless—a tacit complicity in the crime. The sum of it is this: Never has Sherlock Holmes experienced such complete and utter failure and frustration. And he does not know why it is happening, and this is the greatest insult of all."

"And if we knew why, we would, perhaps, solve the mystery?"

"I think it is likely, Doctor."

"Mrs. Masterson, I am stunned by your grasp of Holmes' circumstance."

"Thank you," she said with a smile that seemed almost demure. "It is what I have trained for."

"Do you have any inkling why this has happened, Mrs. Masterson?"

"I do not. I leave that to you. But I must confess, I am frightened."

"For Holmes?

"I am concerned for him. I feel great . . . compassion. But I am not frightened for him. He will recover from this. We will help him, and in time he will recover."

"Then, what?"

"Doctor, despite all of my studies, my tutelage by Dr. Peacham and my internship in Bedlam, I have never had the merest inkling that such a foully twisted person could exist as this monster you seek.

"But I do not fear him, Doctor. I fear what created him."

Chapter 8

Mrs. Masterson's candid insights only served to deepen my sense of foreboding, which had grown with every day that Holmes and I spent on the St. Marylebone case. At least with her on hand, I was gratefully free to come and go as I wanted, and I made it a point to get out for a brief but leisurely walk every day. As much as anything else, I needed exercise and a way to keep my mind as clear as possible. I wanted to be—presumptuous though it may be to say it—in a state of readiness for whatever perils lay ahead. At night, which is when I prefer to write, I also have been free to continue my narrative of our investigation. . . .

Once we had begun our legwork, it hadn't taken Holmes and me very long to learn a great deal about the murdered Alexander Gibbons. A much different picture of the clothier began to emerge.

It became quickly apparent that the esteem in which Gibbons' customers and competitors held him did not extend to those who knew him better, for example, the clerks who worked at the store. Even those who had been in the man's employ for a number of years described him as a cold person and a taskmaster, as likely to dismiss them for a minor infraction of his numerous rules as he was to closely watch the clock when they took their brief daily lunches. They often mimicked his shrill voice, though never when he was on the premises. It was somewhat more surprising that the disdain in which they held him was rivaled only by their ill will for the youngest of Gibbons' sons, Jamey, and the clerks' dislike of him paled beside the outright contempt in which they held the matriarch of the family, Mary; and this they displayed with a rather careless and brazen openness.

In fact, two of the clerks, Alistair Simmons and Gerald Cooke, flatly opined that it was she who killed their employer. We interviewed the two of them over a quiet round of noontime drinks at Randall's, a pub not far from Bond Street.

The two clerks were so animated that it was scarcely necessary for either Holmes or me to ask a question. It was as if they had been storing up and nurturing their information and just waiting for the opportunity to unleash it, like two washerwomen telling each other tales about their masters' households. We listened attentively and occasionally gave the conversation a nudge in one direction or the other.

"Lord knows, they fought enough, the two of them," said Simmons. "I wouldn't put it much past her. The mister and missus were a pair, they were. He'd never pay their, uhm, marital troubles much heed outwardly. It was important to keep up a proper appearance, especially for a man in his position with the public and all. But a couple of times things boiled over, you might say, right here in the store, and that made him all the angrier.

"She's a regular harpy, that one," Cooke said. "Mrs. high-and-mighty she is. We'd treat her pleasantly, of course, when she came into Gibbons', but she'd just snuff her nose at us, as much as to say, 'How dare you speak to me.' "

"Simmons," Holmes asked, "was it possible to deduce the substance of their arguments?"

"Yes, indeed," he said, "for they got quite agitated usually, and you couldn't help but hear them, even with the door to his office closed. 'Twas usually about money, or so it seemed. She was always wanting more than he was willing to provide her. I've a feeling he kept his family on a pretty tight rein, if you get my meaning, sir."

Cooke chimed in. "Oh, there was no mistaking the substance of their feuding, Mr. Holmes. It was either money, or she'd have some gripe with him over their youngest, Master Jamey."

"A damned dummy, that one," Simmons said.

"And on those occasions involving Master Jamey," Holmes asked, "what was at issue?"

"Why, her coddling him like he was a toddler, instead of treating him like a young man of a score and four years.

" 'You've made him a sissy,' Mr. Gibbons would holler. 'He's not fit for work and he's a spendthrift to boot. He's a simpleton with no prospects, and he does not care, and he'll never have to care, as long as you insist on pampering him the way you do.' "

"She'd come right back at 'im, she would," Cooke said, "just like an alley cat that's been cornered. The missus would call him a lout and an unfeeling miser who cared more for his business than his family. 'He's a sensitive and quiet young man,' she'd holler. 'You've never treated him as anything but an oddity, just because he's different from you.'

" 'A freak he is,' Mr. Gibbons'd say. He really had no use for the twit, Mr. Holmes, and I can't say's I blame him overmuch, even if Master Jamey was his own flesh and blood. There's always been something too quiet and, you might say, kind of, well, even scary about him. And it's got nothing to do with his, uhm, private inclinations, if you get my meaning. We seen him many times wearing powder, like a lady, trying to hide his bad skin. He's a few steps over the effeminate side, you ask me. What a young man does on his own is of no mind to any of us. Wouldn't you say so, Simmons?"

"That's a fact," he said. "You can trace that right back to the missus. He was always with her. You'd never see him with his father, always the missus. When he was just a tyke, she'd bring him by the store and his hair would be all in curls. Cute little thing he was, too. Long black curls. But you couldn't tell him for a little boy if it weren't for his shoes, and even then not for a while, until he got older. And by then wasn't he the quiet one; Cooke is right about that. I don't think I ever heard the boy say more than one sentence at a time, and he didn't always make much sense when he did talk. If you ask me, he's got a hard time puttin' two thoughts together at once."

"What of the other son, Albert?" Holmes asked. "How did he get on with his father?"

"Much better than Jamey, I wager," Cooke said. "Jamey couldn't so much as wait on a customer. Just didn't have a way about him. But Albert was always pretty good in that respect, even if he wasn't the most reliable fellow. You couldn't quite count on him to be on time when he did work at the store, but he's always been bright. And not one to fear a day's labor, either. Light work or heavy, never mattered.

"Truth is, Albert takes a lot of pride in his physical condition. He's a very strong lad, and a quick one. Moves like a cat, he does. I remember one time in the storeroom, he had climbed up on a high rack of heavy wooden shelves to get a box down. He was right up near the ceiling when the shelves started to topple over.

"Most anyone else would have fallen and gotten trapped under the weight of 'em, but not Albert. He sensed what was happening and somehow flicked himself backward off those shelves and landed square on his feet on the other side of the room. He wasn't but a whisker clear when those shelves crashed to the floor. It shook the whole building, it did. He just laughed and dusted himself off, picked up the box he needed and went about his business."

Simmons frowned. "He did not just dust himself off, Gerald. If you remember, Master Albert was peeved at getting dust on his suit, and he wasn't able to brush

it off to his satisfaction. So he changed his whole ward-
robe, and *then* he went back to the customers."

"Very well, Alistair," Cooke said with a sigh of
some forbearance. "Very well, but I really don't think
that matters very much to Mr. Holmes . . ."

"On the contrary," Holmes said patiently. "Sometimes the most trivial of observations proves to be
most useful."

"Now that Simmons brings it up, Mr. Holmes, Albert was very particular about his dress, but he had
to be. You see, besides serving the customers, it was
Albert who dealt with all the other merchants in the
Bond Street Civic Improvement Association. Alexander ran the meetings and was in charge of the business, as it were, but it was Albert who had regular
contact with all the principals. And the day those
shelves fell, he was going to be out making his rounds
with them. So it wouldn't have done for him to look
rumpled up, would it?"

"Well, you ask me," Simmons said, "I'd say young
Albert is more than very particular about his dress,
Gerald. He's meticulous."

"Oh, who gives a farthing, Alistair? Honestly! I
don't see . . ."

"Excuse me, Mr. Cooke," Holmes interjected. "You
said 'regular' contact in reference to Albert's visits to
the members of the association? Meaning weekly or
perhaps monthly?"

Simmons looked at Cooke and rolled his eyes as
discreetly as he could, but I caught the gesture and I
was sure Holmes did, too.

"Uhm, well, whenever necessary," Cooke said. "I'd
have no way to know just how often."

"Why would there be a need for contact beyond a
periodic business meeting?" Holmes asked.

"Oh, I wouldn't know, Mr. Holmes, I'm sure," Cooke
said.

Simmons managed to move us off the subject, but
not very artfully.

"Albert and Mr. Gibbons would argue," Simmons said. "Did we mention that? But it wasn't mean-spirited, if you get my drift. Albert's got a head for business, and his own opinion about how things should be done. That's what they'd argue about, usually. Albert would do something one way, and his father would criticize him for not doing it another. But sometimes Albert would be right, and Mr. Gibbons would know it, and he still wouldn't let on or give in to him. Stubborn as a goat, he was."

"Once Mr. Gibbons got it in his mind that something or somebody was a certain way, there wasn't any changing it," said Cooke. "It was that way forever. That was why everyone, all the clerks, were afraid to make a mistake around him. He'd never put it by. He'd never let you redeem yourself, and we're all of us only human, Mr. Holmes, after all. Isn't that right?"

"That's right, Gerry," said Simmons. "You try to do right by people, and to never speak ill of them. That's what I say. Of course, you have to tell the truth."

"Of course," said Holmes. "You have been most helpful, both of you."

We settled our bill, exchanged pleasantries and left the pub.

"Holmes," I asked once we were alone, "what were they not telling us about the Bond Street Civic Improvement Association?"

"I'm not sure, but I suspect we had best make it our business to find out."

"Well, Holmes," I said, "it seems to me that the sooner we meet Masters Jamey and Albert the better, no?"

"In due time, Watson," he said. "In due time. I have sent Albert a note that should bring him round to our quarters tonight at eight o'clock. After that, we will consider Jamey. Before we do anything, I think we should knock on some Bond Street doors and then we should find it most instructive to visit the late Mr. Gibbons' brothers."

"No one mentioned that he had brothers, Holmes."

"I made a discreet appearance at the funeral and saw them. By the way, I expressed our sincerest condolences to Mrs. Gibbons, and I apologized at length for our untimely but necessary intrusion the other night. It was disingenuous of me, of course, but she seemed somewhat surprised and not altogether displeased—which should help us in the long run. Among the more prominently positioned of the mourners were two men whom I correctly surmised to be Gibbons' brothers, Edward and Sidney. I have arranged for us to meet with them individually.

"Meanwhile, let us brace some of the merchants and hope that we find a cooperative soul."

At G. W. Randall's, a shirtmaker, we asked to speak with the proprietor and were ushered to a sedate and well-furnished office off the main floor at the rear of the establishment, where a well-dressed man rose from his desk chair and greeted us enthusiastically.

"G. W. Randall. How may I help you, gentlemen?"

"I am Sherlock Holmes. This is my friend Dr. John H. Watson. We are assisting the police investigation of Alexander Gibbons' death."

"Oh," he said. "Well, anything that I can do to help, of course. A good man he was. A real leader, and we'll miss him sorely. Why, he was the heart and soul of the very district, and I . . ."

"Excuse me," Holmes said. "Why did you meet with Albert Gibbons every week?"

"I . . . uhm . . . association business, that's all. He would stop in and . . ."

"Every week!?"

"It was good business," Randall said. "That's all it was. Just pleasantry. Now, if you will excuse me, I must . . ."

"How much were you paying him?" Holmes asked.

"I beg your pardon, sir?"

"Your hearing seems fine, Mr. Randall. How much were you paying Albert Gibbons every week?"

"I don't see that any of this has to do with the murder of Mr. Gibbons," Randall said.

"You can speak with us or the police, sir," Holmes said. "Which will it be?"

"If the police have business with me, I am sure they will show up on my doorstep," said Randall, his face slightly colored now, his voice as taut as a bowstring. "Meanwhile, I will thank you to leave my establishment."

"Don't get up," Holmes said, and we walked quickly through the shop and out the front door.

"What do you make of that, Holmes?"

"We're on the right track, old boy. We will just have to wear them down."

"How did you know Albert was collecting money from these people?"

"I didn't, Watson. I was running a gambit, but a well-reasoned one. I could simply think of no cause for anyone to make regular visits to these establishments other than to make a collection. Business, after all, is about the making of money. It seemed a reasonable suspicion. I was simply guessing at the payment interval. Let's try another of these fellows, shall we?"

Our experience at the shop of Oliver Bemis, a milliner, was no more fruitful than the first effort, though the response was not as strident. In his questioning, Holmes seemed to alternate rather disconcertingly between polite, icy calm and heated, rude impatience. I wondered if his differing approaches were calculated or whether they were the result of his being emotionally spent. I know that he felt extraordinary pressure, and it was largely the result of his own expectations of himself and, of course, his fundamental anger over the murders. Regardless, the interview with Bemis did serve to convince us that something was very wrong with the Gibbons family's relationship with the rest of Bond Street.

We were about to enter a dressmaker's shop, when we were stopped in the doorway by a tall, broad-shouldered, barrel-chested man dressed in the royal blue jacket and bowler of the association's servants.

" 'Scuse me, gents," he said. "Might I 'ave a word wi' the two o' you?" He spoke softly but used his immense frame to push us out onto the sidewalk. "Let's us 'ave a quiet talk."

I stumbled backward but regained my balance. Holmes, I could see, took three quick steps backward, opening up a small distance between himself and our antagonist. The man's bulk blocked the walkway and the shop door beyond.

"I say, Robert Bledsoe, isn't it?" Holmes said loudly. "I thought you were still in Dartmoor Prison."

Strollers and shoppers heard the discord, and the effect was immediate. Heads turned. Eyebrows rose and then dropped in disapproving scowls. Eyes glared. Noses snuffed. All seemingly in unison. This was Bond Street, after all. Prim. Proper. Any loud display of ill temper or bad taste stood out as an offensive incongruity. An area cleared around us, and suddenly we were as conspicuous as boxers in a ring. I stood about two paces to Holmes' right. The man who was accosting us was twice Holmes' width, and he loomed over the tall detective by several inches.

"So be it, if you want it right out 'ere, instead of peaceful like. We'll teach you better 'n to go about poking your long noses where they don't belong," the man said. He smiled with a malevolence that made his intention unmistakable. Holmes appeared not the least bit ruffled. He was turned slightly to the side, somewhat in the stance that a duelist assumes in order to present his foe with a smaller target. The detective looked up at the man with a smile so broad that I could see his teeth.

"Royal blue is definitely not your color, Bledsoe," Holmes said, again quite loudly. "Yellow might suit you, though . . . or perhaps pink."

The brute's face darkened at Holmes' use of the word *yellow*, and when the detective spat out "pink," the enraged man ran at him with a bellow.

Holmes sidestepped at the latest possible instant, and in the same motion brought his walking stick up with both hands, catching the man in the throat and stopping him as abruptly as if he had run headlong into the branch of an oak. The lower half of the thug's big body kept moving forward. The back of his head hit the pavement with such a sharp crack that I winced. The man clutched at his throat with both hands and made croaking sounds, but could do nothing but lay where he had fallen.

I caught a fuzzy blur of bright blue to the right, in the periphery of my vision. I spun completely around to face the distraction, and as I did so swung hard with my right fist and caught the assailant full in the mouth with a righteous wallop. One of his front teeth broke against my knuckles, and when I looked at him on the ground, I could see that both lips had been splayed open. Blood poured between the fingers of his left hand, which he had clasped over his mouth.

Just beyond the man, at the edge of the crowd, a matronly woman exclaimed, "Oh! Oh!" and then sagged in a faint onto the sidewalk. Her parasol clattered onto the stones.

I had taken my eyes off my attacker for only an instant, but that was all he needed. Still flat on his back, he hitched toward me and scissored my legs out from under me. The back of my head rapped the pavement hard, and I bit my tongue sharply. Through a field of tiny gold and silver lights that floated in my vision, I saw my attacker rise and leap. He seemed temporarily suspended in the air, almost totally parallel to the ground on which I lay. I rolled quickly to my right, and he landed flat on his face. I got up on all fours, shaking my head, and then forced myself upright before he could regain his breath and stand. By the time he was half up, I was in front of him, my feet planted firmly and squarely. I twisted over and down to my right, brought my right fist almost to the ground and then swung straight up toward the roof-tops of Bond Street with the best uppercut I have ever managed, before or since.

My attacker's jaw clacked shut so hard that the sound must have been audible at the back of the crowd. He jerked sharply backward and fell awkwardly in a heap. The crowd was buzzing and murmuring, and from its far edge I could discern loud voices that rang with authority. "Stand back. Move aside. Stand back. I said move. Now!"

I turned toward Holmes to find him standing off to the side, his arms folded across his chest, nonchalantly taking in the action with a bemused expression on his face. In the street just beyond him, I could see that Bledsoe still lay on the pavement.

"The police are coming, Holmes," I said.

Another tough in a royal blue jacket clasped his hand on Holmes shoulder, but doubled over in pain as Holmes jammed his elbow up into his assailant's solar plexus. Holmes then turned around and grabbed the man's wrist in a baritsu hold I had seen him use several times before and flipped him several feet into the front row of the crowd.

Two men were sent sprawling. One of them got up quickly, and broke his walking stick over the head of another man who had been standing, quite innocently, nearby. The tough in the blue jacket kicked him and sent the long stub of the cane flying. It hit a woman behind him in the head, and knocked her beribboned hat to the ground. Her husband flew into a rage and came at the bruiser with both arms flailing.

The blue coat swatted him aside only to be tackled by the man's wife. She had retrieved her hat, pulled a long pin from it and jabbed the brute hard in the thigh as she fell on top of him.

He screamed and cursed and kicked at the woman. His boot caught her in the shoulder. She let out a shrill yelp, and two men from the throng ran at him in retaliation.

From that point on, it was a full-blown melee.

We stood quietly at the edge of the fray, until Holmes looked at me and said with an expression of the utmost gravity, "These people are ruffians, Watson. It is not good for my image to be seen among them."

"You are right," I said with equal seriousness. "I believe it's time we left them to their own churlish devices."

"Good idea," he said. He nodded his head to the front door of the shop.

I looked down at the insensate hulk who lay sprawled at the foot of the steps. "After you," I said to Holmes. I gave him a courtly bow and with a flourishing sweep of my arm motioned him toward the open doorway.

He planted his foot squarely on the fallen man's stomach and then stepped up the short flight of steps. The man roared in pain as I leaped over him and up the steps. I could hear the police behind me, louder now because they had worked their way to within a few rows of the front of the crowd, but they seemed to have been stopped there by the pandemonium that had erupted.

The crowd and the approaching police were blocking our escape, so we entered the dressmaker's shop and moved quickly to the rear of the establishment. The back door was blocked by an elegant woman in a lavender dress. Her feet were spread apart, so that she presented herself as a quite formidable obstacle. She had folded her arms beneath her bosom, which had the effect of somewhat elevating and emphasizing her already ample endowment. She looked at us with a dark and deep frown, but her eyes fairly twinkled, and there was a contradictory, bemused expression on her lips.

"Something in formal wear, perhaps?" she offered.

We couldn't help but laugh, and she did, too. Then she spoke quickly.

"The door behind me opens onto the alley," she said quickly. "Go to the end, take one left and a right, and you're away from Bond Street. If you return in two hours, I will tell you what you want to know."

"And you are . . . ?" asked Holmes.

"Very attractive, don't you think?"

"Indeed," said Holmes.

"Flatterer! I am Madeleine Toussaint.

"Go. Go. Come back by way of this door. Out! Shoo!"

Two minutes later Holmes and I were calmly walking toward Piccadilly as though we owned the day.

"I could do with some lunch, Holmes," I said.

"Good," he replied, and we spent the next ninety minutes over well-deserved steak and kidney pie and a bottle of Tokay.

Given his expert use of the walking stick and his knowledge of baritsu, Holmes didn't have so much as a scratch on him from the morning's tussle. But I had reason to feel weary. My back was bruised from my having landed sharply on the pavement, and the knuckles of my right hand ached from the blow I had delivered.

"I'm getting too old for this business, Holmes," I said.

"Nonsense, Watson. That was as glorious an uppercut as I have ever seen."

"It was, wasn't it?" I replied. It felt good to laugh.

Chapter 9

Precisely two hours after we had left the dressmaker's, we were back at the rear of the shop. I knocked three times, and Mme. Madeleine Toussaint opened the door.

"Come in," she said. "My office, please." Mme. Toussaint gestured to another doorway and called to her clerk at the front of the store.

"Marie, I am not to be disturbed."

"Oui, madame. Très bien," came the reply.

"Sit down, gentlemen. Sit down. Your activities this morning will have marred the public image of Bond Street by the time it's reported in the press. Whatever will the shopping public think? Tssk. Tssk."

"We are assisting in the investigation of Alexander . . ."

"I know all of that," Mme. Toussaint interrupted. "By the time you had made your second stop, Mr. Holmes . . . Dr. Watson . . . George Winston Randall had sent a runner out to all of the merchants warning that you were asking questions about the association. How naughty of you boys. Randall is such a sheep. He makes me ill."

"Madame, you seem to enjoy driving directly to the heart of things," Holmes said, "so let us stop the banter, shall we? Was Albert Gibbons collecting money from all of the Bond Street merchants every week?"

"Not all. I was not among them."

"Why?"

"I refused to pay him a penny."

"There were no repercussions?"

"I paid him in another way," the woman said. "Every week." She paused but looked directly at us. She did not blush. She spoke softly, but clearly and without apology. "I was not always a seamstress, gentlemen."

I was a bit startled, but I rather liked the woman for her unabashed candor. Holmes kept up the pace.

"Madame, how much money was being paid every week?"

"There is no way for me to know, honestly. But it was a great deal of money. The association that Albert's father formed charged everyone on the street three percent of their gross sales every week. The money is used to pay the blue coats' wages, livery services, and external shop improvements. There are, at last count, some thirty businesses in the association, and they do very well, as you can imagine.

"About two years ago, Albert took over the collections for the association, and he told each of us that he was levying a one percent surcharge, but that if word got back to his father, there would be trouble. One of the boot makers on the street, Hubert Jackson, told him to go to blazes. He said he would not pay Albert so much as a shilling more than was already due. Three days later, Mr. Holmes, poor Hubert was visited by that oaf you tangled with this morning: Bledsoe. He broke Hubert's thumbs. The man couldn't work for weeks, and he's still not right. But he's been paying the surcharge ever since. So have all of the others."

"So you believe that Alexander Gibbons knew nothing of the additional sums that his son was collecting?"

"I am sure of it," she said. "Albert always boasted that the old man had no idea what was going on. Alexander Gibbons believed that the increasing subservience the merchants showed him was simply a mark of his effective leadership. Albert was laughing at him behind his back. It was as though it were some sort of game that he liked playing."

"And what would become of this extra money Albert collected? Do you know?"

"He handed it over to his mother. I know not for what purpose, especially since Alexander seems to have always delighted in keeping her on a short leash."

"Madame Toussaint, may I ask why you have confided all this to us," Holmes asked.

"I am no saint, sir, but I am not a bad person, and most of these merchants are not, either. It is time someone found the wherewithal to speak up. Albert Gibbons is a bastard and a cruel young man. Mind, you watch your step with him, both of you. He's as quick as a snake, and a real hand with a pistol. I know; I've seen him use it. I want nothing more to do with him. With his father dead, there's nothing to hold him back. I am afraid. It is as simple as that, gentlemen."

She stood and so did we.

"It has been a distinct pleasure, Madame Madeleine Toussaint," said Holmes. He took her left hand in his, raised it toward his lips and, bowing slightly, kissed it.

She smiled demurely and averted her eyes.

"Good day, madame," I said, and we left by the back door for the second time that day.

Chapter 10

It was past mid-afternoon at this point, and I was already looking forward to the quiet comfort of our Baker Street lodgings. Holmes, however, insisted that we keep to his original plan for the interviews.

"We should just be in time to meet with Edward Gibbons if we move along," he said.

We walked briskly down the Strand to Pennington Lane and into the offices of Edward Gibbons, Solicitor. He received us at once. Gibbons was a short, bald impeccably dressed man of slight build, with silver-framed pince-nez perched on his nose. He tilted his head back so as to look through the glasses directly up at the detective, but said nothing.

He walked behind his desk and sat down. "I do not mean to be rude, Mr. Holmes, but I haven't much time, so please come straight to the point."

"I usually do," said Holmes. "Who had reason to kill your elder brother?"

"Any number of people, I should say. Alexander was a respected businessman, but he was not well liked, as you may already have surmised from the absence of tears at his services yesterday. He was a bully, Mr. Holmes, in his professional life and his personal life, though he generally managed to keep his true temperament hidden from public view. We parted company long ago."

"Who stood to gain from his demise?" Holmes asked.

"Only his son, Albert, and vicariously, of course, his

widow, my sister-in-law, and Albert's brother, Jamey. Though, I expect his widow will be somewhat surprised," Gibbons said.

"How so?" Holmes asked.

"Despite appearances, my brother did not leave much of an estate. I am the executor of Alexander's will, and I can tell you that while my nephew will assume ownership of the family home on Upper Wimpole, there will be no windfall of cash. When Alexander's debts are settled, he will have appreciably less than £1,000, £937 to be exact. Undoubtedly this will seem like a lot of money to Mary and probably to Jamey, though I doubt he could even count that high, but it will not be nearly enough to provide them with the luxuries and conveniences which my sister-in-law believes should be hers.

"Alexander was penurious by nature. He allowed her few trinkets and almost no spending money. She had to ask for whatever he gave her every week, and she was forced to sign a receipt for it. Can you imagine, Mr. Holmes? A receipt! She had to justify every expenditure, every purchase. His own wife! But then, there was no love between them, at least not in recent memory. Who knows what passes for normalcy in the private life of a man and woman, hey, Mr. Holmes?

"Had the store not been burned flat, they could expect to make a livelihood there. I daresay that Albert could have maintained the trade and enjoyed an income good enough to support them all, and that wastrel, Jamey, too. If he is smart, Albert will rebuild Gibbons' Gentleman's Apparel and have a go at it, but that remains to be seen, doesn't it?"

"Why would the family not rebuild?" Holmes asked.

"They all hated the store," Gibbons said, "absolutely detested the business. To Mrs. Gibbons and son Albert, it represented constant work and a preoccupation with service that they always seemed to think was beneath them.

"Jamey hated the place as well, though for entirely different reasons. He simply is not bright, Mr. Holmes, not by half, and it holds no clear future for him."

"Then, it would seem the Gibbons' best interests would have been served by Alexander Gibbons' longevity," I interjected.

"Precisely," said the lawyer.

"Tell me about Mrs. Gibbons, please."

The lawyer sneered. "Irish," he said. "What more is there to say?"

Holmes bristled. "That remark tells me nothing, sir . . . about her," he said.

The lawyer frowned. "I see," he said. "Very well. Her maiden name is McCormick. Put her age at about fifty-seven, though she certainly doesn't look it. She married *up*, as the expression goes. She fled her own kind after the famine. Somehow got to Liverpool as a youngster. She ended up in an orphanage, St. Celia's or something like that. She's a Catholic, naturally. When she was old enough, she managed to get herself taken on as a servant by a good family in Birmingham."

"The name?"

"James. Lord Cecil and the Lady Elizabeth James. Lord Cecil died four years ago, but I believe Lady Elizabeth is still holding her own. Wonderful woman, that, despite her rather unconventional views. It was by association with the James family, actually, that Mary McCormick met Alexander. She had accompanied Lady Elizabeth on a shopping trip to London. They were in the clothing store, and Alexander, just a young man then and working for our father, happened to serve them.

"He was smitten. She responded. One thing led to another, and before you know it, they were engaged. I advised him to break it off, I don't mind saying, and many's a time in the years that followed I am certain that he wished he had heeded my counsel.

"I didn't like her then, Mr. Holmes, and I do not like her now. I would be lying if I pretended otherwise . . ."

and no, not simply because she is Irish and a Catholic, although in most quarters that is reason enough.

"She had a temper, undoubtedly still does, a vicious streak, it seemed to me. Never knew her place, and I thought she was an opportunist."

"I appreciate your candor, Mr. Gibbons," Holmes said. "One last question, please. You spoke earlier of Mary and Jamey Gibbons as profiting 'vicariously' from Alexander's death. Are they not to receive any direct recompense?"

"No, sir. Some little time ago, Alexander took their names out of his will altogether. His entire estate goes to son Albert. I do not quite know why, but it was not my place to ask. All that I cared to know was that it was my brother's wish, clearly expressed, duly recorded."

Holmes stood and thanked the lawyer for his time. "Mr. Gibbons," he asked, "are you at all familiar with the workings of the Bond Street Civic Improvement Association? Or with Albert's relationship with its members?"

"No, I am not," he said. "It has never been brought up in any discussion to which I've been a party. I would remember." He paused, then said to Holmes, "I do hope your inquiries are successful. Even my brother did not deserve so foul a death."

Holmes nodded and pursed his lips quickly in the faintest of acknowledging smiles, and we took our leave.

Chapter 11

Holmes and I boarded a train for Birmingham and settled into our compartment for what I hoped would be a quiet, albeit brief, trip and a chance to nap before confronting Lady Elizabeth James. By most accounts she would be in her mid-eighties now, probably a doddering, dithering old woman, and I did not relish the prospect of listening to her recount the long-ago days in which Mary McCormick was a servant in her home.

We hired a hansom cab at Birmingham Station and thirty minutes later rode up the long set-stone driveway, past the manicured lawns and formal gardens of Breckinridge. The lawns were broad and lush and girded by precisely trimmed hedges of yew. Immense beech trees flanked the manor, but they were dwarfed by Breckinridge itself. The main three-story wing of the light gray stone manor sprawled across the top of a knoll. Sun was burning off the day's haze, which gave the air a lemon-yellow hue and turned the leafless trees into tall and wide silhouettes of lace.

We knocked at the huge front doors of Breckinridge and were admitted by a liveried servant with a pointed nose that seemed permanently trained at a point about thirty degrees above horizontal. He spoke in syllables that were as tightly clipped as the manor's hedges.

"Madame is napping in the sunroom," he said. "I will see if she will receive you."

A moment later he escorted us across the main floor and into a glass-walled room in the south wing. Lady

Elizabeth James sat in an overstuffed chair near the wall, a shawl covering her shoulders, a lap robe draped over her legs.

My misgivings quickly proved baseless. Lady Elizabeth appeared frail, but her blue eyes were bright and alert, her voice strong and clear, and her face rosy. It occurred to me that by the time we are old our faces often have become mirrors of the lives we have led, and I was buoyed by the fact that Lady Elizabeth's face in old age was that of a wizened cherub.

"Good afternoon, gentlemen. I don't get many visitors these days, and I'm always thankful for the company. Do sit down. Please."

She turned to a maid who had been seated nearby and said, "Genevieve, bring us some tea, won't you?"

The servant disappeared quickly.

"I am honored to have two such distinguished guests," she said. "How may I help you?"

"You are most gracious, Lady James," Holmes said. "We are investigating the murders in St. Marylebone that you may have read about."

"Oh, yes. Terrible business. Terrible. I suppose you are curious about Mary Gibbons?"

"Why, yes," Holmes said.

"Oh, you needn't seem surprised. I expected that someone from Scotland Yard would have approached me by now. If Cecil were still alive, God rest his soul, he would have called on the Yard himself. I don't get around much myself anymore. You can understand."

"Of course," Holmes said. "Tell us about Mary McCormick Gibbons, if you would."

"I had need for a personal servant in those days, and having never been blessed with children of my own, I thought it might be nice if I could provide a home for a young girl as well. Cecil agreed most heartily, so we took her in. Right out of the orphanage, she was.

"We knew she was Irish and Catholic, too, but it did not matter to us. In fact, if I am to be perfectly candid, gentlemen, we, Cecil and I and a goodly number of our friends in Parliament, in fact, felt so terrible about the manner in which this country treated its Irish subjects back in the '40's that our taking in an Irish girl was a quiet way of trying to show compassion. I suppose, in our own way, we were asking the Lord's forgiveness.

"Such abject misery and privation those poor people endured, and we sat back and debated and debated and preached self-sufficiency all the while. For all the good that we did, we might as well have had a direct hand in creating the whole tragic affair."

Lady Elizabeth suddenly rose from her chair, as if upset, the lap robe falling to the floor. Holmes and I got to our feet.

"Oh, do sit, gentlemen," she said. "It bothers me to recall all of this, and these old bones stiffen up a bit from sitting, so if you don't mind, I'd just as soon walk about a little."

She held her saucer in her left hand, and used her right to raise her teacup to her lips occasionally.

"I don't mean to lecture, but you have to understand how pitifully the Irish suffered. It is quite literally unimaginable. A million and a half people died of starvation and cholera and dysentery and typhus. Awful. Perfectly awful. And another million left their homeland. They are leaving still, fleeing to the corners of the globe in search of what? Only a decent life. A job. And England just let it happen. Oh, it makes me so ashamed. I do not believe the Irish will ever forgive us for what we did, and frankly, I see no reason that they should, save God's own good grace and in His time.

"I am sure that you already know much of the history, so forgive me if I ramble on a bit. Perhaps it's the lack of company. But I do get upset about it, even now. Dear me. Well, be that as it may, Mary McCormick was the prettiest and sharpest young thing you can imagine. It was our intention that if we took to her and she to us, well, after a time, perhaps we would adopt her. But it was not to be."

"She did not get on well here?" Holmes asked. "It is such a lovely home."

"Thank you, Mr. Holmes. And Breckinridge in those years was a glorious hubbub of activity. A month didn't go by but what we had guests with us, and friends and relatives all coming and going. And the holidays! Good Lord, what feasts we had. It was a busy, happy place.

"Mary got along well enough, but she was never outgoing, no matter what we did or what was going on. We tried to include her in our activities. I took her to London with me often. Shopping. Dining. The theater. Cecil and I did everything possible to make her feel as though she belonged here.

"But she never let her guard down, you might say. She was always very reserved, too reserved, as though she did not, or rather could not, enjoy herself or warm to other people in more than a fleeting way.

"I came to understand, after a time, that it was not us in particular whom she could not abide. It was the English in general, you see, though she would never say so. She would discuss her childhood in Ireland during the famine rather freely, but never would she discuss how it had affected her or her view of the world in which she was then living. It was as though her childhood was an isolated segment of her life, and she would prefer the world to see it as completely unrelated to the young woman she had become.

"We know, gentlemen, that people are infinitely more complicated than that, of course. So let me see . . .

"She was the youngest child in a family of eight. They were tenant farmers in a small town somewhere on the west coast of Ireland. I don't believe that I ever knew the town.

"When the potato crop failed, the McCormicks had no way to pay their rent. They were put out, just like

thousands upon thousands of others. Agents of the
landlord came to the McCormicks' cottage one wet
October morning, pulled them all out into the street
and then tumbled the house into rubble while they
watched.

"They lost what little they had. They were reduced
to begging for work and sleeping in workhouse wards
that were so crowded they had to share lice-infested
beds with all manner of strangers.

"Young children, sirs! Can you imagine? They
barely survived the first season of famine. They lived
on turnip and Indian corn and scraps. Tens of thousands of people died in their county alone. When the
blight claimed the potato crop the second time, that's
when Mary McCormick lost her family. They had
moved out of the workhouse and wandered into the
countryside, begging for food and work. They found
an abandoned pig shed—nothing more than a sty,
mind you—but it had a roof, so they spent their
nights there.

"Mary's father contracted cholera and died. Less
than one month later, her mother failed. Misery,
heartbreak, dysentery and starvation; sitting by helpless while her children wasted away day by day into
pallid, walking little corpses. It would be enough to
drive anyone starkers. And that is precisely what happened. She went insane.

"Mary and her brother, Michael, who was a year
older, left the hovel one morning. They were the only
ones in the family who could still get about, so they
went out to beg for food.

"They came back at nightfall, Mr. Holmes, to find
everyone dead. Rather than continue to watch the
children suffer, her mother had killed all of them. She
cut their throats while they slept, and then she killed
herself.

"Mary McCormick and her brother dragged the
pitiful bodies of their mother and brothers and sisters
into a pile in the center of the shack and covered them

with dry straw and thatch and tinder and set them afire. They went outside and set fire to the shed, and then they stood back in the darkness and watched until the incineration was complete.

"Michael was crying his heart out the whole time, but his little sister, our Mary, didn't shed a tear. 'Not a one,' she said. 'There was nothing left inside me.'

"It turned my blood cold in my veins to think that a child so young could have been laid so low that early in life.

"The Quaker relief workers took the two McCormick children in for a time, may the Lord bless them always. Mary came to England alone. She said Michael did not want her to leave. They exchanged harsh words over the matter, but he stayed behind.

"That is all I can tell you, gentlemen. It is all I know, really. Except that it was readily apparent that Mary McCormick never got over what happened to her family. And after all of the time she was with us, three years I'd say, I don't believe her hatred of all things British had diminished one iota."

"One might ask why Mary McCormick married an Englishman," Holmes said, "and why she lives in this country still."

"One might at that," Lady Elizabeth said. "One just might."

Chapter 12

We headed off to our next interview, a meeting with Sidney Gibbons, owner of Sidney Gibbons, Chemist, on Regent Street. We chose to walk to Gibbons' shop from Paddington Station. I was fond of its ornate vaulted ceilings and cavernous reaches, but as was so in most of the city's stations, the noise from the trains always was jarring. It alternated from the loud rhythmic thrum and clatter of massive iron wheels rolling along steel rails, to the screech and spark and squeal of metal braking on metal. Smoke spewed constantly from the trains' stacks, and it became a dense blue-gray fog that reddened the eyes, made them water and forced many travelers to hold their handkerchiefs over their mouths and noses while scurrying for daylight.

The sun was out, and though the air had a bite, it was clearer for that and refreshing as well. Nonetheless, as the shop was some distance off, I was still chilled by the time we reached our destination.

Sidney Gibbons had the same unfortunate ears as his late brother, but the resemblance between the clothier and the chemist ended there. Sidney was short, lean and stoop-shouldered, with slicked-down white hair, bushy darkening eyebrows and strikingly bright blue eyes. He began talking the moment we walked in, and never stopped. There was something oddly familiar about him, but I could not place it immediately.

"Ah, Mr. Holmes. You're eleven minutes early. No

mind. No mind, at all. And this must be Dr. Watson. Yes. I read all of your accounts, Doctor. Quite good. Quite good, indeed. I particularly enjoyed *A Study in Scarlet*, Doctor. That was the very first, eh? *Beeton's Christmas Annual* of '87. Right? I'm sure of it. Perhaps you'll be writing about this case, soon. I suppose you want to know more about my older brother, yes? Well, he wasn't much good, and it pains me to say so. Never was. He just hid it well, except to his immediate kin, and if you ask me, they were worse. We hadn't spoken for years, the lot of us, until Alexander's funeral, and we didn't have much to say then. Lazy and self-indulgent. Albert's the only exception. Only problem with Albert is, he's quick-tempered. Headstrong. But that comes with youth, doesn't it? Yes, it does. Of course, it does. I was much the same way, I was, when I was his age. Albert. He comes around now and then, and we visit and talk about one thing or another. Never says much about his parents or his brother.

"I feel for Albert, I do. He's in a hard spot in some respects. He's learned the clothing business from his father, God rest his soul, but his heart's not in it. Says he's got no feel for yard goods. Oh, he knows style and fashion and all, but he knows he doesn't have his father's eye for the raw material, and he dislikes the clientele with their superior air. There's them that thinks money and class is the same thing, Mr. Holmes, and we both know that's not the case, eh?

"But brash as he is, Albert's a gentleman. He keeps his own counsel, and he won't speak ill of his family under any circumstances. What Albert'd like to do, he'd like to strike out on his own, in his own business, and I don't doubt he could make . . ."

"Excuse me," Holmes said, "but was Nigel Whitney your brother?" I looked at Holmes, startled, and then I realized at once that he was right: The white hair, eyebrows, protruding ears and bright-blue eyes all conjured up the visage of the murdered tobacconist.

Even the two men's speech patterns were alike. I felt a fool for not noticing the similarities sooner.

"Why, yes," Gibbons said, and for the first time since we had entered the store, he seemed at a loss for words. "He was my brother. Terrible loss, that. Nigel and I were always close. We were born just a year apart. He never used his proper surname, not since '61, when he had the falling out with our father. The old man beat him senseless with a cane and near killed him. Left him with that gimpy leg, he did. The old man never talked about it, but neither father nor son would have anything to do with each other from that day forward. Nigel never spoke of it, either. To this day, I don't know what brought it down to that; such a terrible beating. It was shortly after that Nigel dropped the Gibbons name. Used 'Whitney,' just because he liked the sound of it. He did all right for himself, though. More than all right. Nigel made his money quick in the tobacco business. He always said there's more money to be made in catering to people's wants than to their needs, and tobacco was something they always wanted. Well, he was right. That little shop didn't look like much from the outside, but I'll tell you, my brother was well-off, and he had been for years when he died."

"And his estate?" Holmes asked.

"Well, my share was £20,000, Mr. Holmes. I don't mind telling you it brings a lump to my throat just to think of it, Nigel's gift from the grave. I'd told him he didn't have to do that, you know? I'd rather he were still about." Sidney Gibbons' voice cracked a bit and his eyes teared up. He excused himself and blew his nose into a handkerchief he pulled from his coat pocket.

"Are you going to find the animal who killed old Nige, Mr. Holmes? I hope that when you do, you'll carve . . ."

"We are doing everything we can," Holmes said. "Rest assured. You said 'your' share of Nigel Whitney's estate. Who else received a share, Mr. Gibbons, if I may ask."

"Certainly, you may," he said. "And if I knew I'd be more than happy to tell you, but I don't. I figure it's none of my business, though between us, I can't help but wondering, you know? I had asked Edward on three occasions; but he always refused to say. He's a lawyer, and he can be high-and-mighty about the private nature of his dealings with clients."

"Your brother was the executor of Nigel Whitney's estate?" Holmes asked, his voice rising with incredulity.

"Why, yes," Gibbons said. "If your brother were a solicitor, and a good one at that, Mr. Holmes, why would you go outside the family when you needed a legal service?"

"Of course. I should have realized it immediately. Mr. Gibbons, have the inheritances been dispensed?"

"Late yesterday, Mr. Holmes, as soon as possible after the funeral, which is the way Nigel had wanted it. Edward brought me the bank draft first thing in the morning."

"Watson, we must leave at once. You have been most helpful, Mr. Gibbons. Excuse us, please. We haven't a moment to lose."

Holmes was out the door and into the street waving for a hansom cab so quickly that I banged into the shop's front door trying to stay up with him.

"Watson, quickly. Quickly! We may already be too late."

"Where are we going, Holmes?"

He gave the driver the address and promised him a guinea if he got there in a hurry. "Right you are, guv," the driver said, and cracked his buggy whip so sharply that it was still ringing in my ears when I fell backward into the seat.

Across from me, Holmes sat thin-lipped and angry, his teeth clenched. He whipped the head of his walking stick up against the roof three times, shouting, "Hurry, driver! Hurry!" I doubt the hostler could hear him, though he must have discerned the thumping from within the cab, because the whip cracked again and we picked up speed at once.

The iron-rimmed wheels clacked on the uneven stone paving blocks of the road, and the horse's hooves clomped sharply in concert. The cab tipped first to one side as we rounded a corner, then lurched to the other and finally straightened out. We narrowly missed an oncoming hansom. A passenger in the other cab glared at us as we whizzed by, and its driver cursed us roundly.

"Eeeyah!" our driver shouted, and he cracked his buggy whip again. As the cab skidded and slid around another corner, Holmes reached into his pocket for the fare and gratuity, and gave it to me. He threw open the door of the cab and jumped to the pavement before the vehicle stopped. I paid the driver, and hurried up the steps and through the door to Edward Gibbons' offices. Holmes had flung the door open wide and raced inside to the solicitor's rooms.

Gibbons' door was ajar. A rope was tied around the exterior handle, and it ran up over the top of the door. I pushed it open farther and stepped inside to find Holmes staring at me.

"We are too late, Watson." He pointed his cane toward my feet. I looked down and found that I was standing on a blood-soaked carpet.

"Oh, no," I moaned.

I blanched at the sight of Edward Gibbons' corpse. His wounds were ghastly, and he had been trussed up against the back of the door.

I turned to Holmes, who was standing stock-still looking down at the top of Gibbons' broad desk. The lawyer's waistcoat had been folded into a neat square and placed on the corner of the desktop. In the center of the coat rested Gibbons' eyeglasses.

The detective turned to me and said quietly, "John, please get Lestrade; Gregson, too."

As startled as I was by the unexpected sight of a

third corpse, I was positively stunned by Holmes' use
of my first name; he had never spoken it exclusive of
the last. Never; any more than I had ever called him
Sherlock. As I hurried out the door, I realized that
Holmes, at least for the moment, had been left bit-
terly unstrung.

I knew that in my brief absence, he would comb
the office and examine the corpse for clues to the
killer's identity. But for the first time, I began to worry
how long he could continue on the case without respite. I was so enrapt in my thoughts that I barely
noticed snow had begun falling, quickly and heavily.
This is London, I said to myself. It rarely snows in
London. Good Lord, what next?

Chapter 13

It was 8 P.M. by the time Holmes and I returned to Baker Street, our faces bitten red by the wind, our clothes covered with snow. I marveled at the bright white cloak that had begun to mask the grime of the city. Holmes said nothing. When we were embroiled in matters such as these, he remained focused only on factors that affected the case; his concentration and intense preoccupation left no room for attention to the vagaries of the seasons. Good weather had no salutary effect on him at such times, and bad weather was merely a nuisance.

Mrs. Hudson had prepared dinner for us. We ate in silence, poured ourselves brandies and retired to the parlor. Holmes poked at the fire absently, while I peered out the window at the mounting snow. The detective's discouragement was evident. He was tired and even more peevish than he had been an evening earlier. I repeated my admonition.

"You cannot blame yourself, old man," I told him again. "We're doing everything that is humanly possible."

"And it is not enough," he said, stabbing the coals. "Not nearly enough. We have three murders on our hands.

"While you were summoning Lestrade and Gregson, I used the opportunity to sift through Edward Gibbons' files. Nigel Whitney's will is missing, Watson. And there is no record involving anyone in the entire Gibbons family, not even so much as a ledger entry.

To speak plainly, I half expected that would be the case. Were I the killer, I would be making the same efforts to hide my footprints.

"I also examined Gibbons' office more closely. I very nearly missed finding another gouge in the floor, precisely like the one we found in Nigel Whitney's tobacco shop. The gouge had been made right through the thick carpet. The pile of the rug closed over the mark and concealed it."

"Ah," I said, "the same weapon that was used to kill the tobacconist, then."

"A reasonable presumption, yes," he said. "But in Alexander Gibbons' murder . . ." He was interrupted by two sharp raps on the outer door.

"Aha," the detective said, "that should be Albert Gibbons. I am hoping that a discussion with him will shed some light. I published a message to him in the agony columns of yesterday's papers. I had expected to see him at our door by now. I said eight o'clock. He is already fifteen minutes late; inexcusable."

"But aren't the police looking for him?" I asked.

I heard Mrs. Hudson let the visitor in, and I immediately recognized the voice of Dickie Quinn, one of the street Arabs whom Holmes had befriended and often used for errands.

"I got a message for Mister 'Omes," he said to Mrs. Hudson.

"Here, I'll take it to him."

"Beggin' your pardon, ma'am. I'm to put it in his hand straight away, I am."

"Very well," she said.

Dickie marched into our rooms and handed Holmes a folded piece of paper.

"Thank you, Dickie," Holmes said. "Who gave this to you?"

" 'E din't tell me 'is name, sir. Just asked, could I get this to you, and 'e give me 'half a crown to do it."

"What did he look like, Dickie?"

"Black hair cut short. Dark eyes, an' his face was a

mite funny-looking. 'E looked like some stage actor, ya ask me."

"An actor? What do you mean?"

"Aye, Mr. 'Omes. 'E didn't look quite real. His face, if you know what I mean. It was like he had stuff on it, paint like."

"Greasepaint, Holmes?" I asked. "Is that what he's talking about?"

He disregarded my question, gave Quinn some coins and the boy scampered back out into the storm. Holmes read the note, abruptly crumpled it up and threw it onto the livid coals of the hearth, where it burned to a charred wisp instantly.

"Albert Gibbons will not be joining us tonight, Watson. I am very tired. I think I will turn in."

I bade Holmes good night, but as I turned back to the window and stared into the swirling snow, I couldn't help but wonder why he hadn't related to me the contents of the note.

Chapter 14

Over and over I have thought about the visit from Dickie Quinn, the note from Albert Gibbons and the scene in our rooms that night, for that was the last time I saw Holmes before he was so viciously attacked. More than once, I wished that I had questioned him about the note, and about whether Gibbons gave a reason for not keeping the appointment at Baker Street. But I knew Holmes, and I knew his idiosyncrasies. And in my experience, when he did not volunteer information it was either because the information he had was of no consequence or he had good reason for keeping his own counsel.

Still, I could not help but wonder if by knowing more about the case, I might have been able to prevent the attack, or at least spent my time more productively these past many weeks in which the detective has been recuperating.

The newspapers had pounced on the murder of Edward Gibbons, immediately declaring that with the slaying of the two brothers, it had become apparent that the merchant family had been targeted for mayhem. The killing of Nigel Whitney, while always mentioned in the Marylebone stories, seemed to decline in importance, presumably because it could not be fit conventiently into the notion of family murder. I suspected that it would not be long before reporters learned that Whitney's real last name had been Gibbons, but by mid-March that had not happened, and without additional murders, public interest in the case had subsided somewhat.

Meanwhile, the progress of our investigation had slowed to such a point that it rivaled Holmes' recovery. There had been no sign of either Albert or Jamey Gibbons since the funeral of their father in January, and much to Lestrade's displeasure, their mother had been most uncooperative. The inspector had pressed her about her youngest son's being "away," as she put it the night of the murder, and she finally allowed that he was visiting relatives in Blackpool. Lestrade cabled the household there with notice that at Jamey's earliest convenience, he wished to discuss the circumstances of Alexander Gibbons' death. There was no reply. The police searched assiduously for both young men, but the effort was no more productive than Lestrade's questioning of Mrs. Gibbons.

"Albert and I argued vehemently, Inspector, and he left," Mrs. Gibbons told him. "I do not know his whereabouts. I presume he returned to his flat. I gave you the address before: Harley Street, number 341, just off Cavendish Square. Albert is old enough to take care of himself." No, she told Lestrade, she would not discuss the nature of their argument. "It is none of your business, sir. It is a private matter and has no possible bearing on anything of interest to you and your kind."

Lestrade protested that he would be the judge of that, but she was adamant.

"It is more than a mite suspicious that neither of your sons can be located," the inspector told her. "Much too convenient, I would say, and I want you to know, Mrs. Gibbons, that should they, at some point in the future, be found complicit in any of this business, I will see to it that it goes hard on you for protecting them."

The woman merely clenched her teeth and glared at the policeman. She seemed to realize there was little he could do without evidence that made her or her sons clear suspects in the death of her husband.

"I think," Lestrade told me later, "that we are reduced to waiting for something else to happen."

We didn't have to wait long. A day later, a shirtmaker on Bond Street named Neville Rolfe became the fourth man to die. He was fifty-four, bald, short, thin as a needle and widely regarded as a fine shirtmaker. The man's sister, Alice Felson, who worked for him as a tailor, found him laid out on a fabric-cutting table in the rear of the shop shortly after opening for business. He had been carved up in much the same manner as his predecessors, but the characteristic mortal chest wound was different; it was deadly, without a doubt, but not as deep and bruising as the others had been. When the victim was discovered, his wounds were still fresh, and livor mortis had not yet set in. It was obvious that he had been slain only scant minutes before his sister discovered the body.

Lestrade and I were of the opinion that all four murders shared enough similarities to warrant our belief that all of the deaths were related and, most likely, the work of one person, who may or may not have had a partner.

The newspapers' hunger for fresh news of the Monster of St. Marylebone was made obvious by the speed and ferocity with which it leaped on Rolfe's death. The headlines were positively lurid: "Monster claims fourth victim"; "Savage slaying makes it four in St. Marylebone," and "Horror revisits Bond Street."

Unlike the other murders, however, this one had a witness, or very nearly so, a young street sweeper named Victor Kerr. He told police that shortly before 8 A.M., when many of the businesses opened for the day, he saw someone hurry out from behind Rolfe's shop, turn sharply down Bond Street and run quickly off. Kerr didn't get a good look at the suspect, however. " 'E 'ad a proper cape drawed about 'im," the boy said. " 'At's why I give him notice right from the start, I did. A full black cape, it was. A right nice one with bright red and shiny silver pipin'. I ha'n't seen such before."

Lestrade immediately checked on the whereabouts of Mrs. Gibbons at the probable time of the murder, and was satisfied by the word of her dairyman that she had met him at the door early that morning to accept two containers of milk.

"That puts her in the clear, Dr. Watson, but not her two whelps," Lestrade said. I suspected he was right; still, the fourth murder nagged at me. I felt instinctively that something was awry; some ill-defined aspect did not fit, but upon my soul, I could not say what it was, and in the days ahead, because no amount of concentration, review or reflection was able to alter—or clarify—that fact, I resolved that my misgiving was unfounded.

The newspapers continued with their wild speculations for a while, but the public hysteria surrounding the case slowly subsided, and the murders in St. Marylebone gradually slipped off the front page. That is not to say officialdom or the populace took four brutal slayings lightly. Quite the opposite, really.

Inspector Lestrade ordered everyone associated with the case to maintain absolute silence about the investigation, or be summarily suspended from the force. Lestrade and Lestrade alone would offer periodic reports to the press, and only if and when he deemed them necessary. As a result, however, every word the poor inspector uttered was subjected to the most intense scrutiny and analysis. Depending on which newspaper one read, Lestrade and his Yarders might seem warm, compassionate and friendly; cold, arrogant and efficient; humorous, bumbling and incompetent; bold, courageous and heroic, or some very odd combination of all of the above.

The public was thus entertained, but not informed, and it was just as well, for there was precious little of substance to tell them. Lestrade's public posturing merely masked the fact that the investigation was foundering, and had been for weeks.

There was good news, however: Holmes' condition appeared to be improving, owing, it seemed to me, to the ministrations of his nurse.

Chapter 15

Mrs. Masterson arose before dawn every morning and quietly made her way down to Mrs. Hudson's kitchen to prepare a small pot of strong breakfast tea. By chance, not custom, I awoke early one morning and decided to join her at the kitchen table.

"I love the peacefulness of the hour," she said. "It's a chance to be alone with my thoughts, and I look forward to it."

"Oh, I didn't mean to intrude . . ."

"No, no. Please, Doctor. I was just explaining my morning habit. I like to watch the new day unfold. The world is always a better, easier place this early. It is the one time of day when anything still seems possible. It is really quite magical."

Mrs. Masterson looked directly at me, at least I think she did. In fact, she may have been looking directly through me. She spoke very softly, almost as though she were speaking to herself or, I could not help but imagine, to a lover. The effect was mesmerizing.

"First come the bird songs, even in the heart of the West End like this, the trill of a mockingbird sometimes, the cooing of a mourning dove at others. Then the light slowly brightens. It has different qualities at different times of the year. Some mornings, it is not so much light as it is a kind of illuminated fog, a cloud of light gray or dark gray or yellowish-white wispy smoke.

"When there's a good stiff breeze afoot, the fog moves in swirls and eddies and small dense banks of fluff scudding through the streets as though it had direction and purpose, places to go and things to do.

"When it's to be a soft day full of mist and drizzle, the cooler the temperature, the clearer the air, and the sharper the early sounds.

"On a brisk morning, the horses' hooves make a brittle clip-clop on the pavement, and you can hear the tins of milk and cream clank together when the delivery wagons hit bumps in the road.

"I find the arrival of the poultry wagon a delight. The batch of chickens is always clucking away, and once in a while it's interrupted by the crowing of a rooster, which strikes me as humorous and entirely out of place. It's as though they are all just so many unruly little bumpkins on a trip to the city. Once in a while I pick up the croon of a driver or the murmur of conversation in the street. It's the whole cacophony of morning sounds that I like, don't you, Doctor? Doctor?"

"Um, yes, yes," I said. I had become transfixed by her voice and the images she spun so readily. I sipped my tea quickly. "Quite so," I said. "Your descriptions are almost lyrical."

"Oh, thank you," she said. "When I am well rested and relaxed, it's as though I'm jotting it all down in my daily journal."

"Please," I said, "do continue."

"Very well. When I hear Mrs. Hudson stirring, I warm the oven for biscuits and bread. Sometimes I begin the cooking myself, but I sense that Mrs. Hudson takes some slight offense at this, so I dare not do it often. I do like to cook, but I like it after the fashion of a dilettante, I'm afraid. Being able to prepare a good meal here and there does not make one a cook.

"I think that a woman who can tend a busy household with precision and efficiency, and handle all of its unpredictable wants, and prepare three fine meals a day and afternoon tea as well—and all without so much as the hint of fluster—now, that woman is truly a cook. I am not nearly Mrs. Hudson's equal in that, and I truly do admire her, don't you, Doctor?"

"She is an uncommon woman," I said, thinking to myself that Mrs. Hudson wasn't the only rarity in this household.

"Well said, Doctor. I think she is supremely competent, pleasant and independent-minded. She is proof that a woman's chosen work does not necessarily have to conform to some exalted masculine standard in order for her to be happy; Mrs. Hudson and Mrs. Hudson's work are not altogether one and the same. Oh, dear. I am beginning to sound like one of those New Women proselytizers. I really don't mean to."

"Quite all right," I said. "Mrs. Masterson, it seems silly to me now that we did not get on better at once, and I hope that one instance at the hospital hasn't unduly colored your opinion of me."

"Not at all, Dr. Watson. I see it for what it was."

"Your meaning?"

"A kind of jealousy," she said, with a smile that seemed to hint as much at inquiry as understanding. "It is perfectly understandable."

"Jealousy?" I asked. "How do you mean?"

"Oh, Doctor, don't be thin-skinned now. I simply meant that you and Mr. Holmes have been inseparable friends and adventuring companions for many years, and I think that your kinship has generated a certain proprietary or protective instinct. Undoubtedly, he feels the same, and I greatly admire and envy that.

"Among women it is rare, even in their relations with men. And among most men, what passes for true friendship is usually a mere shallow bonhomie. What you have is to be treasured, I believe."

Mrs. Masterson's candor had left me tongue-tied, but while I did not enjoy the sensation, neither was I altogether displeased. She had again shown herself to be possessed of keen insight, and in this display, at least, I had been the beneficiary. I felt not so much flattered as understood; but I also felt that I had somehow been manipulated and this left me uneasy.

Chapter 16

That night, I was awakened by a loud noise that I took to come from the bedroom shared by Holmes and Mrs. Masterson. I stood by the door, my hand on the doorknob, and asked, "Is everything all right?" When no answer was forthcoming, I entered, though against my better judgment.

Mrs. Masterson's bed was pulled beside Holmes', and she sat upright looking at me in the flickering light from her bedside candle. Holmes was sound asleep in her arms. Her auburn tresses were pulled to one side and lay on her left shoulder. Holmes' head rested silently against her bare ample breasts.

Mrs. Masterson looked directly at me, pursed her lips and held a forefinger to them. "Sshhh," she whispered. "Only the wind against the shutters." She smiled warmly, with no more hint of embarrassment than would a mother with a babe at her breast, though she did pull the blanket up. I, however, found myself nodding repeatedly and stammering for something to say, until I nervously backed out of the room and closed the door.

After a restive night, I was up and out early the next morning, and I determined to busy myself away from Baker Street. Though I had heard Mrs. Masterson and Holmes stirring at first light, I saw neither of them, which was just as well, for our chance encounter the previous night had left me somewhat embarrassed and uneasy.

In truth, I needed some respite in which to collect

my thoughts. I regretted having intruded on Mrs. Masterson and Holmes, although at that moment I had entertained the best of reasons and the purest of motives. She was his nurse, and he her patient, but I could not help but feel as though I had interrupted some tender intimacy, and that made me feel awkward. I am not by nature a distrustful person, and I felt guilty at once for harboring even the slightest notion of impropriety on the part of Mrs. Masterson. But what was I to think? Was it not possible that this beautiful woman was merely some sort of opportunist in fancy dress? Was she something other than she seemed? A manipulative schemer, perhaps? And if so, to what possible end? Or was she guilty of merely being human, of being lonely or of letting her apparently growing fondness for the great detective cloud her professional judgment?

And was Holmes no longer insensible? Was his convalescence being protracted artificially for some reason?

"Watson, you old fool," I said. "Listen to yourself. You are acting like a nanny to a pair of adolescents! Stop this foolishness before you lose your faculties completely." Thus did I resolve to keep my thoughts to myself until I could sort and clarify them. If I was so preoccupied and worn out that I was having difficulty making sense of personal matters, let alone professional, it was clear that I could be of no constructive use in the case until I had rested and had the opportunity to gather my thoughts. I packed my worn old overnight bag, penned a brief note to Mrs. Hudson that I would be away for a spell visiting my friends in Cornwall, and gently tacked it to her door.

I let myself out and walked briskly through the city, soaking up the myriad sounds, sights and smells of which I never seemed to tire. Finding myself at Kensington Station at last, I boarded the train and began my trip to Cornwall. The change of venue, however brief, would do me good, and it had been months since I'd seen my old army friend James Worthy. We

had soldiered together in Afghanistan with the Royal
Berkshire Regiment and had been inseparable in
those days. I had saved his life on one occasion, and
on another he had saved mine. Each of us had been
wounded: I in the leg, he in the shoulder, and after
mustering out we had remained fast friends over all
of the years that followed. We never spoke of the
campaign; as gruesome and harrowing as it was, there
was no need to recount it, and certainly no need to
relive it. I think that is often the case among men who
have been to war together. The experience is a bond
that needs no explaining, no justification.

Worthy had inherited his family's fortune, and with
it a grand seaside manor in Cornwall. We visited each
other once or twice a year, always without formal invi-
tation or prior notice, for it was a matter of pride with
us that such conventions were unnecessary. Occasionally, in his bachelor days, Worthy had stopped by my
somewhat cramped quarters in Baker Street, but it
was usually I who traveled to Cornwall to see him and
his wife, Millicent. She was a pleasant enough woman,
comely despite her plainness, and I felt at ease in her
presence. My relationship with James predated hers,
but never once did she begrudge us our friendship.
Indeed, her naturally good spirits always seemed
buoyed by my visits.

So preoccupied was I that none of the dwindling
cityscape speeding by my window registered as anything but a blur of grays, browns, brick-reds and blues
in dappled sunlight. One moment there were bustling
streets, slums, smoking factories and teeming water-
front docks, and the next there were rolling green
fields and tree-studded hillocks. As the verdant countryside well beyond London stretched before me, I
finally began to relax. My frustration with my own
lack of investigative skill and my uneasiness over the
relationship between Holmes and Mrs. Masterson,
given my prolonged focus on the former and my
sudden concern with the latter, had grown to such

a magnitude as to be disproportionate to their real
consequence in the grand scheme. Such is the effect
of prolonged overwork, I mused. In all things, modera-
tion, the ancients said. It is a lesson as old as Aristotle
himself, and I silently reproached myself for having to
relearn it—though doing so gave me cause to smile,
too, for I also saw this as a sign that I was regaining
my balance.

I had intended to stay in Cornwall for merely a few
days, but at the end of the fourth day, at my hosts'
insistence, I cabled Mrs. Masterson, informing her that
I would be staying on until the end of the following
week. I would return to Baker Street Sunday next,
unless there were developments in the case or a
change for the worse in Holmes' recovery.

Mrs. Masterson sent me a letter by post on the following day:

> *My Dear Dr. Watson,*
>   *All is well here. You will be cheered to learn
> that Mr. Holmes' recuperation is proceeding with
> remarkable speed. I even dare to hope that to-
> morrow, or perhaps the next day, weather per-
> mitting, we shall hire a brougham for a ride in
> the countryside.*
>   *Inspector Lestrade's inquiry into the horrible
> St. Marylebone business continues, but he has not
> had much to report.*
>   *Though we miss your company here, of course,
> by all means please do stay on with your friends
> in Cornwall. I always have found the sun and salt
> air to be invigorating and most refreshing, and I
> am sure you will benefit from the hiatus.*
>   *We look forward to your rejoining us on Sunday.*
>   *Until then, I remain sincerely yours,*
>   *Abigail Masterson.*

The news from Baker Street was better than I had
hoped, and I settled back into my apartment in the

Worthys' elegant home in much-improved spirits. For the first time in months, I was able to truly relax. I spent long hours walking along the cliffs and wading into the icy surf and tidal pools and poking about among the rocks and crevices exposed by low tide.

On one of my meanderings during my second week in Cornwall, I was suddenly aware of the peculiar sensation that I was being watched. I intentionally dropped the rather large hickory walking stick that I used to steady myself as I clambered among the rocks, and when I bent low to pick it up, turned swiftly around so as to catch the watcher unawares. I thought I spied movement in the tall hedgerow of privet situated some thirty yards behind me, but seeing nothing more I continued on my way.

The following afternoon I was out once again, ankle-deep in the bitingly cold seawater with the hot, bright sun of midday beating down upon me, when I turned to look at the shore behind me and saw a black-clad figure standing in the broken shade beneath a towering willow not far from the water's edge. I shaded the sun from my eyes with the flat of my hand and squinted in his direction, but I could make out none of his features.

"Hullo," I hollered. "Is that you, James? I say, James, is that you?"

There was no reply. I took several steps toward shore, and the figure in black moved quite purposefully out of sight behind a tree. I hastened my steps, but when I got nearer, I caught sight of him just passing the crown of the hill, and then he was gone.

The incident bothered me, and I mentioned it that night at cards as James, Millicent and I whiled away the evening over some brandy and a few friendly hands of rummy. My friends were puzzled.

"Our nearest neighbors are the Carstairs," said Mrs. Worthy, "but they've been away for several weeks."

"Even so," said James, "they're not exactly next

door, then, are they? It's a good thirty minutes to their home, and a brisk walk at that."

"Perhaps it was a peddler," I suggested. "Though, I can't imagine why he'd not show his wares and, instead, run off."

"Yes, odd that," James said. "I hope you're not put off, John. You have had a real go of it with these murders in the West End."

"I'm sure it's nothing worth our notice," I said, not quite believing my own words. "I see no good reason to be upset by it. It's true enough that sometimes there is much more than first meets the eye; but then, it's also true that sometimes there is much less.

"I believe it's your turn, James."

"Oh. Yes, quite," he said, and I spoke nothing of the encounter again.

Chapter 17

I can honestly report that when James and Millicent saw me off at the train station in Cornwall, I felt like a new man.

I was well rested and chipper and eager to return to the hunt. So clear and unencumbered was my mind, however, that no sooner had the train gotten up a full head of steam than I drifted off to sleep with my traveling bag half under my arm. I must have dozed deeply for a good many moments, because the next sound I heard was the opening of the door to my compartment. I awoke with something of a start and struggled upright from my comfortable slouch in the window corner of the broad seat.

A stoop-shouldered old man dressed head to foot in black had joined my company. His back was turned to me as he closed the door. He leaned on a stout black cane. It was as straight as a poker and had a ball handle of filigreed silver. As my eyes refocused, I noted that he wore an uncombed salt-and-pepper beard of estimable length and enviable thickness.

"Good morning," I said, with a welcoming smile.

He took a seat directly opposite me. He straightened his back against the cushion with what seemed to me to be no small difficulty. He slowly raised his head, and brought his eyes up to meet mine, saying, "Indeed," as he did so.

The sight of his face made me catch my breath, imperceptibly I hoped. The man was disfigured by a livid scar that ran from the top left side of his forehead down to his upper lip, and straight across his left eye, which had been reduced to a milky-white orb; it was sightless, to be sure.

He did not return my smile.

"And you would be Watson," he said.

"Wha, why, yes," I stammered. "How do . . ."

"Dr. John Haimish Watson, no? Physician, adventurer but mostly lapdog and able scrivener for Mr. Sherlock Holmes of Baker Street. Am I not correct?"

I am no man's lapdog, and so took immediate offense, but I remained calm, so thunderstruck was I by this brazen stranger.

"You have the advantage of me, sir. How is it you know my name? And what is yours? What business have you with me?"

"I do have the advantage of you," he said, "and I shall keep it that way, if you don't mind." As he spoke, he withdrew a single-shot derringer from the pocket of his coat, and from the level of his hip, aimed it at my chest with a smirk. His left hand rested atop the ornate silver ball that was the head of his walking stick.

"What's the meaning of this?" I demanded. "Who do you think you are, to come barging . . ."

The walking stick bobbed upward in his hand so that he held it by its stock, and all in the same motion he dealt me a blow to the side of the head.

"Shut up, Doctor. There's more where that came from . . . so much more." He snickered.

"I regret that we are so . . . confined, as it were. It would be so much more pleasant for me if I could take my time with you. Oh, well, perhaps there will be other, more savory, opportunities, though not with you, I'm afraid. We haven't much time together, you and I. We will be parting company soon.

"Tell me, though, how is your friend, Mr. Holmes? Is he well?" His sardonic smile turned into a laugh so derisively foul and mean-spirited that it turned me cold.

"I've not read of his untimely demise, so I must presume that he is getting along. But in such pitiful shape he must be, eh? Who'd have done such a nasty thing to him? And that ragamuffin boy? Tsk. Tsk. He had a smart mouth, that one. No breeding. Do you suppose he just lost his head? Ha. Ha."

His laughter was positively maniacal. It was calculated to horrify me, I am sure, but it did not. Instead, I grew angry, even as the blow he had struck me began to throb. I touched the side of my head, quite involuntarily, as he spoke.

"Don't worry about that, Doctor. It's nothing, I assure you. But I could do it again just as ably, if you'd like. Though perhaps not so gently. Ah, ah. Don't so much as stir a bone, Doctor. Not a bone, mind, or I'll play a tune on you. Or perhaps I'll just slice off an ear as a keepsake."

He pointed his cane straight toward me so that its tip was little more than a foot from my face. I saw him depress a button just below the shiny head of the cane, and instantly a long and especially thick dagger shot from its tip with a hard metallic ring. No sooner had I been able to focus on the gleaming razor-sharp blade, now no more than an inch from my eyes, than he jabbed the weapon at my cheek. It was a delicate cut, but I could feel blood trickling down my neck almost at once.

"Oh, do use a handkerchief, Doctor. Please. I can't bear untidiness."

I do not recall taking an inventory of my emotions, but I know I was becoming more and more angry. I recall thinking that this was all happening much too fast, and that if I did nothing I would end up just as dead as if I attempted some defense, though the latter course could bring the same result more quickly.

"You do not scare me, you cretinous wretch!" The words seemed scarcely my own, so quickly did I shout them. "Do what you will. You'll never get off this train."

He was startled by my outburst. I lunged at him, throwing my bag straight into his lap, and my body across him, thus diverting another blow from his deadly cane. The gunshot was muffled by the weight of the bag, and I half expected to feel a searing pain as my reward, but it did not come. I was inside of his reach with the cane. I grasped for his throat with both hands, but he crashed the head of his stick against my head and collarbone so many times that I thought I would lose consciousness from the blows. I fell back against the cushions. Still half seated, he used the point of his weapon to pin me where I sat. I felt the steel against my throat, and he pulled his arm straight back to drive the blade home.

It has long been the province of writers to try to express what momentous thoughts pass through one's mind in life's final fleeting seconds. Would that I could report a stolid and peaceful resolve to meet my maker with a clear conscience, no regrets and a silent prayer upon my lips, but in fact, it had all happened much too fast.

I had begun, instead, to mutter a profane oath, when the door to the compartment flung open so quickly that it knocked the sword from my assailant's arm and spun him half around in his seat. He sprang to his feet with an agility that belied his appearance, and thrust himself at the tall angular figure of Sherlock Holmes, who now blocked the door.

"No!" the wretch screamed. And with that, he drove his boot savagely into my friend's groin, even as the detective lunged with his arms outstretched. Holmes doubled over in pain and crumpled to the floor with the man's full beard gripped tightly in his fist. The attacker, suddenly shorn, dropped his head low so as to hide his face in the collar of his coat, grabbed up his sword and, leaping over Holmes, fled through the open door. I heard a commotion outside, a thump and some shouts. "Stop! Stop! You there. Stop, I say!" Then a thud and a scream.

"That was Mrs. Masterson, Watson. See to her." I could barely distinguish the words, for Holmes was writhing from his injury, but he flailed his arm toward the corridor.

I stumbled through the door, and looking down the length of the car, I could see a conductor sprawled on the floor at the far end. The door of the car was open, flapping noisily. Nearer to me was Mrs. Masterson, struggling to sit up against the wall. I rushed to her side.

"Are you all right, Mrs. Masterson? Are you all right?"

"Ooh. Oh. Yes. I . . . I believe I am. He . . . bowled me . . . over. Knocked . . . the wind out . . . I must . . . be a sight."

"Not to me, dear lady. Not to me," I said. "Sit right where you are. I'm going to check on the conductor."

A crimson stain had covered the front of the conductor's uniform and begun to seep onto the floor. I pressed two fingers to his carotid artery, but could detect no pulse.

I returned to Mrs. Masterson and offered my hand. "Here, let me help you," I said. I supported her with my shoulder, and we staggered back into my cabin.

"Is that man dead?" she asked.

"I'm afraid so. Stabbed."

She said nothing. Holmes was seated on the floor with his long arms wrapped about his knees. His face was pallid and drawn, but a tight smile was painted across his lips.

"Well, my old friend," he said with difficulty. "It is good to see you."

Chapter 18

My head ached from the blows I had suffered, but my discomfort was far outweighed by my relief at seeing Holmes and Mrs. Masterson.

"You have saved my life, both of you," I said. "A simple thank you hardly seems adequate. I am overjoyed at your recovery, Holmes."

"I owe that to your diligence, Watson, and to Abigail's ministrations. The score is more than balanced. Furthermore, we did nothing that you yourself would not have done. You are to speak no more of it."

"But what brought the two of you here? How did you know I would be attacked?"

"We did not know for certain, but we began to fear as much when we got a cable from your friend, Worthy. By nature, Watson, you are utterly without guile, and he knows you well enough to know when you are hiding something. In this case he was convinced that the stranger you saw at seaside left you more upset than you were letting on. He told us of the incident on the chance that it might figure into the St. Marylebone business."

"Worthy," I said. "Good old Jim."

"Indeed," Holmes said. "I am afraid I am still somewhat slow in making decisions, but Mrs. Masterson is not. She ordered us down to Cornwall as soon as we got Worthy's message. We took a room in town, and were able to keep an eye on the train station.

"As luck would have it, we saw your visitor watching you. I was disguised as an old man, hunched over in a wheeled chair and tended to by my nurse. It was her plan, and only a few steps from the reality of the situation, I must say. We boarded shortly after the two of you got on the train.

"We took the cabin next to his, but he made his move long before we expected it," Holmes said. "I believed that the nearer we got to London, the more likely he would be to attack. The less time he is on the train after that, the better for him. But I had not considered that at this point he may be moved more by madness and compulsion than by practicality."

"I believe he has come to think of himself as almost invincible," Mrs. Masterson said. "His successful murders had left him thinking that he could, quite literally, do as he pleased."

"But what threat have I posed that he would want me out of the way?"

"You undervalue yourself, Watson," the detective said. "I suspect that our killer sees the two of us—perhaps the three of us—as one."

"And," Mrs. Masterson said, "today's setback will have left him confused and very angry. He may be even more dangerous from this point forward."

I shuddered at the thought.

"We will prepare for that, I assure you," Holmes said. "Meanwhile, I think we have the advantage. He is found out, you see. We are reasonably certain who he is, and he knows it."

I looked expectantly at Holmes, but he was not forthcoming.

"And I suspect that the next time we see him, he'll not be wearing any garish disguise. The scraggly hair and beard and discolored eye and livid scar were a stroke of genius. I spent some little time in this fiend's care, but he was masked then, too. I was not expecting him to continue the masquerade. He is a resourceful fellow."

"You must explain to me all that happened, Holmes.

I have been trying to piece it together, but there are gaps."

"I shall do so, Watson. I shall. It is difficult for me to talk about it, still, but Abigail . . . Mrs. Masterson . . . believes the recounting is somewhat therapeutic, and she is probably correct. Regardless, you certainly deserve to know all. So when we are back in Baker Street and have had a well-deserved taste of Mrs. Hudson's cooking again and a good night's sleep, I will explain everything that transpired. Then, Watson, we will have a go at this bastard once and for all. Never in my life have I wanted to see a man on the gallows more than this one."

Over breakfast at Baker Street the following morning, Mrs. Masterson informed me that she had made arrangements to have her necessaries moved to a room at the Langham Hotel, where she would be taking up residence again at once.

"Mr. Holmes is well now, Doctor Watson, so my work as his nurse is done," she said. "It is no longer necessary for me to stay here."

I nodded and returned her smile. "I will miss your presence, Mrs. Masterson, and for what it is worth, you are most welcome in these quarters at any time. May I trust that we will be seeing you again?"

"In fact, Mr. Holmes has asked for my help on the Marylebone case. He believes that I have some insight into the psychology of this fiend, so yes, you will be seeing me again, rather soon."

Before Mrs. Masterson left, she agreed to meet us for dinner that night at the Holborn Restaurant. Holmes and I bade her farewell, and I took a seat beside the fire. Holmes packed his briar with some of the dottles he had left on the mantel from last night's smoking, an economical habit but one that I found repugnant, and spoke as he lighted his pipe.

"I was very fond of Dickie Quinn, Watson, more than you know. Quite some time ago, I had seen to it that he was removed to St. Stephen's Home for

Boys; I had given the proprietor a modest stipend for his initial care."

"I had no idea, Holmes," I said.

"I never spoke of it. Dickie couldn't have been more than four years old at the time. His mother, Ginny, was of loose morals, and rather well known for it in the East End, except by the boy's father. His name was Patrick Day Quinn. Not a bad fellow, really. A big strapping man who loved the drink, and when he had a snoot full he loved to brawl. But he was an excellent boxer, as well, one of the quickest I have ever seen."

"Wait, Holmes," I said. "Patrick Day Quinn? I have read stories of a boxer in the United States who goes by 'The Mighty Quinn.' Is that . . ."

"Yes, Watson, the same.

"He came home drunk late one afternoon and found his wife naked in bed with a dagger through her heart, and little Dickie tied up in the next room behind a locked door. Quinn went berserk and began tearing the place apart. The Metropolitian Police arrived in force very quickly, too quickly. It took six of them to get the cuffs on Quinn.

"With a little effort I was able to prove that he was nowhere near his home when the murder actually took place. He was acquitted, but the good jury wasn't satisfied. They decided that Quinn's propensity for drinking and brawling made him unfit to raise his son. The boy would have been raised in a workhouse had I not stepped in and taken some little responsibility for his upkeep in a decent place.

"Quinn was brokenhearted to lose the youngster, and he left the country to start over in America. The day after he shipped out, a Malay seaman was found stuffed inside a barrel not far from the docks. He fit easily inside of it because his arms and legs had been broken in dozens of places. He had been beaten to a pulp, and then stabbed once in the heart.

"The police thought of Patrick Day Quinn immedi-

ately because the Malay fit the description one of
Quinn's neighbors had given of a man seen on two
occasions with Quinn's wife.

"There were no witnesses to the Malay's murder,
and police never found the weapon. The coroner said
it probably was a rather commonplace penknife that
was used, but given that all of this just amounted to
another night on the docks, the police weren't going
to press very hard."

The detective reached across the corner of the mantel and removed from it the penknife that he used to
impale his unanswered correspondence.

"Holmes," I asked, "is that knife . . . ?"

"It arrived by post about a month after Quinn's
departure. There also was a note of thanks for my
having saved him from the gallows, and he promised
to send some money for the boy once he was able to
get situated.

"After about a year, he began sending money with
regularity. I just turned it over to the orphanage for
Dickie's continued care, but I made it a point to visit
him when I could. We'd have an outing now and then.
He was a good boy."

Holmes cleared his throat a couple of times, and I
could see his teeth clench down on the stem of his
briar.

"When Dickie brought me the message that night,
I knew at once that trouble lay in store because my
note to Albert Gibbons had required no response. He
may actually have received it, or it may have been
intercepted. The note I received was unsigned. It
could have come from anyone, quite literally. It read
simply, 'Marylebone Mews. Eight o'clock. Come
alone.' I destroyed the message, thinking there was no
need for two of us to risk our lives on this errand,
and ventured out alone early the next morning."

"You should have told me, Holmes. I could have
helped."

"Yes, I should have," he said, "and I think I knew as much when I destroyed the note."

"Well, then, why didn't you do so? We have always faced such things together. I think it was damnably selfish of you." My own words surprised me. Until now, I had not admitted to myself that I had been in the least bit offended by Holmes' actions.

"I was afraid, Watson. I sorely wanted you by my side, but I did not feel that I had handled the case well up to that point. Frankly, I didn't feel that I had earned the right to subject you to such danger. If some harm had befallen you because of my actions or inadequacies, I never would have forgiven myself."

"I am touched, Holmes, but still . . ."

"I would feel as you do, Watson. Forgive me."

I nodded my assent, and he continued.

"I paid no attention to the snow, and that was my second mistake. I could not see three feet in front of me. It was worse than the heaviest fog, because the wind was up and it was driving the snow directly into my face.

"He was cunning, Watson. He used the snow to his advantage. I was bent into the wind peering ahead as best I could and using faint landmarks to mark my way. He clothed himself completely in white. He covered all but his eyes, and he must have stood motionless in the falling snow long enough to be additionally camouflaged by a layer of it.

"I must have walked right by him. He came up behind me, and laid me flat with a cudgel. When I came to, my hands were tied, there was a rope under my arms, and I was being dragged down the street on my back at a good pace. I feigned unconsciousness and managed to work my ring from my finger as he dragged me across the storm drain. I was hoping against all likelihood that it would be found quickly by an eagle-eyed tosher. My captor must have seen me or sensed my movement because another blow on the head left me senseless.

"When I awoke next, I had been trussed up to the post in the stable with my hands tied well up over my head. He had stripped off my shirt, and I believed that if he did not kill me, the cold would.

"I never saw his face. He wore a hood, so that only his coal-black eyes and that cruel mouth showed. And he said only one word in all the time he had me as his prisoner: Abba. Over and over and over, until it became a malevolent chant."

"Did you know that the word means 'father'?" I asked Holmes.

"No, not until rather recently. It was the very first thing I asked Mrs. Masterson."

"And she knew?"

"Yes. She is a surprising woman, isn't she?"

"But what sense does your attacker's use of the word make?"

"I will get to that, but pray, indulge me first. I must get straight through this."

"Of course, Holmes."

"He doused me with cold salt water and beat me repeatedly, but never with his fists. He used his silver-handled cane, Watson, the same one that he attacked you with. Do you remember my noting the gouge in the floor at Whitney's? The same mark was present at Edward Gibbons' office, too. It was made by the cane. That lethal blade in the end of it is spring-loaded into the stock. A button in the handle releases the blade, as you saw, and it comes out behind a heavy spring with incredible force.

"I believe Whitney was killed, literally, with the push of a button. The murderer simply pressed the end of the cane to his chest, over the heart, and pushed the button on the cane. Death was instantaneous. An ingenious and deadly weapon. It has one major flaw, however. The only way to retract the blade is to force it back into position. He stood the cane on the floor and pressed down on the handle with all of his weight and power. That is what created the telltale mark in the floor.

"He used the cane's blade to cut me. He did it slowly, laughing all the while and saying, 'Abba. Abba.' Whenever I lost consciousness, he revived me with salt water. The pain was horrible, and I wanted to scream, but I determined not to utter a word. Not a word, Watson. It was the only way I had to fight back. My silence angered him, and he would torment me all the more.

"The beatings became more vicious. I knew he had broken my ribs, and I could not imagine what a mess he had managed to make of my face. I was weak and frozen beyond numbness, but then when he hit me or cut me, the pain was a kind of searing heat that for an instant each time was almost welcome.

"After hours of this, I became delirious. All I could hear was 'Abba. Abba. Abba.' And then I recognized that it was not my assailant's voice, but mine. I had taken up the chant. Now we said it together. We shared a rhythm, a perverse incantation. He nodded and smiled in pleasure, and we kept saying the word, over and over again, as though it were the only word in the language. Flat. Monotone. Droning. Over and over. It was mesmerizing. Hypnotic. I could no longer feel my body.

"Then he cut a long line down my chest diagonally, and made another, parallel to it, just as carefully. He unsheathed a skinning knife, and delicately joined the two lines at the top with a connecting cut and raised a flap of skin with a quick jerk of the knife. I screamed out in pain, Watson. It was the first sound I had uttered that was not our chant, and it was like opening a floodgate."

Holmes poured us both a brandy. His hand shook as he handed me the glass, and his voice quivered slightly now as he talked.

"Dear God, Holmes. You needn't continue."

"No, Watson. I must. You have to know all, so that

you can understand my hatred. He rubbed a handful
of salt into the raw wound, and I passed out from the
pain. When he brought me around, he continued flay-
ing my chest, an inch at a time, stopping to use the
salt, listening to me scream.

"Then at one point, he stood on a box in front of
me and urinated on me. When he was finished, he
went back to work on the wound. I looked down at
my chest, and his demonic play as though I were dis-
connected from it. I looked at the raw, bleeding line
that stretched to my navel and realized that shortly
there would be another one drawn diagonally from
the other side, and I thought about the work done on
his other victims and it dawned on me then that this
was not an upside-down pyramid, triangle or a vee
at all.

"I realized that what he was carving, Watson, was
a simple letter *A*, which could only stand for Abba.
From any vantage point other than the victim's, the
letter was not easily recognizable. But to the victim,
it is unmistakable.

"I remember screaming one final time when he
ripped the rest of the flesh off that first line. And then
he fell forward on his face, and Dickie Quinn was
standing there in front of me with a club of wood in
his hand.

" 'Lor',' Mr. 'Omes. I'll get you outta this,' he said.
'I'll save ya, Mr. 'Omes.'

"Oh, Watson, dear God, excuse me." And with that,
Sherlock Holmes turned away.

I tried to console him, but it was all I could do to
maintain my own composure.

He was silent for a few moments and then continued.

"The boy had only stunned Gibbons. The monster
uncoiled from the floor like a snake and knocked
Dickie down with one stroke of his cane. He stripped
the boy naked and threw him down in front of me,

all the while laughing at his screams and saying, 'Abba. Abba. Abba.'

"He turned the boy over and beat him into unconsciousness with that infernal cane of his. Then he stopped and looked at me, and I stared into his eyes, at the well of hatred and insanity there, and I said, 'I am going to kill you.'

"He was startled at that, and for a moment I thought I saw panic. But then he laughed a low, maniacal laugh and turned back to Dickie Quinn.

"He carved the 'A' into Dickie, but he didn't kill him. The boy had passed out again, so he threw water on him and slapped his face until he was conscious. But Dickie had been beaten so severely that he could barely move. The monster walked out of my sight and when I saw him next, he was carrying an ax.

"I knew what was about to happen, and I screamed against it, but nothing would stop the fiend. He cut off the boy's head with one stroke, and the heart went out of me altogether. He picked up the severed head, stuffed a rag in its mouth and set it in front of me on the floor while the blood drained out of the boy's corpse like a river.

"My attacker could have killed me then, and for a good long while, Watson, I have wished that he had done so. I did not want to live with the memory. That was the way he wanted it. That was why he tortured me and committed a bestial murder before my eyes. He wanted me to know the kind of despair and black chaos that occupies his thoughts day in and day out. He wanted me to long for my own death as something preferable to hopeless insanity. And he left me alive to live with the longing for death. He had ample time in which to kill me. One stroke on his way out the door would have done it. But he knew that living would be infinitely more difficult.

"He stepped up to me and stood so close that I could smell his fetid breath. He grabbed my hair in his fist, and slammed my head back against the post.

He put his mouth to my ear and bit it hard, and then he whispered to me, Watson. He whispered the way one lover might whisper to another, softly and affectionately, his bloody tongue and mouth caressing my ear.

"He whispered, 'Make her stop' "

Chapter 19

I was so shaken by Holmes' tale of what had happened to him that I slept very little that night. By early morning I had given up all pretense to slumber and left my bedroom to find Holmes seated before the parlor window enveloped in a dense cloud of tobacco smoke. I presumed, accurately, that he had been up most of the night lighting one bowlful of shag after another while his nimble mind examined and reexamined the facts of the case in search of answers.

"For God's sake, Holmes," I said with a laugh, "throw open the window, won't you? I can't see the wall for the smoke. I thought you were on fire for a moment."

He smiled good-naturedly, raised the sash and let in the morning's spring air. It was the first time I had seen him smile of late, and the fact of it was reassuring.

"You seem in a good mood, Holmes."

"I find that I am thankful to be alive, Watson. As silly as it may sound, until now I have always taken my well-being for granted."

"As well you might, Holmes. You had no reason to contemplate your own mortality until now. Had I not faced death several times in Afghanistan, I would have felt the same way, I assure you. It is only natural."

"I suppose so, yes. But I must say that Mrs. Masterson has had an effect upon me as well, Watson. She has helped to restore my vitality, somehow. I am somewhat embarrassed to say it, because it seems so, so sentimental, but she has made me feel as though my life is more important than I believed it was."

I smiled. "My good man, you don't suppose that you are in love, do you?"

"No," Holmes said, but rather too quickly. "Although I will say that she is quite unlike most of the women I have encountered. She is not bound by convention and expectation and entitlement to such an extent that she ceases to be a real person. She has a mind of her own, and she speaks it, and she takes action, and yet, she is every bit as feminine a creature as ever walked this earth."

"Oh, Holmes, you do have a case of it, old boy."

"Watson, are you laughing at me?" Holmes asked with an uncertain smile.

"Not at all," I assured him. "I am delighted, but I must say that it seems good to see you wrestling with matters in which I am rather well versed for a change. As much as I admire and respect your expertise in matters of reasoning and deduction, Holmes, you can't know how tiresome it can get always being an understudy. But here, at last, is an area in which I am more experienced than you. It feels good, though odd, to be in such a place."

"Don't be smug, Watson." His voice was sharp, but his eyes fairly danced.

"Nonsense, Holmes. I will be as smug as I bloody well please, and there's nothing you can do about it. In fact, I may well turn out to be insufferable on the subject."

The detective gave out a hearty laugh, and it was a good sound to hear. I could not recall having seen him in better spirits, despite the horror he had faced.

"Is that what you've been doing all night, Holmes? Trying to fathom your feelings for Mrs. Masterson?"

"No, most certainly not," he said. "I have been poring over the murder cases. Just before dawn I came to the conclusion that I have rarely overlooked as many important points in an investigation as I have in this one."

"Surely, you are being too hard on yourself."

"Not at all, Watson. Not at all. Think back to our discovery of the room in which Nigel Whitney was trussed up. We both stood there looking at a rather large pool of blood in the middle of the floor. . . . Indeed, I was on the floor beside it trying to determine its age . . . and neither of us noticed that there were no bloody footprints anywhere."

"I'm not certain what you are driving at, Holmes."

"This, Watson: Nigel Whitney was hung from a rope thrown over the beam in the middle of the storeroom and then he was cut up. But we found him in the front room."

"Yes?"

"Well, it is not difficult to imagine that one person could string him up, but how could one person cut him down without standing in the pool of blood beneath the body and then leaving a trail?"

"By thunder, you're right, Holmes."

"It could only have been accomplished by two people, Watson. One person on either side of the pool. One pushes the body into a swinging motion; the other grabs it when it's clear of the pool, and while he's holding on to the corpse, the other cuts it down, probably with that damned cane."

"So the killer did not act alone?"

"Obviously not, and I should have realized it at once, Watson. Other facts point to the same inescapable conclusion."

"Such as?"

"Such as the fact that we know there were already at least two other people besides Nigel Whitney in the tobacconist's shop when our surly stranger arrived. Quincy Morton, of course, was one. Do you recall Tobias Gregson's interview with him? Morton noted there was another person in the room, but could not tell whether the stranger was a man or a woman. That is just a trifle odd, wouldn't you say?

"Let us suppose for a moment, that this androgynous creature was waiting for our killer. And if that is so, it seems likely that this party is someone who was known to Nigel Whitney. A tobacconist's shop is not a clothier's, after all, or a hat shop, where a customer can spend time shopping. In a tobacconist's shop, a customer simply goes in, gets what he wants and leaves. To do otherwise is to loiter or arouse suspicion—unless you are a friend of the proprietor."

"But, Holmes," I said, "you assume too much, do you not? Why couldn't the unidentified person simply have been a stranger waiting to consult with Whitney? The stranger wants a particular blend or needs to inquire about a pipe, or the repair of one or, I suppose, any number of other possibilities."

"I think not, Watson."

"Holmes, there is something you are not telling me here."

"Yes. Look at this, Watson." And with a flourish, he removed a newspaper from the deal table by which he had been standing. In the center of the table was quite a large photograph of the Gibbons family.

"Here are the late Alexander Gibbons, his widow, the raven-haired Mary McCormick Gibbons, and their issue, Masters Albert and Jamey, taken not eight months ago. Lestrade saw it at the house, noted the name of the photography studio and Voilà! He had images of his suspects to show the other Yarders. It is a good photograph, is it not?"

"Holmes, please. This has the air of a magic show."

He laughed. "Indeed it does," he said. "Watch." From beneath the family portrait he removed a paper cutout and carefully positioned it over the photograph. Satisfied that the overlay was in place, he motioned me to come closer.

I bent over and peered at the photo.

"Good Lord!" I exclaimed. "The likenesses are extraordinary, Holmes."

"Exactly. By silhouetting out the hair on the mother and her sons, it becomes obvious, does it not? They have almost precisely the same faces, despite their differences in age and gender. Notice, too, that they are all standing and that, while Alexander is considerably taller, mother and sons are all about the same height."

"When did you notice this?" I asked.

"Oh, several hours ago," he said. "It is not readily apparent because of the positions the family members have taken in the photograph: mother and father at the center, one boy on either side. I daresay that if the mother and sons were side by side, the resemblance would be clear immediately. It must be undeniably obvious when the three of them are together in person."

"Well, not quite," I said. "For your purposes, you have removed Mrs. Gibbons' hair. That is not as readily accomplished in life."

"And why not, Watson?"

"What are you saying, Holmes?"

"I am saying, what if Mary McCormick Gibbons' beautiful raven tresses are merely artifice?"

"In other words, a wig?"

"Yes," Holmes said. "A wig. Not even a novelty on the Continent, and fine ones are readily available in London at any number of salons, not to mention from costumers, though not of such quality. As you know, I have a few myself that I use in disguise from time to time."

"Yes, of course. But why would Mrs. Gibbons don a wig?"

"The wrong question, Watson. We need to ask why she would take it off."

"I beg your pardon?"

"Without the wig, she could quite readily pass as either of her two sons."

"And with it," I said, finally following the detective's reasoning, "either of them could pass for their mother."

"Just so!" Holmes said. "Just so!"

"But why would they want to do so? Are all three of them murderers?"

"I do not think so," he said. "But if two of them are involved, I would bet a tidy sum that one is Mary McCormick Gibbons. Her involvement also is suggested by her actions at home the night of Alexander Gibbons' murder."

"You are referring to the fact that she cleaned up the murder scene and moved the body?"

"I am referring to the fact that she was able to move the body at all," Holmes said. "You saw Mary McCormick Gibbons, Watson. Though I would hardly call her frail, she is a smallish woman, is she not? Her husband was a big man, much too big for her to easily move about on her own. I daresay that she could not possibly move or even drag his deadweight without some assistance."

"Of course," I said. "How could we have overlooked the fact?"

"How, indeed, Watson? But we did. We most certainly did."

"So you are saying that she may have been an accomplice in both murders?"

"It is likely, Watson; yes. But we are still missing pieces of this puzzle. What has been Albert's role in all of this, if he did, indeed, play any role at all? If he does not figure into the crimes, then how are we to view him? If he is innocent, he may well be dead by now, for all we know. And precisely the same points may be made about Jamey Gibbons, no?"

"And," I said, "we haven't even considered the murder of Neville Rolfe, the shirtmaker."

"Oh, there's a good reason for that," Holmes said.

"Really?" I was bewildered. "Pray, what might that be?"

Chapter 20

Holmes' flair for the dramatic never ceased to surprise me. We promptly hailed a hansom cab, and the next thing I knew we were alighting outside "Rolfe's" on Bond Street, where Lestrade, Gregson and the boy, Victor Kerr the street sweeper, were already conveniently waiting.

"Right on time, you are," said Lestrade. "I always appreciate punctuality."

"Shall we, gentlemen?" said Holmes. I was getting peevish; it seemed that everyone here knew what was going on but me, although I was quickly developing an idea.

Lestrade and Gregson marched through the front door like soldiers, Holmes right behind, then the boy and me.

"Police," Lestrade said gruffly to the startled clerks, and walked through the showroom and straight into the back room. There were five people busy at their work, and Alice Felson was one of them. She was leaning far over the cutting table nearest us, the very same platform on which Rolfe's body had once lain. With a pair of long, sharply pointed scissors, she was cutting snow-white broadcloth from a big bolt of fabric.

"Ahem!" Lestrade said sharply. "Mrs. Alice Felson is it?"

The woman was startled. She turned and, seeing a knot of us standing not five feet away, visibly caught her breath. And then she burst into tears, dropped the scissors and, quite literally, collapsed at our feet.

"Watson," Holmes said.

I quickly knelt beside the sobbing, obviously hysterical woman. Discreetly, with the toe of his boot, Gregson drew the scissors away from her toward himself, and then, handkerchief in hand, carefully picked them up.

"Mrs. Felson," Holmes said in a low voice. "You must come with us. You know that, don't you?"

She nodded and snuffled. "I hadn't a choice," she sobbed. "No choice 't all. My own brother taking after my little Toby like that. I warned him to leave my boy alone, but no, he'd a turned him into some little fay, just like himself, if I'd not stopped him. I warned him. I did. I warned . . ."

"That's enough, Mrs. Felson," Holmes said. "We know. Come now. Is that your cape there, with the red and silver trim?"

The woman nodded.

"Victor, would you be a good lad and fetch Mrs. Felson's cape for her?"

The boy did as he was asked, picking the cape up off the floor and looking it over all the while. He looked at Holmes and nodded, sadly I thought.

Holmes took the cape from him. I helped Mrs. Felson to her feet, and Holmes draped the garment around her.

"I couldn't help but notice your cape," he said to her. "It is a beautiful garment. Oh, I see that it has no store label. It was privately made?"

"Aye," Mrs. Felson said. "And one of a kind it is. I made it. There's none other that I've seen like it."

"Beautiful, indeed," Holmes said.

"Come along now, ma'am," said Gregson, and he and Lestrade and the boy left Bond Street with Mrs. Felson in tow.

On the way back to Baker Street, I asked, "How did you know, Holmes?"

"I didn't precisely, but from the coroner's report at the inquest, I was quite certain that the murder weapon, while similar in shape, was not the same as what we've seen in the other murders. In point of fact, it was somewhat larger, but it was not wielded with nearly the same force. That fact led me to suspect that while there was not a coiled machine spring behind the blade, such as the one you got a close look at on the train, neither was it likely that there was a man behind it.

"Victor Kerr had seen someone running from the scene at a time police later realized was shortly after the murder. But the boy, given all the time he spends having to sweep mud and dirt out of the way of some of the fanciest clothing London has to offer, quite naturally noticed more about the stranger's cape than he did about the person—a peculiarity that worked to our advantage in this instance."

"I hope the courts take her motives into account, Holmes; protecting her little boy and all."

"I'm sure they will, Watson, and when they do, she will swing without a doubt."

"What?"

"Six months ago, Neville Rolfe complained to the Yard that he was being blackmailed. It took great courage, because in order to do so he had to explain to police *why* he was being blackmailed. He was a homosexual, Watson, but not a pederast. He told police he suspected the blackmailer was his sister; they hated each other, and always had. It all fit. Lestrade had the pieces of this puzzle in his pocket all along, but he didn't know it because he insisted on trying to connect Rolfe's murder to the other cases.

"Had he kept an open mind, he might have done what I did, which was to have one of his minions follow Alice Felson to work. I saw her fancy cape, and thought we had our murderer. Very simple, really, though I hadn't expected she would give in so readily."

"What do you suppose pushed her to kill her brother?" I asked.

"I'm sure the police will find out, that is, if they question her properly, though there's no guarantee of that unless Gregson does it. Maybe Rolfe lost hope that the police would trap her, and he decided to confront her. Perhaps it was as simple as that."

"And she maimed him to make it look like one of the Marylebone murders?" I asked.

"Yes," Holmes said. "What could have been more timely?"

Chapter 21

At Holmes' request, the Yard managed to keep the arrest of Alice Felson quiet for quite some time. Of course, Lestrade had ample incentive to do so; he was not especially eager for anyone to know that he had been gulled—and by no less than a woman, a point that the ever-conventional inspector found most nettlesome.

"Well, Holmes," I said, "by so effectively clearing away the chaff among these cases, you have left us with the wheat, have you not? I think we should confront the Gibbonses, force their hand and be done with it."

"Absolutely not, Watson. We have only suppositions and suspicions, and no real evidence. We could confront them and hope they will fall apart like Alice Felson, but I think that is not much of a likelihood. No, Watson. These people are cold-blooded murderers, as vile and calculating as the worst that we have ever encountered. They may be *the* worst; if they are not, I am not sure I want to meet their superiors. We must continue to build our case somehow, and then we will brace them."

"I think we should grab these two before they can wreak more carnage, Holmes. You are being much too cautious. Forgive me for saying so."

The detective looked hurt. He turned away from me and reached for his beloved violin.

"Holmes, I mean no insult, man. I am sure you are right. Sure of it. It's just that the thought of these

wretches left loose . . . Shouldn't we at least have
another parley with Lestrade and Gregson to review
the developments?"

"Watson, you always have trusted my methods,"
Holmes said, "and you must do so now. Trust me
when I tell you that I must ponder the problem. I need
to think matters through. I do not want to conduct so
much as another interview until I have had a chance
to refresh my mental processes."

"I understand, Holmes," I said, "but I cannot help
worrying that by not moving swiftly, we are risking
disaster. The killers could flee and never be found. Or
there could be more murders."

"That is a risk we must take," he said. "I need to
have my wits about me, and considerably more energy, to go further. Right now, I have only some of
the former and precious little of the latter. And,"
Holmes said, somewhat cryptically, "I want to let
things simmer a bit."

"Simmer?" I sputtered. "Holmes, what do you
mean 'simmer'? Good Lord, we're awash in a boiling
cauldron as it is."

"Trust me, Watson. Dammit, man! Trust me. But
be wary. We are in deep waters. I don't want matters
complicated by anything else."

"Speak plainly, Holmes."

"I am saying be patient and supremely cautious at
all times. You have been carrying your service revolver since the assault on the train, have you not?"

At no time had I displayed my trusty Webley Double Action, though I had, in fact, made it my constant
companion of late. I knew better than to be surprised
by Holmes' powers of observation, but I did ask him
how he knew.

"The concealment of a weapon requires at least a
modicum of talent for duplicity, Watson, and you have
very little. You always betray concealment. It is simply
not in your nature to do otherwise. At two of the
more harrowing points in my story of my experience

with the killer, you reached to your side unconsciously; there could only be one reason: to be assured
of protection.

"On another occasion, I detected the slight, but unmistakable clink of brass when you put your hand in
the left pocket of your overcoat. Undoubtedly, some
loose cartridges."

I smiled slightly and nodded. "Very well, Holmes."
I still thought that for some inexplicable reason he
was stalling, but it was clear there was not much that
I could do to change his mind. And I was certain that
he did, indeed, need some rest. It was an odd position
for me. It has always fallen to me to admonish Holmes
to seek some respite from his work, but now here I
was, pressing for action.

Holmes had taken the chair by the window, and the
next thing I heard was his violin. The music seemed
more haunting and mournful than usual, and it made
me wonder if his interest in Mrs. Masterson had not
somehow undermined his customary aggressiveness. I
had seen it happen to others: A decisive man falls in
love and is riddled forever after by a heightened need
for self-preservation. It's as though love makes a man
too vulnerable for his own good. Perhaps it does. I do
not know. I am not a philosopher. But for the first
time in my long association with Holmes, I had to
wonder if, for whatever reason, he were not simply
scared.

Chapter 22

The next morning, Holmes left Baker Street early. He took a hansom cab to the Langham, where Mrs. Masterson joined him in the downstairs restaurant for a leisurely breakfast. I had been invited, but I demurred, knowing full well that although Holmes was making an uncharacteristically thoughtful effort to include me, what he wanted most was to spend some time with Mrs. Masterson. For this, he could hardly be blamed. He did relate to me the events of that meeting, however.

"You look tired, but well, Mr. Holmes," Mrs. Masterson said. "Those gray eyes of yours are sparkling."

"Thank you, Mrs. Masterson. I might say much the same of you."

"I am tired," she said. "I stayed up late writing in my journal. It's an old habit, and I'm afraid that I am compulsive about it. The day does not truly come to an end for me until I have set down my most private thoughts. Once I have done so, I am free to sleep. But even so, I have not slept well since I left Baker Street."

"Why is that," Holmes asked.

"I worry."

"You must not. What can I do to allay your fears?"

"Nothing, I'm afraid," she said. "I probably will not rest well until this business is done."

"Nor I," Holmes said. "I worry, too."

"As well you might," she said.

"No. Not so much for me. I fear for your well-being, your safety . . . and Watson's. I owe the two of you a great deal, and while I may be unalterably self-centered in some respects, I am not so egocentric as to want either of you exposed to further danger. I must insist that after tomorrow our contact be minimal . . . at least until I have brought this business to a close."

Abigail Masterson said nothing for a long moment. She sipped her tea and looked off toward the front of the restaurant. Then she turned back to Holmes, and looked intently at the detective.

"Mr. Holmes . . ."

"Sherlock . . . please."

"Very well . . . Sherlock . . . I will be blunt. Please do not 'insist' that I do, or not do, anything, or surely I will lose respect for you."

"It is only out of reasonable concern that I do so," Holmes said. "You must understand that."

"I do," she said. "I accept that your motives arise only out of fond concern, and I am touched. Truly. But are you making the same demand of Dr. Watson?"

"No, I am not," Holmes said. "He knows the danger, and he accepts the risk, as always."

"And why do you insist on treating me differently? You are being unfair. Damn you!" Abigail Masterson exhaled deeply, as if to vent steam.

The detective bristled. The very notion of being criticized was alien to him, and it left him ill at ease, if not angry. He started to speak, but stopped and, for the instant, could do nothing but look away from the woman.

She reached across the table as if to put her hand on his, but then withdrew it. "Oh, Sherlock," she said. "Hear me out. Please.

"I won't accept lies of any sort, even when it is kinder and more civil to prevaricate than to embrace the truth, and this chauvinism of yours is a kind of lie. It presumes that I am somehow incapable of taking care of myself. More than that, it presumes that I am not an adult, fully able to make my own choices and live with the consequences.

"I will not be ordered about for any reason, not by you or any other man. I will not have you acting as though you must shield me from life, even its most unsavory aspects. You must not presume to become my guardian angel. If there is danger to me, so be it," she said. "I suspect that it is inevitable in this line of work, and I freely accept the consequences. I got myself knocked down and bruised on the train the other day when we ran to Doctor Watson's aid, did I not?"

Holmes nodded.

"Well, you've not heard me complain, despite the fact that the experience left me with some rather sore bruises. And I would not complain. I accompanied you of my own accord, after all."

Mrs. Masterson lowered her voice so that it was little more than a whisper. "Besides, Sherlock, I am armed. I have a two-shot derringer laced to the outside of my right leg just above the knee."

The detective's face colored briefly, but she continued.

"It is well hidden by my skirts, but I can reach it quickly. It's an over-and-under, and it's loaded. The weapon is quite accurate up to about twenty feet. After that, you'd best have practiced a good deal. I am an excellent shot."

"You are a woman of infinite surprises," Holmes said.

"My work sometimes has exposed me to harm," Mrs. Masterson said, "sometimes by virtue of the neighborhoods that I have had to visit as a nurse; but sometimes, even in hospitals, and particularly when I was working in Bedlam. I long ago came to the realization that I had to rely on my own wits when confronted by trouble. A good many men in the medical profession fiercely resent professional women and will do nothing to help them, even under the most trying and precarious of circumstances."

"How often have you had to defend yourself?" he asked.

"A couple of times," she said.

"And when was the last?"

"About a year ago, in Spitalfields. I had been asked to tend to a boy of about twelve who had contracted cholera. I did so, but by the time I left the family's flat, it was after ten o'clock. The fog was heavy, as always. I walked quickly away from the building and continued for about two blocks. I had just walked by 'the Gypsy's,' which, as you know, is a notorious bar, even for the East End, when two men stepped out of the gloom. One of them grabbed me, and I kicked his shin as hard as I could. He reached for his leg in pain, but pushed me down hard on the roadside as he did so.

"Actually, being flat on my back made it somewhat easier to reach my pistol. While he was cursing me, his compatriot came at me. But by then I had the gun in my hand. I shot him straight through the right kneecap."

"What of his friend?"

"He was so enraged, you would have thought I had shot him. He charged at me like a bull, but by then I was on my feet. I sidestepped at the last instant and tripped him. He fell on his face, and I fled—none the worse for the experience."

"I see," Holmes said. "The modern woman. The new woman. No man need apply."

"Stop it, Holmes," Mrs. Masterson said. "Have you not heard anything I have said?"

"Yes, I have," Holmes said, "and don't raise your voice. The other diners are starting to pay attention. I have been listening, and yes, Mrs. Masterson, I have been hearing, and I have heard you explain that you need no one but yourself."

"I can, and do, manage on my own," she said, "but that is not the point. That is not the point at all. Oh! I thought you would be different, not just, just . . ."

"Just what, pray?"

"A man."

"I cannot help that, Mrs. Masterson. And I won't apologize for the fact."

"Any more than I can change my being a woman, Sherlock Holmes. Nor would I apologize for that!"

"What do you want from me, Mrs. Masterson?"

"I want you to understand and accept that I am your equal. Not as a detective, of course. Any more than you are my equal as a nurse or doctor. But equal as another person, regardless of my gender, and entitled to the same freedoms and the same respect."

Holmes was silent for some time.

"I give you my word that I will try to do so. I will try. There. Will that suffice?"

"How could I ask for more?"

"Most women seem to find a way," Holmes said.

"Any sentence that begins with the words 'Most women' deserves to be disregarded," she said.

"I suppose you are right," Holmes said. "You are angry?" he asked.

"Frustrated, perhaps."

"I did not mean to ruin the day," he said.

"Oh, you haven't. Friends should be able to argue and then quickly recover, don't you think?"

"I suppose that I do, Mrs. Masterson. In fact, I rather like the notion. Yes, I'm sure of it. We will speak our minds to each other without fail from this point on."

"You show considerable promise, Mr. Holmes."

"In that case, would you care to join your able student for a ride in the countryside?"

"I would be honored."

"Honored? I think probably not."

"Very well. Pleased, then."

" 'Pleased' will suffice," Holmes said.

Chapter 23

I saw little of Holmes for two days, and upon his return to Baker Street, it was obvious that his holiday had served to revitalize him. The spring sun and fresh air had returned some color to his features, and he seemed in a better frame of mind.

"You seem refreshed, Holmes."

"Yes. It was good to get away, however briefly," he said. "I think there is no better place to clear one's senses than on the South Downs; Mrs. Masterson had never been there before, and . . . Ah, but it's time that we returned to the business at hand, Watson. I suggest we review at least two points that we have not paid much attention to so far pertaining to the murder of Alexander Gibbons."

I was relieved to have Holmes back in the hunt, and to see that no matter what he had been doing, the murders had not been far from his mind. This was the Holmes I knew.

"First," he said, "there's the extraordinary violence of the crime to consider. All of the murders have been macabre and brutal, to be sure, but Alexander Gibbons' corpse was very nearly unrecognizable by the time his murderer was finished. The handiwork in the other slayings was more precise, but I would say that in the case of the clothier, the work was frenzied. There is evidence of a passion at work here. I have already told you what I think of this. The work evinces a deep-seated and savage hatred, sentiment bred only by the most elemental of wellsprings: love, sex or money; too little or too much. This points to family, as if we needed another indicator, for who but an intimate could be said to harbor such emotions?

"Secondly, Watson, do you recall the way Alexander Gibbons' hand was extended to such a degree that it made his fingers seem like talons?"

"I do. I believe we agreed that was the result of his agony."

"Yes, we did," Holmes said, "but without agreeing on the cause of it."

"Well, we presumed that because he was so horribly mutilated . . ."

"Presumed, yes, Watson. Presumed. Dammit, man! I was a dunce. My descent into the killer's madness must have affected my brain. I had presumed that the reason I did not find that telltale gouge mark in the floor around Gibbons' billiard table was simply that I had not had an opportunity to adequately search for it.

"I realize now that I would not have found such a mark if I had spent an entire day searching for it."

The look of puzzlement that I affected served as a question.

"The answer, Watson, has two parts. And the first is so simple as to be laughable. I would find no telltale sword mark on the floor because it was the Gibbons' own home, and one does not deface one's own property, and even if one were inclined to do so, one's mother would not allow it."

I laughed, but more in admiration. "That does fit, Holmes, doesn't it? As nasty as the slayings have been, there is a sense of meticulousness to them, and a fastidious treatment of the clothing that is removed, and . . ."

"And, Watson, whose first impulse was it, guilty or no, to scrupulously clean the murder scene?"

"Mrs. Gibbons, of course," I said. "She was particularly pointed about that with Lestrade, as I recall. So whoever used that blade probably took the instrument outside to force the retraction of the point, probably against pavement or a rock."

"Now, Watson, the second reason for the absence of the telltale mark . . . Consider the agony that Alexander Gibbons suffered in his death. What if its source were other than that abominable slashing? What if that bit of savagery came after?"

"It seems academic, Holmes."

"Not at all, Watson. What else might cause such horrible agony? You are a doctor, Doctor."

"Well, rat poison, would do it. Strychnine."

"Precisely, Watson. Strychnine causes the victim to convulse violently. It is an awful, furious death, and it causes the victim to expend energy so savagely and rapidly in his death throes that rigor mortis, or something very nearly identical to it, is instantaneous.

"This also would explain why the corpse stiffened so quickly. You will recall that merely three hours passed between the probable time of the murder and our examination of the body, and that at that time, Gibbons' corpse was rigid. You know as well I do that in the absence of any other inducement, rigor mortis is not plainly evident for a good four hours, on average.

"The inducement here was strychnine. I am sure of it. And how would a man ingest rat poison? It would have to be administered surreptitiously, would it not? And who would be in a better position to do so in a man's own home than his wife or children?"

"That certainly is plausible," I said. "That may, indeed, have happened. And given the mutilation of the body, the coroner could be expected to not look for evidence of poisoning. But why would they have poisoned him instead of just attacking him, stabbing him through the heart with the sword cane the way they did Nigel Whitney and Edward Gibbons?"

"Because, Watson, they were afraid of Alexander Gibbons, though it is not entirely clear why. But that was not the case with the other two."

"Rat poison is easy enough to acquire, Holmes. Any chemist in London would have it. You don't suppose . . ."

"Perhaps, Watson. Stranger things have happened. Let's go speak with Sidney Gibbons and see if he has sold any rat poison to his relatives recently."

Chapter 24

It was after 3 P.M. when Holmes and I finally arrived at the chemist's shop. Sidney Gibbons was busy with customers. Holmes excused himself for interrupting, and passed Gibbons a note.

"Whyn't you join me for tea at four o'clock, gentlemen?" Gibbons said in response. "That'd be good, wouldn't it? Is that all right? I can close the shop for a few minutes, and we can talk in private, eh?"

"Very well," Holmes said, and we left the shop.

Holmes looked abruptly up and down High Street and then turned to me. "We have forty-five minutes to waste, Watson. I suggest we have a glass of sherry."

"Capital," I said.

Over drinks, Holmes asked if I recalled our earlier discussion with Sidney Gibbons, and did he or did he not say that, with the sole exception of Albert, he had had nothing to do with any of the family for years until Alexander's funeral.

"That is what I recall, Holmes; yes," I said. "I am sure of it. I remember being taken somewhat aback by his remarks about the lot of them."

"Then, if he sold any of them rat poison, he will have been lying to us for some reason."

"Why, yes, Holmes. Of course, but why?"

"I do not know yet, though I have my suspicions. And there is another point that bothers me where the good Mr. Sidney Gibbons is concerned. His dislike of the family seemed to include his brother Edward. So we may infer that Edward was included in Sidney's insistence that he had no dealings with any members of the family—again, with the sole exception of young Albert Gibbons. Correct?"

I nodded my affirmation.

"And yet," Holmes said, "Sidney Gibbons had, in fact, made contact with Edward. Sidney's own words were 'on at least three occasions.' Further, Watson, he made it clear that he knew the terms of Nigel Whitney's will, at least as it pertained to him. Do you recall Sidney's saying that he himself had told Nigel that no bequest was necessary?"

"Right again, Holmes. We should have been paying more attention to Sidney Gibbons' story. The inconsistencies should have been obvious at once."

"They were, Watson. I was not unaware of them. But you will recall that the fate of Edward Gibbons was of more immediate concern, and his death certainly bore that out."

"So far, Holmes, the entire Gibbons family is not what it seems to be. I've never seen such a greedy and deceptive clan. Lord knows what they have done, every damned one of them."

"Yes, Watson. Ironically, the solicitor alone may have been without guile. We have not yet considered Albert or Jamey Gibbons, however. At any rate, we must be off. It would ill behoove us to be late to tea."

Less than a block from the chemist's shop, Holmes stopped abruptly, turned out of the wind, and lighted his pipe. I stopped short so as to not leave him behind.

"We are being followed, Watson. You have your service revolver, I trust?"

"Of course, Holmes," I told him. This cloak-and-dagger business was something new, and I did not welcome it. As we arrived at the chemist's shop, Sidney Gibbons was escorting the last customer out the front door.

"Ah, gentlemen," he said. "Come in. Come in. I've already put the pot on. We'll have tea in just a moment. How may I help you. Anything I can do, you need only . . ."

"You could help us, Gibbons," Holmes said abruptly, "by telling us the truth."

The remark took him by surprise.

"Why, Mr. Holmes, what do you . . ."

"You know my meaning very well. Do you take me for a fool? Your brother—to whom you were so close, you say—dies a wretched and untimely death, and you do not seem to have shed so much as a tear. 'A terrible loss, that,' you said, as though you were commenting on some turn of events in Parliament. Is that what passes for a brother's grief in the Gibbons family?"

I had not seen Holmes so aggressive in his questioning, and it took me quite by surprise, which was much the effect on Sidney Gibbons as well.

"See here, sir. You will leave my . . ."

Holmes took two steps forward, grabbed the man by the collar of his shirt and fairly threw him off his feet and into a chair just a few feet from the small stove where his teapot steamed and burbled.

"I'll not leave until you answer my questions, Gibbons. I am rapidly tiring of the lot of you. Now, when did you sell the strychnine to Mary McCormick Gibbons?"

"I didn't . . ."

Holmes turned to me abruptly. "Watson, is the front door locked? I'm going to give Mr. Gibbons a taste of the Marylebone Monster's methods. Fetch me that boiling water from the stove will you?"

I knew that Holmes was intensely angry, but I had never known him to lose control. I was sure he was running a gambit, so I quickly moved to the stove and reached for the iron teapot. Sidney Gibbons' eyes went wide, and he began stammering. "No. No, please. Don't. I didn't know . . ."

"You didn't know what?" Holmes shouted. "You didn't know that your brother's neighborhood is one of the few in London that has not been plagued by rats for years? You knew why she wanted the poison, didn't you? Didn't you?"

"Yes." Sidney Gibbons blurted it out. "Yes, I knew. Yes. She said that by the time they finished, no one would ever suspect it. Don't hurt . . ."

"They? Mary and the boys?"

"Yes. Her and that foul son of . . ."

"Did you ever speak of any of this with Jamey or Albert?"

"No," Sidney said. "Only the Missus."

"How much did she promise you from Alexander's estate?"

"Another £20,000."

"A princely profit, Mr. Gibbons. You made £20,000 from Nigel's bequest, and then stood to double your gain by helping to dispense with Alexander."

"I didn't kill him. I didn't kill him."

"How much did Nigel leave in his will to the love of his life?"

I looked incredulously at Holmes, who was towering over Gibbons as though he would reach for his throat at any instant.

"How much did Mary get?"

Sidney Gibbons looked up at Holmes with a mixture of fear and hatred in his eyes. "All of the rest. All of it. About £80,000."

"You're going to swing, you know."

"I didn't kill him. I didn't kill him."

"Oh, stop it," Holmes spat out. "You sniveling little coward. You murdered your brother as surely as if you had poured the poison for him yourself and then wielded the blade that mutilated him. You'll have a hard time convincing a jury of anything else."

"I didn't kill him."

"I think instead of waiting to see you hang, Gibbons, Watson and I will find a way to inform your dear sister-in-law and her son that you have given them over. How does that sound? There won't be enough pieces of you left to put on the gibbet."

"No!" he screamed. "No. They're crazy. Both of them. No, I beg of you. Don't do that, they'll . . ." The man broke into tears, and it was obvious from the odor and the spreading stain on his trousers that he had soiled himself. But Holmes did not relent.

"How long do you suppose they will let you live, Gibbons? I half expected to find you trussed up and carved like a Christmas goose before we could confront you. Surely, the prospect must have occurred to you. Nigel is dead. Edward is dead, so he can't point the police toward Nigel's will. Only you remain, and you can prove that they killed Alexander.

"Do you suppose they're going to wait for you to take that knowledge to a natural and distant grave, Gibbons? How much longer do you think you have? Another day? Two days? A week? A month?

"And you really believe they are going to hand over the £20,000 you've been promised from Alexander's will? You are a fool, Gibbons! Whether we turn you over to them for the turncoat and vermin that you are, or we walk out of here and say nothing, you are already dead. The only unanswered question is how much your nephew will make you suffer before you die. He is quite adept at it, you know. He doesn't like to dispatch his prey with any speed. He prefers to play with them. He'll cut . . ."

"Stop it," Gibbons shrieked. "Stop." The chemist fell from the chair to his knees as though he were melting. He clutched Holmes' legs, and raised his head to the detective. "Oh, God, please!" he screamed. "Help me, please."

Holmes stood in silence for long moments, watching without expression while Sidney Gibbons sobbed and groveled.

"There is another option," Holmes said calmly. "Tell me what I want to know right now, and we will let you leave here. We will wait two hours before going to Scotland Yard."

"Anything, yes. Yes," Gibbons said. "Oh, yes. Please. Anything."

"Did Alexander Gibbons know of Nigel's love for Mary?"

Gibbons was quiet at first. He sucked in his breath a few times and sat back down in the chair, looking away from us.

"Yes, he knew. Not at first, but by the time Albert was born, he'd figured it out, and confronted our father with it. The old man told him the truth. My father had caught the two of them, Nigel and Mary, in bed. He had come home unexpectedly from the store one afternoon and surprised them. Mary and Alexander were engaged to be married at the time. My father flew into a bloody rage. He beat Nigel to within an inch of his life and threatened to expose her for the slut that she was.

"Nigel was deeply and passionately in love with her. He left the family, changed his name and all, but he never gave up on the witch. She didn't love him. Didn't love anyone or anything.

"But she preyed on Nigel. Years after Jamey was born, she went to Nigel and told him she still loved him, that she had always loved him, but she couldn't disgrace the family by leaving Alexander. Truth was, as soon as Alexander had found out about her and Nigel, he had made strict and complex provisions in his will that would have prevented Albert from contributing to the welfare of his brother *and* their mother in any way. And just to be sure that he would have his revenge if anything happened to Albert, he cut Jamey out of the will, completely. Alexander had come to believe that Jamey wasn't his son, but Nigel's.

"In effect, Alexander left everything to Albert. It was a secret. I had to wheedle it out of Edward. While he was alive, Alexander gave Mary barely enough to run the household on, and he made Jamey beg for whatever he wanted. So she kept meeting with Nigel on the sly."

"And how was that accomplished?" Holmes asked sharply.

"Easy," Sidney Gibbons said with a smug look at Holmes. "She'd take off that grand wig she wears. Her real hair is close-cropped like her boys', so she'd walk right over to the shop looking for all the world like Albert or Jamey just out and about."

"So Nigel gave her money every month, and she gave him her affections in return?"

"Aye," Sidney Gibbons said. "That's it. Nigel really loved her, the poor old fool; he was blind to everything. He'd been her lover for years, and she was still milking him and nobody knew it."

"But you did," said Holmes, "and so did Albert."

"Yes. Jamey doesn't have a normal thought in his head, that one. He never knew what went on. All he knew was that he hated his father for the way he treated him, and especially for the way he treated Mary. God only knows what goes on between that woman and her sons. As far as Jamey is concerned, his mother's some Madonna that fell out of a painting. Only Albert knew the whole story."

"How?" Holmes asked.

"I told him. He was troubled by his parents; his brother, too. But he knew Jamey had never had a right moment. Albert couldn't fathom why his mother and father hated each other so, and it was driving him to distraction."

"So as his loyal confidant, you explained it to him, eh?" Holmes asked.

"I did. Seemed only right," Gibbons said. "I felt for the boy. Somebody had to look out for him. Somebody had to tell him the truth."

"But you didn't tell him the complete truth, did you, Gibbons? You didn't tell him that you were blackmailing his mother, did you?"

Holmes might as well have struck the man; the impact was that visible.

"No," Gibbons said in a barely audible voice.

"What threat did you use, Gibbons? What did you hold over her?"

"I told her . . ."

The man's head was bowed, and his voice was soft.

"Speak up!" Holmes demanded.

"I threatened to go to Alexander, to expose her for the whore she still was. He already hated her for the relationship she had had with Nigel. Alexander beat her whenever the spirit moved him. If he had known she was still seeing Nigel, he'd have killed her."

"Get out of my sight," Holmes said. "Go! You have two hours. And then we go to Scotland Yard. Get out. Now!"

Holmes stood with his arm outstretched, pointing toward the back door of the shop, like a self-appointed God casting Lucifer into the darkness. Sidney Gibbons cowered before him. He rose from his chair, turned quickly away and ran out of the shop, into the labyrinth of alleys behind the storefronts on High Street.

"Incredible," I said. "How did you know all of that, Holmes? I can't believe that after figuring it out, you'd let that miserable bit of offal escape."

"He won't escape, Watson," the detective said, rather obliquely I thought. "As for the rest, I have often said that when you eliminate what is possible, what remains, however implausible, must be the truth. Sidney Gibbons' complicity was, in the final analysis, the only thing that made sense."

"But I don't . . ."

My words were cut short by a piercing scream. Though it was some little distance away, it was unmistakable.

"Great Scott, Holmes! What was that?"

Holmes looked directly at me. His teeth were clenched so hard that his lips quivered when he spoke. "I believe that was justice, Watson—calling on Sidney Gibbons."

Chapter 25

We found Sidney Gibbons not two blocks away. He had been impaled atop an eight-foot cast-iron gate that blocked the alley and faced the street. An ornate picket protruded from the back of his neck. His scream had drawn attention, and two policemen were on hand already. Lestrade had been notified and was on his way, presumably.

I stood watching as the policemen extricated Gibbons from the gate with considerable difficulty, and then quickly covered the corpse. It struck me that the man was as pitiable in death as he had been in life, but then I had another realization, and the enormity of it hit me like a boxer's fist.

"You knew," I said to Holmes. "Bloody hell, man! You knew something like this would happen. You were expecting it. You knew that someone was watching us and waiting."

Holmes turned and eyed me coldly. "Yes, Watson. I thought as much, but the game needed some little time in which to play itself out. I needed to be certain. Mrs. Masterson and I were followed yesterday from the time we left the Langham until we gave our watcher the slip in Paddington Station. We took a train down to Sussex and hired a coach for our foray into the Downs. It was made all the more enjoyable by the fact that the watcher had no idea where we were going or why.

"His actions did convince me, however, that we had to brace Sidney Gibbons as soon as possible. Until this moment, I thought it was one of the Gibbonses who was following us; now I know that it was not. But I knew that someone was, and that he was bent on doing harm."

"If we were not being watched and followed by one of the Gibbonses, Holmes, then by whom?"

"Right now, I know only that elementary physics precludes Albert and Jamey Gibbons having anything to do with this murder."

"A big man, then?" I asked.

"And a strong man, and one who is in a murderous rage."

"And you sent this wretch, Sidney, straight out to meet this . . . this killer, all the same? I do not believe you, Holmes. I cannot believe you could undertake something so diabolical. Why, you probably would have poured that boiling tea water on Gibbons, too!"

The detective spun around on his heels, and for a moment I thought he was going to strike me.

"Don't be naive, Watson! Sidney Gibbons was every bit as guilty of grisly murder as Jack the Ripper. He helped set four killings in motion. And need I mention to you, Doctor, that when I close my eyes at night, I still hear my own screams at the hands of a tormented maniac? Or that I see Dickie Quinn, a boy of thirteen, an orphan of these streets coming to my rescue, only to be savaged, violated before my eyes, and then slaughtered?"

The detective's face was livid. He was trembling with rage.

"Did you think for a moment that I would be satisfied merely to play by Marquis of Queensbury rules and hand such fiends over to the courts? Did you!? That is my last resort, Watson, my very last resort. I am going to see them dead. If I have to do so, I will wring the life from their worthless bodies with my own hands."

He was silent. I was dumbfounded. When next he spoke, he was calm and under control.

"For what it's worth, Watson, I intended only to scare Sidney Gibbons with that kettle of boiling water. I would not have engaged in torture. But as for the rest of it, understand that neither you nor anyone else will stay my retribution. If you want to remain with me, then please do, for I need you and I value your help and, God knows, your friendship. But with you or without you, I am going to see them dead. I am sworn to this."

My own voice trembled now. I put my hand on my old friend's shoulder and said, "May God forgive you, Holmes." And with that, I left the great detective watching after me as I stepped from his side and walked out of the alley.

Chapter 26

I did not return to Baker Street for several hours. I briefly contemplated not returning at all, but decided, at length, that I had no choice. My friendship with Holmes, and my sense of loyalty and honor, binds me to him. But I have determined that regardless of how understandable or justifiable his revenge might be, I will not become an accomplice to murder. I will help him do whatever is necessary to put the killers on the gallows, but I will not become a vigilante; for then I would be no better than our quarry. Moreover, I determined that if it were at all possible, I would prevent Holmes from sinking to those very same depths.

Holmes and Mrs. Masterson were seated by the fire when I entered the room.

"Watson. Good. I had begun to worry," Holmes said. "I am glad you are here. Will you help us fathom through this business? Mrs. Masterson arrived only moments ago, and we were just talking about our friends the Gibbonses."

"What of them, Holmes?" I asked. My response must have indicated a measure of indifference, for they both looked at me with some surprise.

Holmes frowned his disapproval, and his words had a curt and angry edge to them. "Specifically, I am wondering what additional role the enterprising young Mr. Albert Gibbons has played in this affair."

"Well," I said, "beyond helping his mother to extort thousands of pounds from the members of his father's civic improvement association, I don't know, I am sure. That alone will land him in prison, no doubt. It would seem entirely plausible that he had something to do with the murders."

"Why do you say that?" Holmes asked.

"Because every member of that awful family seems guilty of one great misdeed or another. We already know that Albert and his mother are crooks. It just seems that the odds favor much deeper involvement."

"Hmmm. Well put," Holmes said.

"I believe I have persuaded him to visit us this evening. I told him that if he did not come, then we would go directly to Scotland Yard with details of his Bond Street activities. He knows that police throughout the city are driving themselves to distraction trying to find him as it is, and he knows that I have found his lair."

"Albert Gibbons is back in the city?"

"He never really left, Watson. He has simply been in hiding, which is what I suspected. I put the Irregulars on his trail, and Wiggins reported yesterday that they had located Albert. Gibbons had accurately divined that after Scotland Yard had finished at Nigel Whitney's and the place had been boarded up, the rooms over the tobacconist's shop would be a better hiding place than most.

"Unfortunately, however, Albert Gibbons will not be able to tell us who killed Sidney Gibbons. I may have that answer, Watson, but I am not sure. It seems too fantastic to discuss yet. We must wait for more developments."

No sooner had the detective finished speaking than Mrs. Hudson knocked on the door to say that we were wanted downstairs.

Holmes and I hastened to the front door, where we were met by Wiggins and his friend Tommy Jacobs. A rolled, somewhat lumpy, carpet lay at their feet.

" 'Ere's yore package, Mr. 'Olmes," Wiggins said.

"Ah, thank you, Wiggins," said Holmes, giving each of the boys a coin.

As they left, Holmes turned to me and said, "Help me, would you?"

I gave him an uncertain look.

He took one edge, nodded for me to take the other end of it, and with a great pull, together we unrolled the carpet. Out tumbled one Albert Gibbons.

"An unconventional way to travel, wouldn't you say, Watson? But it has proven to be a safe one."

I did not know what to say.

"Are you quite all right, Mr. Gibbons?" Holmes asked.

"Yes, I think so," said the young man. "It was pretty stuffy in there."

The young man who stood before us was generally handsome, lean of build, with his mother's jet-black hair, though his was close-cropped, her pallid complexion and the same piercing dark eyes.

"I regret that this subterfuge was necessary," Holmes said.

Gibbons nodded. "Maybe some good will come of it," he said, "but I did get rather mussed."

He followed us upstairs to our rooms, brushing dust and carpet fibers off his jacket as he went. He was still plucking at his clothing when Holmes introduced him to Mrs. Masterson.

"My pleasure, ma'am," he said distractedly.

Mrs. Hudson brought us tea, and we all sat. Albert sipped from his steaming cup and continued to dust off his clothing with the flat of his hand.

"Why have you not gone to the police?" Holmes asked.

"I . . . I have not wanted to bring shame on my family, Mr. Holmes, either through my own actions or those of my family . . . and I have feared for my life."

"One would think that sooner or later the fact of the latter would outweigh any concern for the former," Holmes said.

"I haven't known just what I should do," Albert said.

"I think you are without much spine, young man," Holmes said. "Furthermore, you are a thief, an extortionist. You have been squeezing extra funds from the association members."

The young man bristled in protest, but tears welled up in his eyes. "What you say is true, Mr. Holmes. Before all that is holy, I am ashamed, and I have resolved that when this business is settled, I will do whatever is necessary to restore the money to the association members. And if needs be that I go to jail for what I did, then I will do so. I will pay my debt in full, Mr. Holmes. That is my intention. Please do not judge me so harshly."

"What have you done with the money?" Holmes demanded.

"I've done nothing but hand it over to my mother and Jamey, sir. Every pound," Albert said.

"For what purpose?" Holmes asked.

"I do not know."

"You do not know, Mr. Gibbons?" Holmes asked. "Really? Do you expect us to believe that you have collected untold sums of money and even been party to the breaking of a tradesman's thumbs, without knowing the reason? You disgust me! Do you take us for fools?"

"I do not, sir. But the Lord's own truth is that I was merely doing what I was forced to do. I had no choice in the matter. You have no idea what he is like, Mr. Holmes. You can't possibly know."

"Oh, I have a good idea, Albert. But why don't you help us to understand? Tell us about Jamey. Have you always feared him?"

"For as long as I can remember, sir. He is twenty-six years old, two years my junior, and I . . . I have always been afraid of him." He looked down at the floor, wringing his hands. "He delights in causing pain. When we were boys, he would capture small animals and torture them. Sometimes he would set them on fire. I tried to stop him every time, but he was always very strong and quick."

"Did your parents not know this?" Abigail asked.

"My father did, and whenever a reason presented itself, he would take a strap to Jamey; but it never did any good. Jamey told me once that he got more pleasure from the beatings than he did from his 'playing' with the animals. And my mother always sided against my father. She'd say it was just Jamey's way, and he'd grow out of it, and there was no need to treat him so cruelly. They fought over him often. But then, they fought over everything. Jamey has always been her favorite."

"There were never two brothers but that one didn't think the other was his parents' favorite," Holmes said.

"I suppose that's true, sir. But theirs has never been what you would call a normal relationship." Albert's face colored, and he looked away from us again. "Begging your pardon ma'am, but some of what I have to say is . . ."

"Off-color?" Mrs. Masterson suggested.

"Yes."

"I will not be offended," she said, "nor will I think ill of you."

"Very well."

"My father spent a good deal of time with me when I was a boy growing up, but almost never with Jamey. He taught me the business, but I don't have the knack and instinct for it that he did. My mother insisted that Jamey be allowed to work in the store as well, but it was disastrous. He couldn't even stock shelves to my father's satisfaction. There were always scenes. My father would explode at him and strike him. That hurt Jamey because I think that, at least at first, Jamey really wanted to have a hand in the business and to have our father's approval. But he couldn't get it. No matter what he did, he could barely get a kind word from him.

"I learned years later from my uncle Sidney that Jamey's real father was probably my uncle, Nigel, or at least that's what my father believed. And that was the real cause of the warfare between my parents. That and the way mother treated Jamey, like he was a prince of some kind. I think the harder my father was on Jamey, the more my mother cared for him, as if to compensate for my father's cruelty.

"And it *was* cruelty, Mr. Holmes. There's no other way to describe it. I argued with my father about it more than once. But it was never much of an argument. It always ended the same way. He would tell me to mind my own business, and that my brother was his problem not mine, and if I wanted to stay in my father's house, I had better keep my own counsel."

Albert's face was contorted with emotion at various points in his story, and more than once his voice faltered and his eyes teared up. Holmes, however, betrayed no emotion. He sat smoking his briar pipe or sipping tea and listening intently, sometimes with his eyes tightly closed. When Albert paused, Holmes said, as he had more than once during this account, "Pray, continue. Leave nothing out."

"When Jamey was a youngster, my mother always dressed him in fancy clothes and curled his hair. My father would have at her for it, but it did no good. To this day, she still calls Jamey her 'Sweet' or her 'Pet' or 'Little Prince.' She even calls him 'Plaything.' " Albert looked away again.

Holmes' eyes blinked several times in rapid succession, and he puffed on his pipe more vigorously. "Mr. Gibbons, the truth always requires courage. Rest assured that you have it. It only needed some prodding. We do not judge you unkindly for that. Pray, continue now."

I looked at Mrs. Masterson and found her looking with fond admiration at Holmes. I could not help but envy him. His compassionate interjection was precisely the right thing to say to the young man. His flair for dramatic good timing was always impeccable, but the sentiment was no less genuine for that.

"Thank you, sir," Albert Gibbons said. "I firmly believe that my parents hated each other. In some ways, you could say that Jamey was the battleground upon which they fought their wars. But they—Jamey and my mother, that is—always feared my father. He drank a good deal at night, and he would fly off at them all the quicker when he was in his cups. And he'd threaten to turn them out, divorce my mother and disown Jamey."

"Are you aware that your father left his entire estate to you, Albert?" Holmes asked.

The young man nodded. "My uncle Sidney told me."

"Was your mother aware of the changes in the will?" I asked.

Albert was silent. He looked at the floor, and then at Holmes and me.

"Yes, she knew. I told her as soon as I found out."

"And her reaction?" Abigail asked.

"She was furious," Albert said. "But I told her not to worry, that despite the provisions in the will, I would find a way to take care of her and Jamey. How could I do otherwise? They are . . ." The young man paused and choked back tears. He cleared his throat and continued. "They are my family, my mother and brother. Mr. Holmes, how could I not see to their needs?

"My mother was still very angry. One night the following week, she confronted my father over the change in the will. She told him she would fight it in court if she had to. He had been drinking again, and he lost his temper. He jumped up from his chair and swatted her onto the floor like a bug. Then he kicked her in the side. I ran to get between them, but Jamey stepped into the room just then, and my father stopped. I think he was starting to fear Jamey.

"Apart from that, in the weeks just before his murder, there hadn't been much trouble at all. Just one other time, one incident. He had walloped my mother hard, and both of us, Jamey and me, tried to get between them, and he thumped us a few times, too, but that pretty much took it out of him.

"My parents slept in separate bedrooms for as long as I can remember, and the next morning when my father awoke and set his feet on the floor, he got his feet cut in several places. During the night, pieces of broken bottle glass had been spread all around his bed on the floor.

"Jamey had done it, and my father knew it. I think my father realized right then that he had gone too far too many times, so he eased up. So for the few weeks before he died, it was like there was a truce of some kind. But then the store went up in flames, and that changed everything.

"My father was distraught over the fire. He seemed, all of a sudden, like a broken man. It is a terrible thing to watch your father come apart emotionally, Mr. Holmes. He was sullen and morose, and after a day in which he said very little to anyone, he accused my brother of setting the fire.

"My brother cried, 'How could I do such a thing, Abba? Why would I . . .' "

Holmes interrupted him. "He called your father Abba?"

"Why, yes," Albert said, seeming somewhat surprised that Holmes had fastened on the point. "That was Jamey's reference to him. It always has been. My father hated it, but Jamey insisted on using it. 'Abba' is from the Bible. The word is synonymous with God, but it is a common sign of reverence for the father. Jamey always used it. The word has almost mystical significance for him."

"Are you a religious family?" I asked.

"My father was raised a Presbyterian, but once his father died, he announced that he had never believed in the church's doctrines and hereafter would have nothing to do with it. He said he only kept up appearances because my grandfather insisted on it.

"My mother is a Catholic, but she is not devout. Only Jamey pays any attention to it," Albert said. "He carries a Bible with him wherever he goes. He is always reading it. I think it's a kind of escapism, myself, but Jamey has always found comfort and meaning in it, especially the Old Testament."

"He always carries a Bible?" Holmes asked.

"Yes, sir. He is never without it. Never. In the past several years, I have not seen him so much as walk around the house but that he had it in his hand."

"I have diverted you," Holmes said. "Please go back to the confrontation over the fire at the store."

"Ah, yes. Jamey protested that he would never have done such a thing, but my father would have none of it. He knew how much Jamey and my mother hated the business. He said he was going to the police and that he would have Jamey arrested."

"Why did your mother and brother hate the business so," Holmes asked. "It was your father's devotion to the business that brought prosperity for the family, was it not?"

"Yes, of course, sir. I knew that. So did my mother, but she wanted no part of any business that had service as a precept. She felt that it was demeaning. I never agreed, but that was how she felt. She also resented the amount of work and time that the business commanded. It left my father very little time for anything else."

"And this was Jamey's opinion as well?" I asked.

"It was," Albert said. "I think he hated the business even more than my mother did, but of course he would never let on. To Jamey, the store was a reminder of his failure in his father's eyes. He believed that if he could have been good enough to work in the store, he would have had his father's affection, but he could not handle the work, and so the place taunted him somehow. He hated it all right."

"Enough to burn it?" Abigail asked.

"Oh, I should say so," Albert said. "Yes. I do not doubt that he burned it. He would see it as a hellfire, a punishment of wickedness."

"You are not at all religious yourself?" Holmes interjected.

"As I said, sir, no. I am not. I have come to understand some things about religion. Jamey's preoccupation raised my curiosity, you might say."

"Mr. Gibbons, in each instance of murder, the eyes of the victim were destroyed," Holmes noted. "What do you make of that from a religious point of view?"

"An eye for an eye, perhaps? That is a precept of the Old Testament. I do not know. The eyes as the mirror of the soul? By destroying the eyes, the murderer was annihilating the soul? Is that a possibility, Mr. Holmes? Dear God, such delusion. It is so sad." The young man appeared gripped by despair. He alternately wrung his hands and seemed to pick at some dust on his trousers, though I could see none.

The detective was silent. He puffed on his pipe and, finding that it had gone out, rose from his chair. I watched patiently as he performed the ritual I had come to take for granted. From the fireplace mantel, he plucked the pocketknife that he used to keep unanswered correspondence pinned in place, pushed it back onto the shelf, scraped the ash and sediment from the bowl of the pipe, emptied it into the fireplace and stuck the penknife back into the mantel. Then he opened the Persian slipper that hung from the mantel, dipped the pipe, bowl first, into the toe of the slipper and repacked the instrument with fresh tobacco. As he relighted his briar, the detective looked at us and then directly at Albert Gibbons, puffing as he spoke, smoke rising in small white billows that came between breaths.

"It may be simpler than a biblical interpretation," Holmes said. "It has long been suspected that the last image a person sees before death is frozen in his eyes."

Albert seemed startled.

"Yes, of course," he said. "I believe I have read as much. So by slashing his victims' eyes, the killer was trying to hide his own identity?"

"Perhaps, " Holmes said, "but if so, then the killer is an imbecile, a blundering, moronic and incompetent fool." Holmes spit out the insult.

Gibbons sat stiffly upright, with a noticable jerk.

"One of the inspectors at Scotland Yard only last year rather effectively disproved the worth of the theory," Holmes said. "He was assigned, as were many others, to investigate the so-called 'Ripper' slayings. He convinced his superiors that he should be allowed to photograph the eyes of the dead prostitutes so that he might thereby get a glimpse of the murderer. The experiment failed miserably. But it was not reported in the press because by then the commissioner had fairly well stifled all such reports in the interest of investigative confidentiality."

"I see," Gibbons said.

"And why, Mr. Gibbons, do you appear to take some offense at my insult to the murderer?"

"I do not mean it to seem so," he said with an earnest, almost hangdog frown. "The truth is, I am protective, even now, of my brother, Mr. Holmes. I did not mean to give you the wrong impression, but I fear that my brother is the so-called Monster of St. Marylebone, and I pity him for that."

"Of course," Holmes said. "In fact, your brother's future as a free man right now would seem to be in considerable jeopardy. Let me ask you, Mr. Gibbons, does Jamey ever wear woman's cosmetics?"

"Yes, sir, he does. Powder. When he was in his teens, he developed that skin condition which so often afflicts young men. Acne, I believe it is called. It left his face, and his back, too, quite scarred. He is very self-conscious about it. When he ventures out, he usually wears some makeup in an effort to mask the condition."

"I see," Holmes said. "I have one last question, sir. Did you and your mother argue shortly after your father's funeral?"

"We did, sir, with some vehemence. She insisted that I move back into the family home on Upper Wimpole Street, and I refused. I told her that I could not, and that I feared for my own safety there."

"And her response?"

"She felt insulted, and she was angry, but I stood my ground."

"Well, Mr. Gibbons, thank you for mustering the courage to tell us your story. You will have to repeat the substance of it for the benefit of Scotland Yard at some point in the immediate future."

"Of course, sir," said Albert Gibbons.

"Have you anything further to add?"

"Only that I . . . I loved my father, despite all of this. And I feel bad for my family, or rather what is left of it. Is there any chance at all, Mr. Holmes, that the courts will exercise some mercy in Jamey's case? And my own, for what I have done? I can be held liable, I know, but I wonder if my brother can be held accountable for his own actions."

"I cannot engage in guesswork, Mr. Gibbons. There is no way of knowing what the courts will do or, for that matter, what the future holds for any of us. That is a condition of life—precarious, uncertain, without guarantees of any kind."

"How will you go back home tonight?" I asked Gibbons.

"I've decided, Doctor, that I am simply going to walk out the front door and onto Baker Street and then to my late uncle's rooms. Tomorrow, I will move back into my flat on Harley Street. If I am arrested by the police, then so be it. I will atone for my sins. I will accept whatever comes my way. Speaking with you has emboldened me."

"Good for you, young man!" I said. "That's the spirit."

"You will be safe tonight," Holmes told the young man. "The youngsters who collected you will be following to be certain no one troubles you. If they spot the police, they will whistle as a signal."

Albert Gibbons nodded and turned to leave. He opened the door, but before he could exit, Holmes called out to him sharply: "Here! Mr. Gibbons. Don't forget your walking stick."

Gibbons began to turn back toward us, but stopped abruptly. After a pause, he turned to face us. He looked directly at Holmes, his black eyes flashing like hot rivets. A tight smile crossed his lips. He spoke softly.

"I did not bring a cane with me," he said.

Holmes fixed him with his own stare . . . and an equally tight smile.

"Forgive me," he said. "I am in error."

Gibbons nodded curtly and with that, left our quarters.

I walked over to the sideboard and poured three brandies.

"Well, Holmes, Mrs. Masterson, a remarkable story, wouldn't you say?"

"Oh, it is that," he said. "It is quite remarkable, indeed."

Mrs. Masterson said nothing. She looked upset. Despite the usually calming effect of brandy, the color had drained from her face.

Chapter 27

Holmes escorted Mrs. Masterson back to the Langham, and I was half asleep by the time he returned.

"What do you think of Albert Gibbons?" I asked.

"Until tonight I was not absolutely certain of our murderer's identity," Holmes said. "Now there can be no doubt."

"I expect that Lestrade will be somewhat shocked," I said.

"Lestrade is always somewhat shocked by the solution of a crime," Holmes said.

I laughed. "Yes, to some degree, I suppose. But he will have his hands full with this one, even though it is you who will have brought his case to a close once again. And the newspapers will have a field day with it."

"Yes, I suppose they will," Holmes said. "I am going to stay up for a while, Watson. I have some thinking to do. But we must be at Scotland Yard early, so be sure to wake me if I'm not up already when you arise."

In fact, by the time I awoke, Holmes was halfway through a hearty breakfast. "Get moving, Watson. Your breakfast grows cold, and we both will need some stamina today."

We ate in silence. Holmes quietly shuffled through the day's newspapers as I struggled to push away my grogginess. We were putting on our overcoats preparing to leave our Baker Street lodgings when Mrs. Hudson called to us.

Holmes shouted back impatiently. "What is it, Mrs. Hudson? We are going out."

"Sorry to bother you, sir. You have a visitor."

"We can't see anyone now, Mrs. Hudson. We are leaving in one minute." He sounded perturbed.

"It's Mr. Mycroft, Mr. Holmes."

"Mycroft here? Very well," Holmes said. "Send him up, please."

The tall and wide frame of the detective's brother nearly filled the doorway to our apartment.

"Mycroft," Holmes said, "what prospective calamity in Whitehall brings you here?"

"I see that you have had recent dealings with the unfortunate Mr. Sidney Gibbons," he said with a tight smile.

I was startled, but not as much as I might have been were this the first time I had been witness to the brothers' gamesmanship. The detective always insisted that Mycroft was every bit his equal in the art and science of deduction. It was only Holmes' energy and aggressiveness that gave him the edge, he said.

"That poisoner's handbook lying open on your desk, Sherlock, indicates that, as usual, you did your homework. I am aware of your work on the Marylebone case, of course, and I know that the Gibbons family figures prominently in it. The only Gibbons who is a chemist, or rather, *was* a chemist, is that man Sidney. Hence, my conclusion."

"Good, Mycroft. Elementary, to be sure; but very good, nevertheless."

"I presume it was not you who killed Gibbons, Sherlock?"

"You know better, Mycroft," the detective said, "and Sidney Gibbons was not merely killed; he died horribly."

"I know," Mycroft said. "I know. Dreadful business."

"Mycroft, the fact that you chose to walk here this morning—by way of Portman Square, I might add—instead of taking a hansom cab would indicate a lack of urgency to your visit. And yet, the fact that you are here at all and not in your office in Whitehall, your rooms on Pall Mall or the sepulchral chambers of the Diogenes Club presages something of moment, I would say.

"You are quite right on all counts. I presume you noticed the red clay dust on my boots; the repair work in Portman Square."

"Precisely," Holmes said, "and I'm glad to see that you weren't seriously hurt when you tripped and fell."

Mycroft smiled and waited for his younger brother to continue.

"Well, the toe of your left boot is scuffed; it's noticeable even though you have tried to rub off the mark. There is a slight touch of dark red on the right knee of your trousers, and the knuckles of your right hand have been recently scraped. Your left foot caught on something, probably the corner of a paver, and you used your right arm in an effort to break your fall, but your knee hit the ground."

"Yes. There is a reason I don't make it a habit to amble about the city very much. I tend toward clumsiness. Obviously, your health is vastly improved, Sherlock, and you are back in good form. I am glad. Let me come to the point."

"Do," Holmes said.

"Late last night, we received word that one of the Crown's most reliable agents was found dead in Ireland. His name was Peter O'Reilly, Sherlock. He had infiltrated a cell of the Irish Republican Brotherhood quite some time ago, and ever since had proved himself to be a most reliable source of information.

"His last message to us, only a few days ago, was startling. He reported that for the past three years, the lion's share of financial support for these terrorists has been coming from London itself."

"I am not surprised, Mycroft," the detective said.
"One man's terrorist is another man's patriot."

"Be that as it may, Sherlock, the source of the
money appears to be none other than Bond Street."

"Ah, yes," Holmes said. "The Bond Street Civic
Improvement Association, no doubt."

"No doubt," Mycroft said.

"Frankly, I had already deduced as much," Holmes
said. "Albert Gibbons collected the money every week
and then handed it over to his mother. He insists that
he had no idea of the collections' purpose, but
whether he did or not really is of little consequence.
Mary McCormick Gibbons knew exactly what the
money was for."

"Indeed," Mycroft said, "it was for her brother."

Holmes raised his eyebrows.

"Michael McCormick, one of the leaders of the Irish
Republican Brotherhood," Mycroft said. "He's been
in the thick of it for many years. He's a brutal, merci-
less scoundrel. We think it was he, in fact, who killed
our agent, broke his neck and sent him floating down
the Liffey."

"I have no quarrel with Michael McCormick,"
Holmes said. "As for the rest of his family, that is
another matter altogether."

"McCormick is an enemy of the Crown, Sherlock.
Do you recall reading of the parade bombing in Dublin that killed forty-eight people?"

"I do," Holmes said.

"Thirty-six of the dead were British soldiers. Twelve
were natives, his own people, Sherlock. Irish men,
women and children. Michael McCormick and his
henchman planted that bomb, and it was not their
first."

"He is the Crown's problem, Mycroft, and if I know
the Empire's history at all, and I assure you that I do,
I would guess that we had a hand in creating him, this
Michael McCormick, terrorist. Do not expect me to

undertake the Queen's business in this. I have my own score to settle here."

"You are an Englishman, my brother," Mycroft said softly.

"I am the Queen's most loyal subject," Holmes said, with a most obvious edge to his voice, "but I am not her assassin."

"Nor are you expected to be," Mycroft said.

"Then, why are we arguing?" Holmes replied.

"We are not," Mycroft said, "but I am warning you, Sherlock: Be careful with this. There is grave danger here. I . . . I do not want to visit you in the hospital again . . . or worse." Mycroft Holmes looked uncomfortable.

"Thank you, Mycroft. I know that when I was in Dr. Peacham's care, you were never very far away," Holmes said. "That matters a great deal to me, you know. And I appreciate your concern now. Trust that I do."

"Very well," said Mycroft, turning to leave. "Good day, Dr. Watson.. You have been warned, Sherlock. Godspeed."

Chapter 28

A short time later we met with Lestrade at the inspector's office. At Holmes' request, Inspector Gregson had also joined us.

"It is time, gentlemen, that we arrested the Monster of St. Marylebone," Holmes said.

I presumed, accurately as it turned out, that he had decided the pieces of our puzzle were as clear as they ever would be, and a case finally could be made against the Gibbonses. Lestrade and Gregson listened intently as Holmes recounted, almost verbatim, Albert Gibbons' story from the previous night. He said nothing, however, of Mycroft's early morning visit.

"Well," Lestrade said when Holmes was finished, "what you are telling me, Mr. Holmes, pretty much confirms my own thinking in the case. We were about to make a move in that direction ourselves."

I started to speak. I wanted to protest Lestrade's statement as ludicrous and self-serving, but Holmes gave me a piercing look and I turned my words into a rattling cough, instead.

"I am sure that you were closing in fast," Holmes said, his lips pursed in a tight and quick smile. "May I accompany you to the Gibbons home on Upper Wimpole?"

"I don't see why not, Mr. Holmes. Always good to have you along."

"Perhaps I can pick up some pointers, eh, Lestrade?"

Gregson smirked and quickly covered his mouth.

"I didn't mean it that way, Mr. Holmes," Lestrade said.

On the way out the door, I turned to Holmes and asked where Mrs. Masterson was, and he said that she planned to meet us on Upper Wimpole Street.

"She seemed ill when she left us last night," I said. "Was she all right?"

"Yes. Listening to Albert's story, she became more acutely aware of just how awful life was behind the facade of the Gibbons family's pride and respectability. More to the point, the certainty of the murderer's identity had registered as something of a shock."

"She is made of stern stuff," I said.

"Yes, Watson, stern enough, I hope."

Moments later we arrived outside the stately Gibbons town house on Upper Wimpole Street. We looked up and down the sidewalk, but Abigail Masterson was nowhere in sight. Holmes' gaze fell on a single lady's glove on the sidewalk.

"Quickly, Lestrade," he said, alighting from the police coach. "I only hope we are not too late."

The four of us ran to the heavy front door, and Holmes pounded with the large brass knocker. There was no answer.

"We'll have to break it in," Lestrade said, but by the time he had finished speaking, Holmes had used his walking stick to break the front window and was knocking out large pieces of jagged glass. He slipped through the window, and we followed quickly.

The house was as silent as the grave. We moved noiselessly through the first-floor rooms. All of us but Holmes had a handgun at the ready.

Holmes and I neared the stairwell to the second floor at the same time. We heard a soft noise upstairs.

"That sounds like . . . like crying," I said.

Holmes said nothing. He climbed the wide stairs, two and three at a time, up to the second floor. I took the same strides and quickly joined him on the second-floor landing.

The crying was more distinct now. It seemed to be coming from the second bedroom on the right. We tried the door knob, and to my surprise, it turned. I flung it open from a crouched position, not knowing what would greet us on the other side.

I thought that at this point, I was prepared for anything. I was wrong.

Before us, a young man sat crying on the bed. A small thumb-worn Bible with red leather covers sat beside him. In his arms he was gently cradling the limp, broken body of a cat. The boy was weeping inconsolably. It was Mildred, the fluffy black and white cat Holmes and I had seen when we first visited this house. In a wooden box by the bedside, her four kittens mewed incessantly and stepped all over each other trying to escape.

When Holmes spoke, his voice was soft. "Did Albert do this, Jamey?"

The young man nodded several times and looked up at Holmes through his tears. His face bore the ruddy, healed-over scars of his adolescence, but otherwise he looked very much like Albert. In fact, the resemblance was uncanny between brothers who not only were not twins but who had been born two years apart.

"Why? Why did he hurt Mildred? Mildred was a nice kitty. She never hurt anyone. Why did he hurt Mildred?"

"Your brother is very sick, Jamey," Holmes said. "There is something wrong inside his head, and it makes him do these things."

"But Mildred never hurt nobody, mister. Who's going to take care of her kittens now?"

"We'll help you take care of them, Jamey. We will help. But you have to help us," Holmes said. "Albert has always done things like this, hasn't he?"

The boy nodded his head and snuffled. "Albert likes to hurt things," he said. "He hurts me. He beats me sometimes. I think he hurt my daddy real bad so that

he died. I think Albert did that. I tried to teach him
what the Bible says about hurting living things, and
about hurting people, but Albert always made fun of
me and he wouldn't listen.

"Mommy didn't listen, either, and she's a Catholic.
She should know better."

Lestrade and Gregson stood silently in the doorway,
stunned expressions on their faces.

"I don't think she's a good Catholic. I pray for her
all the time, you know? But she hurt me, too."

"What do you mean?" Holmes asked.

"She would hold me down sometimes while Albert
hurt me."

"That's over now, Jamey." Holmes' voice cracked
audibly when he spoke. "They're gone."

A look of surprise, a smile and then sheer and utter
panic seized Jamey.

"Gone? They're gone? I'm alone? Am I all alone?
I don't know if I can take care of Mildred's kittens
alone." He began to sob.

Holmes sat beside Jamey on the bed and put his
arm around the boy's shoulders.

"You won't be alone from now on, Jamey. We'll
see to that. I promise you. But you have to tell me
where you think they might have gone."

Sobs wracked the boy so that he could scarcely
catch his breath. Holmes whispered softly in his ear.

"Jamey. Listen to me. Listen to me. You have to
say where they went. We have to know."

"Am I all alone?" the boy asked, trying to wipe
his tears.

"Jamey. Listen. Where did they go?"

"Home," Mommy said. "She said I had to stay
here."

"Where is home, Jamey? Where?" Holmes asked.

"A girl's name. It was a girl's name. She told it to
me a long time ago, but I forget."

Holmes was silent. He stared intently at the wall,
and then looked around the room. His gaze fell on a

chiffonier set against a far wall, and then at a fine lace
runner laid over the top of it.

Mrs. Hudson always insisted that some of the best
lace in the world came from the west of Ireland.
Holmes and I spoke at the same time. "Clare?"

"Was it Clare? County Clare? In Ireland? Jamey!
Was it Clare?" Holmes persisted.

The boy's eyes widened. "Yes. Clare."

"Damn!" Holmes exclaimed. "Lestrade, we've got
no time to . . ."

I could see Holmes' lips forming the words, but I
couldn't hear his voice because at that instant an ex-
plosion occurred that shook the entire house as if it
had been rocked by an earthquake.

Chapter 29

The blast knocked me off my feet. Lestrade and Gregson fell just as quickly, too. Holmes sprang up off of the bed and, leaped over us as we regained our senses. He raced out into the corridor.

Holmes looked down from the top of the stairs and found the entire first floor engulfed in flames. The blaze began to lick up the stairwell. Holmes raced back into the bedroom and threw the door shut behind him.

"Quickly. He must have set off a fire bomb on a delayed fuse. We have no time. Watson, knock out that window."

I grabbed a wooden chair and threw it straight through the window and out into the yard. I knocked the loose shards of glass clear of the window frame and looked down over a drop of nearly twenty feet into a hedgerow of yews.

"It's not bad, Holmes. What about the boy?"

"Jamey, listen to me," Holmes said. "We're all going to have to be brave and climb down out of here over a rope. Mildred's kitties are depending on you, Jamey. You're going to have to put them in a pillowcase and carry them down with you. Can you do that?"

Jamey Gibbons' eyes were wide with alarm, but he nodded his head vigorously.

While Holmes was speaking, Lestrade and Gregson were already emptying the chiffonier in a search for sheets and blankets other than what were on the bed. They found two sheets and quickly knotted them to-

gether and tied those lengths to the sheets and blanket
already on the bed. They then tied the whole length
fast to a post of the bed and pulled it tight to the
window.

I could hear the fire roaring outside the bedroom
door, and in the distance through the open window,
fire bells announced the calamity.

"Gregson, you go first," Holmes said. Gregson
climbed out the window and descended hand over
hand into the yews. Lestrade was right behind him.

Smoke was pouring in around the doorjamb, and I
looked at Holmes.

"You're next, old man," I shouted. "You have a
load to carry." Holmes would have protested if he had
had the time, but he didn't. I could see the muscles
in his jaw knot together.

He turned from me and shouted at the boy, "Let's
go, Jamey!" Holmes crouched on the end of the bed
with both hands clasped onto the rope and his back
to the window. "Put your arms around my neck,
Jamey. Bite the end of the pillowcase together with
your teeth and hold on to me. Do it now. Do it now."

The young man put his Bible in his coat pocket and
did as Holmes had instructed. The detective backed
out of the window and lowered himself down the rope
with Jamey on his back; but the sudden weight of the
two men was too much. The bed jerked up off the
floor, snapped the bedpost in two and sent it hurtling
against the open window. It jammed crosswise momentarily, long enough, I knew, so that after a frightful lurch, Holmes and Jamey Gibbons should be fairly
near the ground. The post held fast for another moment, then slipped down the casing and flew through
the window. With it went my only means of escape.

I stood staring at the window, momentarily numbed
by my plight, and only vaguely aware of the crackling
and roaring of the fire beyond the bedroom. The noise
had grown ominously louder, and now, suddenly, it
seemed all encompassing. I turned toward the closed

door, only to see flames washing and licking around the inside of the jamb. The air was growing more and more smoky. In an instant the flames flowed across the door and then covered it. I was frozen to the spot, fascinated by the growing inferno. The flames defied gravity and all natural law. They seemed to skip and glide and then effortlessly roll from the top of the door to the edge of the ceiling. In the next instant, an adjoining wall was transformed into a seething, undulating, almost liquid field of bright reddish-yellow and blue-tipped orange. The flame seemed alive and in a race with itself, as, indeed, it was; the open window was feeding the conflagration a supply of much-needed oxygen. The opposite wall went next. And now the fire was pushing dense, charcoal-gray smoke ahead of itself. The smoke filled the room and washed over me, surging in billows out the lone window, which was now barely visible. Indeed, I could see very little in the room at all. My eyes hurt, but I finally discerned a bright grayish-white rectangle where I remembered the window should be.

I pulled the mattress up off the bed, embraced it as though it were a soft shield and stumbled toward the gray light. I was coughing so hard that it hurt my ribs. The smoke was cloying, and the heat and sudden density of it seared my lungs. Every cough was difficult, and hurt more than the last. My lungs were beginning to feel as though they might explode, so I tried not to breathe at all. I buried my face in the top of the mattress and clutched it tightly against my chest. I staggered clumsily up onto the windowsill, balancing my weight in a crouch against the awkward bulk of the mattress. I nearly fell backward, but managed to force the mattress through the opening. The door behind me gave way with a deafening blast, and I could feel the heat of the flames licking at my back and neck as I lurched forward from the window, clutching the mattress, flattening my body against it.

Chapter 30

Providence was with me, for I landed atop the outer edge of the hedgerow, with the mattress acting as a buffer between my body and the old stiff yew branches. The branches gave under my weight, but sprang back hard and spun me out away from the house. The mattress landed on top of me when I bounced to the ground, which was not precisely what I had hoped for, but it was good enough. I was alive.

My overcoat was scorched, and the back of it was smoldering when Holmes pulled me to my feet and ripped the coat from me. I was coughing, wheezing and gasping for breath. My eyes stung badly, my lungs hurt, and my shoulder ached from the fall, but I was otherwise unharmed.

It wasn't until I got to my feet and looked up at the window from which I had jumped that I truly appreciated just how close I had come to meeting my end.

A red and orange plume of flame filled the window, and fingers of color now flicked from every portal on the first and second floors. The roof of the house started to smolder, and then the very center of it exploded with a deep, hollow, resonating noise that sent slate shingles and splinters of roofing boards flying through the air like missiles from a cannon. Bricks were shocked loose from the tall pilastered chimneys at either end of the house. The noise drew a startled gasp from the crowd that had gathered out in the street, and the onlookers screamed and ran. Debris fell among them, missing most, but not all. A fireman trying in vain to douse the inferno with water was knocked senseless when a spinning board caught him in the back of the head. One poor woman died instantly when a flying brick crushed her skull. Others, children among them, suffered numerous cuts from flying glass or splintered slate roof tiles. At least one boy was hurt when he was knocked to the ground and trampled by the fleeing crowd; I believe his right collarbone and left arm were broken.

The twin chimneys of the house collapsed into the gaping hole that now yawned like a mouthful of jagged teeth at the center of the roof. The bricks crashed into the flames that had consumed the house. A shower of sparks and flaming embers flew skyward, carving trails of orange light through the gray and black smoke that filled the neighborhood like a fog.

I was thunderstruck by the horrific display. Following, as it did, so closely on the heels of my escape, I could not immediately comprehend what had happened.

As if to answer my silent question, Holmes said, "A second firebomb. This one obviously was planted in the attic. It had to be even larger than the first. They didn't want to leave anything to chance. Some flammable liquid, probably coal oil, must have been sealed up inside a large container. Come, Watson. Let us leave this hellhole."

Holmes guided me down the street some distance before he said, "I am eternally in your debt, my friend."

"Oh, well," I sputtered. "Thank you, Holmes. Most gracious of you." My voice was a rasp. A fit of coughing forced me to stop talking for a moment, and then I resumed briefly. "Nothing you wouldn't have done, I'm sure," I said. "Is Jamey . . . ?"

"He's upset, but otherwise fine," Holmes said, "and so are Mildred's kittens. Gregson has taken them and the boy to the Yard. The ladies of the St. Marylebone

Benevolent Association will be called, and for now, they will tend to Jamey and his charges. He'll be in good hands."

"Mrs. Masterson?"

Holmes looked crestfallen. "They've taken her," was all he said.

"You're sure, Holmes?"

"Yes. Jamey said there was a pretty woman with reddish-colored hair standing behind his mother. As best I could gather from Jamey, Abigail's hands were tied behind her."

"The newspapers were right all along," I said.

Holmes looked puzzled.

"The Marylebone Monster. The description was not overblown."

"No," Holmes said. "It was not. We must get back to Baker Street and pack. We have a desperate trip to make."

"We do, indeed," I said.

In three hours' time we boarded a train out of Paddington Station. An express would take us across country overnight to Liverpool, and from there we could voyage to Dublin. It would be another day's trek west across the country to County Clare. The trip would take time that we did not have. Our only consolation was that it would take the killers just as long to reach their destination. Holmes' most conservative estimate put our quarry about seven hours ahead of us.

We spoke little on the first brief leg of the trip. The day's events had already been exhausting, physically and emotionally. When we were seated alone in a compartment on the express to Liverpool, however, I asked Holmes when it was that he knew for sure that Jamey Gibbons was not the killer.

"After the interview with Albert," Holmes said. "Up to that point, I had been thrown off by Albert's use of cosmetics. Jamey may use it legitimately to mask his acne scars. In fact, I would bet on it.

"When Albert used it, however, he did so in order to draw attention to the fact of the cosmetics, in other words, so that we would look for some man who used it. Once we discovered that Jamey used it, we would have one more reason to believe that Jamey was the murderer.

"But in the interview, Albert made two points that greatly outweighed the importance of the powder, and led me to realize who the killer really was.

"He told us that Jamey liked to torture small animals. I instantly recalled seeing the cat, Mildred, when we were at the Gibbons home after the murder. No house cat could have prospered in the same house with a torturer of small animals, Watson.

"Obviously, it was Albert, not Jamey, who had grown up tormenting small animals. His mother suggested that breed of cruelty is something that children outgrow, but I think not. It is clear that in Albert's case, at least, the penchant for cruelty only worsened. More to the point, it was clear from looking at that healthy, nursing cat that nobody was currently mistreating her. Albert had to be lying. And the only reason could be his effort to draw the noose even tighter around his own brother's neck.

"But he was most clever. As fantastic a tale of depravity as he painted, there was some truth in every bit of it. The best liars always include truth in their tales. But what gave him away, finally, Watson, was a trait of his character that he simply could not disguise."

"What was that, Holmes?"

"His fastidiousness. When he trussed me up like a goose for carving last winter, he took the time to carefully fold my clothing and set it aside while he did his work. The killer did the same in the attack on Nigel Whitney. His shirt had been removed, folded and set in a square at the end of the counter on which we found his corpse. And then Edward Gibbons. His waistcoat had been folded ever-so-neatly and placed on the corner of the desk. His eyeglasses were set atop the coat, perfectly centered atop the fold.

"Fastidiousness, Watson. A compulsively meticulous attention to detail, to a superficial sense of order amid chaos, as if this mere imposition of will in the simple act of neatly folding a bit of clothing and setting it safely in its place, somehow is enough to restore the wreckage of a life.

"Last night, in our rooms, Albert constantly picked at dust and carpet fibers on his clothing. I looked carefully, Watson, as I am wont to do, and save for a few strands of fiber that he had brushed off at once, I thought he looked as neat as a pin, even after traveling inside of a rug. And, of course, there was the matter of his reaction to mention of his walking stick."

"I should have noticed," I said.

"No, Watson. Not necessarily. Albert Gibbons is very clever, and he had a perfect scapegoat—a poor, harmless simpleton whose only crime in life was being born into the Gibbons family. All Albert had to do was to keep feeding us clues that were tailored to fit the traits ascribed to his brother.

"He did not count on our moving as quickly as we did. Had we been a few moments later, the family home would have burned up with Jamey in it. The boy never would have survived. As it was, he was confused and very hurt by Albert's having broken Mildred's neck, probably while Jamey was in the room. That left the boy distraught, quite literally paralyzed by his grief. The fire was calculated to add fear and more chaos to the mix. Left alone, Jamey surely would have perished in the flames.

"I carried the boy to safety, Watson, but it was you who allowed it, by putting us ahead of your own safety. You have always had my respect, Watson, though it has not always been obvious; you may not know that you have my admiration as well, but you most certainly do.

"As for me, it is my natural inclination to contemplate and thoroughly plan my every move. In fact, there are times when I would do better to act first and think later. Fortunately for me, Watson, you are a good and most patient teacher in that regard."

I was choked with emotion. I suppose I also was exhausted from the morning's ordeal, but the best I could do was to utter a simple, "Thank you, Holmes."

When I had regained my voice, I asked him, "Did Mrs. Masterson come to the same conclusion about Albert?"

"Yes, Watson. She did. That was why she was so upset when she left us last night. The realization that Albert Gibbons truly is a monster had just seized her as well."

I turned and stared out the window, and watched the night flicker by. I tried to concentrate on the soothing droning and rumbling of the train as it wound its way across England.

"Does it not bother you," I finally asked, "that you passed up a chance to grab the real killer. We had him within our grasp. With the three of us there, we certainly could have bested him, Holmes."

"It would have spoiled the chase," he said.

I was exasperated. "Holmes! You don't mean to say that you deliberately let him go just to satisfy your own . . . your own . . . need for adventure?! I can't believe that you would . . ."

"I am not being serious, Watson. Don't exercise yourself. I *am* bothered by the fact that such a notion even occurred to me. But, in truth, it took all of my dramatic skills to be civil to Albert Gibbons, let alone refrain from putting a revolver to his head and pulling the trigger. But I could not take the risk.

"What do you suppose would have happened to Jamey, had Albert not returned? I suspect we would be examining his corpse right now. And Mary McCormick Gibbons would still have fled."

"She seems as evil as any creature imaginable," I said.

"She is, indeed," Holmes said. "She is, indeed. In fact, it is pure conjecture whether she is more villainous than Albert. This very aspect of the case was something that I discussed at length with Abigail. I was a while returning from the Langham, you will recall?"

"Yes, but I had presumed . . . well, you know."

"Aah, I see. You think I am some schoolboy with a fever, eh?"

"Not at all, Holmes. I just meant that . . ."

"I know. I know. Actually, the restaurant lounge was still open, so we ordered some wine and sat off in the corner to discuss Mary McCormick Gibbons. It is apparent, I think, that she has been the malevolent force behind this entire twisted affair.

"She cruelly used her own son, Jamey, to satisfy her sordid voyeurism. She actually held the boy down on any number of occasions while Albert beat him and tormented him. Jamey was her 'pet' and 'plaything,' according to Albert, but I did not know enough to start taking him literally until he dared utter those very words.

"Abigail's reaction crystallized my opinion. She said it was likely that sexual aberration had played a part, at least in a fashion, for quite some time. That was not to be doubted, in her opinion. All that was unknown was the precise form her perversion had taken. And Jamey made that clear to us.

"We know, too, that she used Nigel, and we know how; her renewed profession of undying love and devotion was enough to leave him duped for an eternity.

"She also managed to use Sidney as well. He supplied her with the poison she needed to render Alexander, if not dead, then helpless."

"But she could have gotten strychnine anywhere."

"True, Watson. But Sidney was already keen to the whole business. She pulled him in by promising him £20,000. But I believe she needed Sidney for another reason, too."

"What was that," I asked on cue.

"Cocaine. Yes, Watson, that drug which you have so often chided me for using. I have used it in a relatively weak dosage, a seven percent solution, during my bleakest moments of boredom and lassitude. But I believe that Master Albert Gibbons is incurably addicted."

"How do you know this," I asked.

"He tried to hide it during my captivity, but I feigned unconsciousness at one logical juncture, and he broke from the torture long enough to give himself an injection. The fun truly began after that. He was even more vicious. And his eyes, which I could see clearly enough though his head was hooded, were dilated to a wildness that I recognized intuitively, one user observing another. Sidney had to be the supplier. What better source than a trained and licensed chemist who uses the drug legitimately as a component of some of his prescriptions?"

"Did she use it as well?"

"I have no reason to think so. I believe that she provided Albert with all of the cocaine that he wanted, or at the very least, with enough of the drug to keep him under her control. That was one of her crowning achievements. She rendered him totally and completely subservient."

"The son as slave to the mother?"

"Very much so. She has, in some respects, freed Albert to do what he has always longed to do. He is at liberty to torture and kill not merely with impunity, but with the approval of the only person in his life who has ever mattered to him: his mother."

"Good Lord, Holmes. How perfectly diabolical."

"Yes. Albert has been her weapon," Holmes said. "All she had to do was aim him at the target."

Chapter 31

I do not consider myself to be particularly naive, but I was left speechless by the realization that Albert Gibbons' every dastardly move had been orchestrated by his mother. I became silent as the enormity of her crimes sunk into my consciousness. I could not—and even now, I cannot—square the emerging true picture of Mary McCormick Gibbons against the notion of motherhood to which I have always been accustomed. Mother: the giver of life, the nourisher, the nurturer, the keeper of home and hearth. Mother: the one word, the single notion and image that embodies all of the homespun and eternal verities that are supposed to be sacred enough in our culture to momentarily soften even the most jaded and calloused of hearts.

But in the person of Mary McCormick Gibbons, Holmes and I were faced with a bestial perversion of the ideal: a woman, a mother, who not only was a vicious killer, but a woman who was capable of manipulating, twisting, tormenting and even slaying the issue of her own loins with no more feeling of remorse or regret or compassion than a butcher has for an animal brought to the slaughter.

The very notion was so foreign to me, so horrifying and repulsive, that I truly could not comprehend it.

Holmes interrupted my macabre reverie. "I quite agree, Watson," he said, "there is nothing in the average person's experience, and not even yours or mine, that has prepared us for the truth about this woman. She is a Medea reincarnated."

"How in blazes . . . ? That is precisely what I was thinking."

"Of course, Watson," he said without a smile. "Your brow was furrowed and your face, if I may be so bold as to interpret it, bore an expression that seemed part anger and part puzzlement. But I could see sadness in your eyes as well.

"Mary McCormick Gibbons had to be the focus of your thoughts. Nothing else in our recent adventures could possibly engender such a confluence of emotions. What's more, my good man, your consternation mirrors my own.

"I can scarcely contemplate the evil that moves such a woman, Watson. It is very nearly beyond me, and that fact alone leaves me unsettled. I am much less frightened by the prospect of running Albert Gibbons to ground and dealing with him face-to-face."

"If I may say so, Holmes, it is not like you to talk of being frightened in either event."

"As you have noted, Watson, I have had a glimpse of my own mortality. Perhaps that has made me too cautious. At any rate, I do not want to be the butt of some ludicrously ironic turn of events wherein I am dispatched from this life only because I proved too timid to act in time."

"I have every confidence that when the time comes, Holmes, you will rise to the fore. I do not doubt it."

He smiled wanly but said nothing as the train swayed and shot across the quiet, darkened countryside. I had never seen Holmes quite so introspective. I had not lied to him; I really did believe that in the end he would make a good accounting of himself, as always. I was a bit unsettled by his self-deprecation, modesty never having been one of Holmes' more noticeable attributes.

"I am puzzled by other aspects as well, Holmes."

"Go on," he said.

"Well, is it not safe to presume that Mrs. Gibbons and her son believe that Jamey and his would-be rescuers have all perished?"

"That certainly is what they hoped for, yes."

"If that is the case, Holmes, why have they taken Mrs. Masterson hostage? I see no point."

"Security, I expect," he said. "While they certainly intended that we all be incinerated in that blaze, there is no way that they can know for sure whether we managed to escape. If we did, we would be after them, of course. They know that because they have Abigail as their hostage, we would be forced into a different kind of play from what we might have undertaken otherwise. Simply put, they won't be looking for us to do anything that would further jeopardize her safety."

"And, of course, we won't," I said.

Holmes gave me a look that chilled me to the bone. "We will do whatever we have to do, Watson. Mrs. Gibbons and her son will not escape me, regardless of the price."

"Holmes," I protested. "You don't mean that you would deliberately expose Mrs. Masterson . . ."

"She trusts me to do whatever needs to be done, Watson. I am confident that I only am doing what she herself would have me do. Believe me, I would take no unnecessary risks with the woman's life in the balance, but if we are unable to move quickly—for whatever reason—then they will kill her without flinching.

"Frankly, though, I have high hopes. I think we do have the element of surprise working in our behalf, at least to some extent. The fact that Abigail was already there on Upper Wimpole Street waiting for us to arrive would suggest the timing of the firebombs was deadly accurate. The Gibbonses probably are too clever to be taking our untimely demise entirely for granted. But I think they will still be somewhat surprised to find that we are very much alive and onto them."

"I hope so," I said. "We need an advantage."

"We do, indeed, old fellow."

We lapsed into a long silence. When I looked at Holmes, I half expected to find him napping, but he was not. He looked puzzled.

"What is it, Holmes?"

"Oh, I was just musing at the interconnectedness of things, the irony, I suppose you would say."

"I don't understand," I said.

"This whole business has its roots in Ireland. The motive for the murders. The use for which the Gibbons' extorted money is intended. And here we are on the trail of two killers who are seeking refuge in Ireland. And as if all of that were not enough, I, meanwhile, have been nursed back to health by an Irishwoman."

"You are serious, Holmes? Abigail is Irish?"

"Indeed, I am," he said. "Her maiden name was O'Reilly. She grew up in a town called Ennistymon."

"I don't believe I've heard of it, Holmes. Where is it?"

"In County Clare, Watson. In County Clare."

Chapter 32

Mrs. Masterson later related that she saw the two figures walking toward her on Upper Wimpole Street, where she stood waiting for me and Holmes, and knew that it was Albert and his mother, Mary McCormick Gibbons, approaching.

The woman no longer wore her wig, and thus shorn, the flinty hardness of her features was more obvious. There seemed to be nothing in her eyes but a cold empty blackness that was repulsive and frightening.

Albert's features were remarkably similar, at least from a safe distance. He had his mother's coal-black eyes, but they did not rival hers for emptiness. His were now opened unnaturally wide, as if in fright, and they were rimmed with red. The pupils flit back and forth like moths at a candle, as if to announce the frenzy that ate at him constantly. Mrs. Masterson realized in a glance that Albert Gibbons probably was as insane as any inmate she had ever seen at Bedlam.

She stood staring, transfixed, as they came closer. In an instant, Albert had both of her wrists in a one-handed grip that was like a steel cuff. His mother quickly tied the young woman's hands in front of her with a cord and then wrapped them in a fashionable muff of light fur, so that the prisoner looked like any proper lady out for a stroll with her friends.

They escorted her in that fashion even aboard the packet to Dublin. When his mother stepped out of sight, Albert leered at his captive and, as discreetly as possible, for there were other passengers on deck, tried to paw her body. She spat in his face. He snarled, "Bitch!" under his breath, and turning to shield her body from their view, drove his knee hard into her abdomen. She reeled and retched over the side of the ship, appearing to be no more in trouble than any frail passenger who had lost her sea legs.

Albert put his arm around her in a show of solicitousness, and whispered in her ear. "Once more, and you'll go over the side." His mother, who bent over so as to appear equally concerned, looked into Mrs. Masterson's eyes and said, her voice flat and cruel, "There's no one left to help you. Do you understand? There's no one left to care."

Mrs. Masterson caught her breath and held it and let the woman's quiet words linger without making a further sound. Then she stared directly into Mrs. Gibbons' face, forced her gaze to go out of focus as if she were in shock, and exhaled deeply. She hung her head as though in abject resignation, and vowed to herself that she would live long enough to avenge Holmes' death.

Moments later, it occurred to her, however, that if the Gibbonses were certain that their pursuers were no longer a threat, they would not have kept her as hostage. It would have been much easier and safer for them to have killed her before they boarded for Dublin. Nor would they be acting with the sense of urgency that seemed, when she bothered to study them, to mark their every movement. Thus buoyed, Mrs. Masterson remained numbly submissive for the duration of the voyage.

In Dublin, the three went directly from the docks across the city and down Merrion Row and Lower Baggot Street, a long lovely avenue full of great row houses built in the Georgian manner, with grand and colorfully painted doors, to a public house called O'Keefe's. In the pub, Mary McCormick Gibbons spoke briefly with the barman, who went directly into a back room and then returned and motioned them toward him.

Inside the room a man sat alone, his back to the wall. His big, hamlike hands were folded in front of him atop a small wooden table, and he wore a tweed cap at a jaunty angle. He had a big head, curly jet-black hair, a square jaw and dark eyes that bore a look of ineffable sadness. He looked at Mary McCormick Gibbons and gave her a bright white and toothy smile, but the sadness never left his eyes. He spoke softly.

"Are you well, Mary?"

"Aye, Michael. And you?"

"It's been many years, has it not?"

"Aye."

"And this must be young Albert."

"It is."

"How do you do, Uncle Michael?"

Without rising, the big man took Albert's hand in his huge paws, pulled him down to within an inch of his face, and stared straight into Albert's red-rimmed eyes.

"You're on it, are you not?"

"Ye . . . yes. I can manage. My mother helps me with it. I can manage."

"Aye. You look like you can manage. You've got eyes like a white rabbit, and your nose is as wet as a week-old calf's. You cause us trouble of any sort, and you'll be floating in the Liffey. Is that clear?"

"Yes."

"Say, 'Aye,' not 'Yes,' like you was one of her royal majesty's foot soldiers."

"Aye," Albert said.

"Better," said Michael McCormick, and he looked directly at Mrs. Masterson for the first time.

"And who's this," he asked.

"Her name is Abigail Masterson," Albert said. "She's Sherlock Holmes' whore."

Michael McCormick rose slowly to his feet and towered over his company. He did not take his eyes off

Mrs. Masterson. "Well, he has good taste, this Holmes fella." And without looking at Albert, he hit him square in the mouth with the back of his hand and sent him sprawling into the corner. Albert never dropped his black walking stick.

"I know you're me blood sister's son," McCormick said, "and more'n that I understand from her letters that you've been helping us collect those thousands of bloody British pounds, but you'll not use language like that in the presence of ladies, let alone one of 'em bein' me darlin' sister and your blessed mother.

"Do you understand that? I'll loosen all of your teeth with the next one, so help me I will."

Albert nodded quickly, and wiped blood from his lips. He stood off to the side, glowering, but out of Michael McCormick's reach. Mrs. Masterson could see Albert clenching and unclenching his fist. The knuckles of his right hand were white against the embossed silver head of his cane. His palpable fury increased the already oppressive tension in the room.

"Why'd you bring her here, Mary?"

"Insurance," she said. "I think we got this Holmes and his friend when we burned the house, but we could not be there when it went up, so we couldn't be sure. If they did make it out and they've followed us, they'll be thinking twice before doing anything to put this woman in harm's way."

McCormick never raised his voice above a whisper, but he did not have to. His words were darkly emphatic. "You shouldn't have brought her," he said. "We don't need a crazed lover on the hunt for revenge. You're a fool, Mary m'dear. I've a good mind to do her now and have it over with, but I've never been one for intentionally hurtin' a woman. Not even an Englishwoman."

"I am Irish," Mrs. Masterson said. "O'Reilly, from Ennistymon." Mary McCormick Gibbons' mouth fell open.

"Are you, now?" Michael McCormick said. "Are you?"

"Aye," Mrs. Masterson said. "And I'm no man's whore. Mr. Holmes is a friend, that is all."

"I see," Michael McCormick said. "And it's Ennistymon you're from? Doesn't that beat all, then? Ye must know how many died at the big stone workhouse there in the famine?"

"Near on to twenty-six thousand," she said, "my grandparents among them."

"Then, you're with us, are you?'

"In my heart, I am," she said, "but it ends there."

"And how can it end there, woman? How? To have yer country in yer heart is to have yer country in yer soul. And if Ireland has yer heart and yer soul, then she has yer mind."

"My mind is my own," the captive said. "I am a doctor in training, a healer, and I am sworn to it. I cannot countenance revolution."

"And neither could I, at one point," McCormick said. "I hate the violence, though I have become a violent man. For a right-thinking person, there is no longer a choice in the matter, none. We all come to it, sooner or later. The Brits respect nothing else. They've shown us that time and again.

"Aah, enough," he said. "I'll not be justifyin' myself to you."

"I did not ask you to, Mr. McCormick," Mrs. Masterson said. "I am not your judge, but if you are not mine, you will order me released. I mean you no disrespect, and I'll bring you no harm."

Mary McCormick Gibbons was incensed. "No, Michael! Don't listen to her. She's one of them, as sure as I'm standing here. Sherlock Holmes won't stop with me and Albert. He's a detective and well known. He's a meddler with ties to the government. He'll be your undoing if you don't help us."

"Woman, you come here because you wanted to come home to Ireland after all of these years, when you never should have left in the first place. You left me alone with no family and beggin' you to stay with me where you belonged. But no, you'd have none of it. And now I've agreed to let you and your spawn buy your way back. Well, I'll not be going back on my word, but don't think for a minute that you'll be telling me what to do.

"I've no fight with this Holmes, and neither do the Boyos. If he's chasin' you, it's fer the butchery you did on yer own to raise the money and get free of the Brit you were fool enough to marry.

"There's a small cottage for you up off the west coast, in Lahinch."

He stopped to write on a scrap of paper, which he handed to his sister.

"You contact that man. He's one of ours. It's a quiet town in a whole county of quiet little towns; Ennistymon's just one more. Everybody knows everybody else in these places, and nothin' ever happens out of the ordinary. He's been tellin' the locals his family from America is comin' to stay. So your bein' there won't be unexpected."

Her eyes blazed at him as she took the paper. Her mouth moved as if to form words, but she said nothing.

"That's all, then," McCormick said. "Keep your prisoner if you want, but I'll not see you again under any circumstances. We'll have no contact after this moment. Ever."

"I am your sister." She moved forward, her head angled up at him sharply, and spat the words as though they were venom. "I have given the cause a king's ransom, and this is the thanks I get!?"

"Aye. And it's all that you deserve," her brother said. "You did only what you were bound to do by your nature, and you know it! The money has bought the two of you a future when you had none, unless you want to count the gallows. Our cause, you say? *Our* cause! You abandoned yer own country long ago, woman. And you abandoned me. You went to mother England to find a proper husband.

"We're takin' a frightful chance just findin' you a home. Yer worried about this Holmes character bein' after you. We're lucky you haven't brought half the bloody British Empire down on us already. This Holmes is the least of your trouble.

"Leave now," McCormick commanded. "Ian," he hollered. "Ian Donovan, come in here." A short wiry man opened the door. "Take our visitors and go," McCormick told him. "By way of the Burren. Be off now."

McCormick turned toward Albert, who had moved nearer, and backhanded him across the face again. Albert reacted as though he had half expected the blow. He didn't blink. He reeled from the force of the assault, but stayed on his feet this time and immediately turned back toward McCormick with hatred in his black eyes. Ian Donovan whipped a pistol from beneath his jacket, and Albert stopped.

"That's for what yer thinkin', spawn!" McCormick said. "If ever you see me again, you'd better have a big gun, 'cause yer'd be nothin' in a fair fight, even with that stick of yours. I know yer kind. You have no spine, and you kill for the love of it. I can see it in yer eyes. Now, get out."

He tipped his cap to Mrs. Masterson and smiled a roguish smile.

"And a good day to you, ma'am."

Chapter 33

"I doubt that the Gibbonses will go directly to County Clare on their own," Holmes said. "I think they have no choice but to make contact with McCormick first. And so shall we. In Dublin."

Mycroft's last intelligence before the Crown's Dublin agent had been murdered had identified O'Keefe's pub as one of McCormick's regular haunts. We edged our way into the crowded room, ordered Guinness and stood talking idly. Holmes nodded toward two men who were standing outside a room off behind the bar area.

"Rather obvious, don't you think?" Holmes said.

"I would say so. What now?"

"I have to get into that room," Holmes said. "It will require a diversion. Are you feeling fleet of foot, Watson?"

I smiled. "I'll be waiting for you at the northern edge of the green we passed."

I drained my glass, moved toward the front door and, as inconspicuously as I could, picked a rumpled newspaper off the end of the bar and walked outside, smoothing it open and pretending to read it. I set one foot atop a small barrel, slowly lighted my pipe, and looked up and down Baggot Street nonchalantly.

The opposite side of the way appeared empty, and the nearest person on this side was half a block away and headed in the opposite direction. I struck another match and lighted the newspaper afire. I dropped it inside the barrel, and as smoke began to rise, I picked up the barrel, hoisted it over my head and with a running lunge, threw it straight through the window of O'Keefe's. I pulled my revolver from my pocket and fired two quick shots into the top of the doorjamb, took off my hat so as to not lose it in the street and began running as fast as I could.

Behind me I could hear shouts of "Fire! Fire!" and I knew Holmes had added to the confusion. Someone shouted, "There he goes!" I stopped just long enough to fire one more shot intentionally wide of the bar. Two men who had run outside threw themselves to the pavement, and I cut between two buildings, vaulted a wooden fence at the end of the alley and kept going.

Holmes told me later that when the flaming barrel broke through the window, the publican ducked behind his bar and came up with a shotgun with foreshortened barrels. A tall man who had been standing at the bar not far from Holmes snatched a half-empty bottle of whiskey and clobbered the bartender, grabbed the shotgun and ran straight at the guards who were blocking the closed door at the back of the room.

The stranger slammed the stock of the shotgun into the nose of one of the guards, and as the man went down, rapped the other hard across the teeth with the gun barrel. Holmes was right behind him.

"Good to see you again, Mr. Quinn."

"And you, Mr. Holmes," the big man said. With one straight-legged kick, Patrick Day Quinn knocked the door open wide and barged into the room, almost knocking McCormick over.

"Well, now," said McCormick. "That's British hospitality for you. Is this to be the way it goes? All for the bounty on me?" The big Irishman moved to the center of the room with his fists on his hips, staring at Holmes and Quinn.

The boxer leveled the shotgun at him waist high and cocked both hammers.

Three men from the outer room rushed into the doorway. McCormick waved them off; if anything happened to Quinn, McCormick would die instantly. "It's all right, lads," McCormick said. "We're just getting acquainted."

"We don't have time to play with you," Quinn said. "You're Michael McCormick, and I'll cut you in half if need be, but I don't want to. The government sorely wants your head, but I don't give a damn. That's their business, not mine. I am Patrick Quinn. This is Mr. Sherlock Holmes. Now, tell us where your visitors went."

McCormick grinned. "You'd mean me lovin' sister and her darlin' son? Oh, and yes, Abigail O'Reilly Masterson . . . lately of Ennistymon. Go to blazes, the both of you."

Quinn dipped the barrel of his shotgun quickly, pulled one trigger and blew the table in two. McCormick shied backward, trying to duck splinters.

"Don't waste my time," Quinn snarled.

"Lahinch is where you'll find them, Brits. Lahinch."

"When did they leave?"

"Two hours ago, maybe three."

Quinn nodded and eased down the other barrel's hammer.

"Let's go for a walk," Quinn said.

"You won't need me for a hostage," McCormick replied. "Nobody'll touch you. Let me at the door." He slowly walked to the doorway and called out across the room. "Boys, these two gentlemen have my permission to leave. You'll not be stopping them. Is that clear?"

Then he turned to Holmes and Quinn. "I appreciate you didn't kill me when you had the chance, but now you've had the better of me in front my friends. It's a thing of honor that I come after you proper. No hard feelings. Matter of pride, you see. And family. My sister betrayed me. Her country, too. But I can't just let you have her. Do you understand that?"

"Do what ye have to do," Quinn said, "if you can."

"I'd probably feel the same, McCormick," Holmes said. "Until then."

"Aye," he said. "Until then."

Chapter 34

Near St. Stephen's Green, Holmes hurriedly introduced me to Patrick Day Quinn, and the three of us broke into a stable and led three sturdy mounts out of their stalls. We didn't like having to steal the horses. Quinn said that in parts of America horse thieves were summarily hanged. Holmes nailed a most generous payment to the wall of the stable, and we saddled up quickly.

"We've got a long ride ahead of us, gentlemen," Holmes said, "and by the time we get to Lahinch, we'll have Michael McCormick at our backs and maybe his friends as well. This isn't going to be easy."

"Then, we had best get on with it, Holmes," I said.

We mounted the horses, and Holmes turned to Quinn.

"It *was* you who killed Sidney Gibbons?"

"Aye," the big man said, "and I'd do him again for the hand he had in my boy's butcherin'. I was listenin' at the alley door. Simple killin's too good for the lot of them, Mr. Holmes. 'Sides," he said with a sly smile, "I couldn't be lettin' two toffs like you soil your hands with it, now, could I? I came sailin' back home soon as my sister sent word about Dickie. I know'd you'd a not just let it happen. I figured somebody'd put you down fer good. And I'm glad I was wrong, I am. I owe you, Mr. Holmes. If not for you, my boy would have had it much worse in his blessed short life."

"If you owed me anything," Holmes said, "the debt

is well paid. You should go back to America now, before the Yard figures out that you have returned."

"It's too late for that, Mr. Holmes, and ye know it well. I've followed ye this far, I'll not be tarnin' back until justice is done." His eyes were dark and hard, his square jaw set, and it was clear there was no room for argument.

Holmes nodded and we were off.

We traveled as fast as we could to make up for the disadvantage we faced in not knowing the country. We had scant provisions, which we had to replenish along the way, but we had brought stout oilskins, for we knew the weather could be unpleasant even in springtime. After three days of hard riding, we had made our way west to Naas and Kildare and Mountmelick and across the Slieve Bloom Mountains to Birr and Portumna, where we rested the horses for a time, and ate fine fresh salmon at a small tavern on Lough Derg.

I was taken by the gentle and varied beauty of the land and its emerald-green rock-studded fields, but I was saddened by the poverty of it, even by rural standards. We passed many whitewashed stone cottages with thatched roofs and roses in bud along lichen-covered stone fences, but nowhere was there a sign of real comfort, much less any degree of affluence. Indeed, many were the ruins and rock piles that once had been family homesteads. All too vividly they called to mind the story that Lady Elizabeth James had told us about the widespread evictions that had taken place during the famine decades ago.

It had been years since I had seen as many sheep as I did in this country. I delighted in watching them, particularly when they were being herded by a Border Collie under the watchful eye of his master. But we had no time for sightseeing. We moved on to Gort and then Corofin, and the following day we reached the southern end of the strange region known as the Burren, a landscape of sprawling, rolling limestone terraces, outcroppings and upwellings so broad and vast as to seem altogether like another country.

We were greeted rather warily by strangers, but nearly everyone displayed a simple and decent hospitality that was matched, at least in my modest experience, by no other nationality. Time and again we were invited to rest, partake of hearty tea and a stout Irish stew of mutton, potato and vegetables, though I had no doubt that our hosts could ill afford to be feeding three hungry strangers. Twice we slept in warm, sweet-smelling haymows, and twice we were treated to the comforts of a guest room and a cozy peat fire, and for no other reason than we were three travelers in need of food and shelter.

On the main street in Ennistymon, which was not far from our destination, we stopped at a butcher shop with a handsome painted sign in front that read "O'REILLY'S."

A counterman was busy wrapping a purchase for a customer, and behind him an older man sliced bacon from a flank of pork.

"I'm looking for William O'Reilly," Holmes said.

The counterman looked up and said, "Who'd be askin'?"

"Good friends of his cousin, Abigail."

The man at the rear smiled and put his cleaver down. "Ya don't say?" He walked over to the counter wiping his hands vigorously on his bloodstained apron.

"I am William O'Reilly," he said. "I've not seen Abigail in years, but she's certainly me cousin, God love her. What news have you? Is she well?"

"Could we talk in private, Mr. O'Reilly," Holmes asked. "It's very important."

His smile disappeared immediately.

"This here is me son, Gavin. I've no secrets from him. Gavin, go lock the front door for a moment, and pull the shade."

He picked up his cleaver and slapped the back of the blade into his palm as he spoke.

"Say what's on yer mind, mister, for yer startin' to concern me."

"Mr. O'Reilly, my name is Sherlock Holmes, and these are my companions, Dr. John Watson and Mr. Patrick Day Quinn. We have traveled from London to find Abigail. She has been kidnapped by two killers, a woman and her son who have murdered several people already. We are trying to save Abigail and bring them to justice. You must believe me. We haven't much time. She is being taken to Lahinch. We need you to take us there as quickly as possible, or to at least find us fresh horses and tell us what we need to know about the town."

William O'Reilly said nothing for a moment.

"Gavin, get me coat and hat, and come along. Quickly. Mister, if it's as you say, we'll do whatever we can. Family is family. But along the way, you'd better do a fine job of explaining this."

Gavin rode Holmes' horse beside me, while O'Reilly and Holmes rode ahead of us in the butcher's light wagon, so the detective could explain all that had transpired. Quinn stayed several yards behind us.

"This is bad business, Mr. Holmes," O'Reilly said when Holmes had finished his tale. "You painted it true, you did, but there's something you'd best be knowin' right now. Michael McCormick's a hard man and a good one, and I'll not cross him if it comes to that. Nobody in these parts will. He's the Irish Republican Brotherhood, and even those of us who aren't with 'em, aren't opposed to 'em, if you get my meaning. He's a patriot, as sure as I breathe, and if there were more like him, maybe we'd be havin' our freedom from your country sooner."

"I understand," Holmes said. "I will not ask you to turn against your own. Were the situation reversed, I would not do so. Nor would I expect it of any man."

"Good," O'Reilly said. "So long as we understand each other. But those two who've got me cousin Abigail, that's a different matter. Aye."

"I just need to find them, Mr. O'Reilly. I don't expect you to tackle them. Watson and Quinn and I have been waiting for just such an opportunity for some time."

"I see," O'Reilly said. "Well, who would Michael McCormick have his sister lookin' up in Lahinch, now? Most likely, it'd be Guinan, Robby Guinan. He's a hard one, too, and an old friend of McCormick's. And he's the only man I know in Lahinch who owns more property than what he can live in at one time. He has a nice little cottage back up off the cliffs a ways. It's in Liscannor, truth be known, but everyone thinks of it as Lahinch because Liscannor's just a mite of a place."

"That would be the Cliffs of Moher?" Holmes asked.

"Aye. You know them, then?"

"No," Holmes said. "I merely know of them. Geography is one of my interests."

"Ah," said O'Reilly. "Well, then, you know those cliffs are as fine and grand to us as your White Cliffs in Dover. When they're not fogged in, you can see for miles, all the way to the Arans and well beyond. They run about five miles north to south, and they're near onto seven hundred feet high in some places, the cliffs are, and way down below the top of 'em, the ocean rolls and swells in mighty waves that'd crush a good boat in the blink of an eye.

"When the wind is up, it makes a sound along those cliffs like a t'ousand banshees. It's a deep, low moaning at first. Very long and slow like, and then as the wind picks up, the moaning turns shrill, and that's when it starts to bother you some. You can't think in it, and you can't hear noothin' else for the sound of it. And when it gets real bad, it's all a shriek, like a high-pitched wail that makes your ears hurt. It goes right through you, it does. It's enough to turn you ice-cold on a warm night. Like banshees, I tell you.

"There's a story about a farmer who once tried to

graze a good herd of cows up there when the wind came up like I was telling you, and it lifted six of 'em right off the cliff and deposited 'em way over on Inishmore. That's the westernmost of the Aran Islands."

Holmes looked at O'Reilly and raised his eyebrows.

"Well, I don't vouch for the veracity of that tale," said the butcher, "but it does get the point across, doesn't it, now?"

Holmes laughed and O'Reilly continued.

"Now, the only building right near the cliffs is O'Brien's Tower, up at the northernmost end. You can't miss it. It's the only building that's tight to the cliffs. Big round tower what was built back in 1835 for the mariners and the sightseers."

"I'm surprised it hasn't blown away," Holmes said.

"It did, you know. We just hauled it back up there."

It was O'Reilly's turn to laugh at himself. "Naaaw, I'm pullin' yer leg. That one's built of big stones, it is. Hasn't moved an inch in sixty-four years. We should be in sight of it pretty soon."

We could hear roaring surf as we rounded a rising curve in the road minutes later, and the stone tower immediately became visible in the distance. Far more impressive was the landscape that greeted us, broad and rich rolling green fields to the right, the angry steel-blue sea off to the left and magnificent striated cliffs zigzagging along the water's edge for as far as the eye could see. Seagulls soared above us and hovered on currents of air below us, off the cliff's edge. A needlelike pinnacle of rock jutted up out of the water off the cliffs, and the sea roiled white all around it.

"That's called Breanan Mor, that rock stack is," O'Reilly said.

"I see why this is a beloved spot, Mr. O'Reilly," Holmes said. "It is, indeed, magnificent."

"Aye," he said. "Now, Guinan's cottage is just a ways off to the east."

We could see wisps of white smoke curling up over the green rise in that direction. The smoke rose to a point just above the crest of the hill and then was snatched and quickly dispersed by the hard wind that had begun to blow in from the west.

"I think this is close enough for us in daylight," Holmes said.

"We've a couple of hours until dark," O'Reilly said. "What say we repair to the town and have us a couple of pints?"

"A welcome idea," Holmes said, and I was glad to hear it, for I was more than a little hungry myself. What's more, my nether parts were sore from all of the riding we had been doing.

Once we reached the town, we took a large table off to the side of the main room at an establishment called Doyle's Pub and ordered sandwiches and drinks.

"How will you handle it? Have you decided?" O'Reilly asked.

"No," Holmes said. "I have to be sure that Abigail is safe before we do anything."

"Aye, but how will you be knowing that?"

Holmes paused and O'Reilly continued. "I think me and Gavin should go up to the cottage and see what gives. If we can get a look inside, it'll be a help."

"I can't ask you to do that," Holmes said.

"No," O'Reilly said, "but I can volunteer. Abigail's me cousin, after all. So let's be done with it, then."

It was dark by the time we left Doyle's, and the wind was up. We pulled the collars of our coats around our chins, mounted our horses and allowed O'Reilly and his son to lead the way. We stopped below the crest of the hill, and they drove on to Guinan's cottage. The wind was as loud as O'Reilly had promised, and cold besides. We dismounted and in silence stood together between our horses, using them to block the wind as best we could. We didn't have long to wait.

The two men returned shortly, and we followed them back toward town for a distance so that our voices would not be carried in the wind.

"There's only the woman there, Mr. Holmes," O'Reilly said. "Michael McCormick's sister. No sign of Abigail or the other one. We told her we was friends of Robby Guinan's, and we saw the peat smoke and decided to come by, thinking Guinan was to come home for some reason.

"She's not the most hospitable type, that one. She was suspicious right away. I could tell. So as soon as it was clear we had made a mistake, as it were, we made our apologies and left, but we had a good look inside. It's just one big room, and she was the only one in it, I can tell you that much."

"Thank you," Holmes said. "You have done much. We'll take it from here."

"Best of luck to the three of you then," O'Reilly said. We all shook hands, and the two men left, for home I presumed.

"I'll stay behind a bit," said Quinn. "I want to be sure that witch stays put, at least 'til you're out of sight. Then I'll follow."

Quinn apparently had figured out Holmes' next move, but I had not.

"Let's go, Watson," the detective said. "I only hope we're not already too late."

"Where, Holmes?"

"There is only one other place they could be up here, Watson. Come on, man! O'Brien's Tower. There's no other possibility. I am sure of it."

Holmes wheeled his horse around and was in a full gallop by the time I was mounted, but I whacked my horse hard on the right flank, and caught up to him quickly enough. The distance between us and the tall stone tower was deceptive; as is always the case on open ground. The wind was blowing harder, and the sound of it had taken on a shrill edge that was as eerie and unsettling as I had imagined from O'Reilly's description. I could hear nothing but the wind, not even the galloping of our horses as we approached the tower.

A light flickered dimly through one of the open windows. We dismounted and stole up to the building, quietly by habit, though the wind made stealth unnecessary. We slipped through the main door, which had no lock, there being no conceivable need for one out here, and stepped inside.

The sight that greeted us turned me colder than any salt wind could have accomplished. Abigail was trussed up against a wall, the way Holmes had been tied to a post in the mews. Her face was haggard and bruised, and there was a bright red welt across her left cheek; but she was conscious, and her eyes were open wide in terror. Albert stood before her, his stiletto-tipped cane in one hand, a leather riding crop in the other.

"There's more where that came from, dear," he said. I had never heard a more crazed, malevolent voice in all my life. "We'll take our time and get to know each other, I think. But I need to see what you really look like first."

He slit the bodice of her dress from the throat to the waist with the tip of his cane, then reached up and ripped it half off, exposing her undergarment and the tops of her breasts.

"Ooh," he said. "You're going to be fun to look at." He had raised his cane again when Holmes stepped out of the darkness. I stood beside him, my pistol at the ready.

"Defenseless women and little boys, Albert? That's your speed, is it?"

Gibbons spun around and faced his adversary.

"Holmes!"

"And I'm not even tied up, Albert." Holmes moved toward him as he spoke. "And look," he said, holding his hands palm-outward from his sides. "Nor am I so much as scorched by the fire you laid for us."

A look of panic passed over the man, but it was fleeting. In an instant, his black eyes resumed their horizontal dance, that maniacal, constant flitting that marked him, even at a distance, as in the throes of addiction and crazed. He kept licking his lips, as though they were parched. He raised his cane until the tip of the blade was pressed against Abigail's throat.

"If you come closer, I'll slit her from ear to ear, and you can watch her slowly bleed to death. Don't come any closer, I said."

Holmes' voice was calm, flat and tightly menacing.

"Albert, I do believe you are shaking. You should be. I am going to kill you, Albert. And you can't even guess how, can you? Look at me, you insignificant little bastard! You don't see any weapon, do you? And yet I am going to kill you, just as sure as you are standing there."

"I'm warning you," Albert said. "I'll do her, and you'll watch."

"That will leave just you and me, then, won't it?" Holmes said. He glanced at Abigail and nodded almost imperceptibly. "Either way, Albert, you're going to lose.

"We could trade, Albert, me for her and . . . Now!" he shouted, and Abigail jerked her head away from the blade and kicked upward furiously at Gibbons. Her foot caught the maniac in the shoulder. The blow didn't hurt him much, but it did make him lurch to the side and pull the stiletto further away from her throat.

That was all the opening Sherlock Holmes needed. He had taken two running steps as Abigail had kicked Gibbons, and before the man could regain his balance, Holmes had leaped upon him, his arm outsretched, reaching for the cane. The force of his attack brought the younger man to the floor with Holmes on top of him. Gibbons flailed at the detective with the riding crop that he held in his free hand, but the blows fell harmlessly on Holmes' back.

Gibbons swore and screamed in pain as Holmes

managed to twist the cane from his grip, and his face turned a deep shade of red when Holmes' right hand clenched tightly around his throat.

Holmes brought his left fist back and drove it squarely into the man's nose; blood began to spurt immediately. Holmes brought his arm back again for another punch, but Gibbons arched his back and flung his leg over Holmes' head and across his neck, propelling him backward.

Gibbons wriggled free as quick as a snake and sprang to his feet, but Holmes was already standing. The detective grabbed the cane and, with one deft swipe, severed Abigail's bonds. She slumped to the floor, but began loosening the ropes from her wrists.

I extended my arm and aimed my service revolver at the struggling men, waiting for a clean shot at Gibbons to present itself. A voice startled me. "I won't hesitate to kill you if you pull that trigger." I turned just in time to see Michael McCormick's big fist as it thundered into my jaw and sent me flying across the floor and my pistol skittering into the corner.

McCormick quickly stepped between Holmes and Gibbons.

"You've got to go through me, Holmes."

"Out of the way, McCormick. I've no quarrel with you. Your nephew's a fiend, and he'll answer for it."

"All he did was kill some Brits," McCormick said.

"Among them his own father and a thirteen-year-old boy he beat and tortured first. Do you condone that?!"

"No, but you'll not be the one to kill him . . . unless you do me first."

He swung wide and hard from his shoulder with a roundhouse punch that caught Holmes on the side of the head and sent him reeling. McCormick closed in with more punches even as the detective was falling to the floor.

Holmes hit the floor hard but swung his right leg in an arc that caught McCormick in the side of the knee with a horrible crack. The big man roared in pain, and it was apparent that Holmes had broken his leg. McCormick tried to stand, yelped in pain and fell to the stone floor hard on his good knee.

Gibbons turned and ran for the door.

Holmes saw him go, but could not stop him. He punched McCormick hard twice in the face, first with a right cross, then with a left. The man's head jerked from side to side with each punch, but with his right hand he was able to pull a pistol from his coat pocket and take aim directly at Holmes' chest.

The shot sounded sharp and flat, but it echoed so loudly in the stone chamber that I flinched at the sound. A look of stunned confusion froze on McCormick's face, and he fell forward. Blood seeped from a small hole that had appeared at his right temple.

Abigail exhaled loudly and dropped her small derringer from her hand. Holmes rushed to her side.

"Gibbons is gone," she said.

"I know," Holmes said. "We'll catch up with him. Will you be all right?"

"Yes. Yes. Be careful."

He nodded and turned to me.

"Watson, grab your revolver."

I had it in my hand already. We ran for the door.

Chapter 35

There was a half-moon, but it was hidden much of the time by dense, fast-moving clouds, leaving the night black and cold. The east wind was blowing harder and louder than ever. In the darkness I got my bearings by focusing on the sound of the breakers beneath the Cliffs of Moher, but even that was barely audible.

Holmes leaned off his horse and cupped his hand so as to direct his voice straight at me.

"The cottage," he shouted.

I nodded, and we turned our horses to the east and rode off after the Gibbonses.

As we neared the cottage, we heard the unmistakable sound of a gun shot. We dug our heels into our horses' flanks and sped up the road. We dismounted and charged at the front door. We burst into the room, and in the light of an oil lamp found Albert lying facedown in the middle of the floor.

"Damn her!" Holmes exclaimed. "She has cheated me. Come on."

No sooner had he spoken than we heard the whinny of a horse and the sound of hooves clomping fast on the roadway.

We ran to the door to catch a glimpse of Mary McCormick Gibbons charging off to the cliffs to the south, whipping her horse hard.

We quickly remounted. I raised my hand to slap the horse's flank with the reins, and felt a searing pain in my head, even as I heard another gunshot. I turned back toward the cottage and began falling, and as the ground rose up to meet me, I could see Albert standing in the doorway, a pistol in his hand still pointed in my direction.

"Holmes!" I shouted. "He tricked us. Look out."

Holmes leaped from his horse and was beside me almost as I hit the ground.

"I'm all right," I told him. "I think it just grazed my head."

He clapped me twice on the shoulder and ran toward the cottage.

Albert aimed his pistol and fired twice, and then a third time, but in his desperation was unable to hit the detective as he ran toward him. With a shout, Holmes leaped onto Gibbons in the doorway, and the two men fell back into the cottage grappling. I half ran and half staggered dizzily in their direction.

They were struggling in the center of the room. Gibbons had his deadly cane in hand and was using it like a sword, thrusting at Holmes one instant, slashing at him the next. Blood stained the left arm of Holmes' coat, and his left ear had been nicked as well, but he was bobbing and weaving quickly, looking for an opening.

I felt a huge hand on my shoulder, but before I could turn I was pushed hard to one side. It was Quinn. He charged through the door with a shout.

"Sorry to be late, Mr. Holmes. I was detained," he said, with a gesture to a nasty-looking gouge in the side of his head. "Move away, Mr. Holmes," Quinn shouted. "Move off now. Do it!"

Startled, Holmes stole a quick look at Quinn and straightened up. Gibbons used that fleeting moment to take a fearful arcing slash at the detective, and he would have found his mark had Quinn not thrown himself in front of the blow.

The fighter took the full force of Gibbons' stroke on the meat of his upper left arm. He bellowed in pain, but lashed out hard with his right fist and caught the madman in the side of his head and sent him sprawling.

Dark blood drained from Quinn's wound and covered his lower arm, which hung useless by his side, but he moved in a boxer's shuffle straight for Gibbons, who had risen to his hands and feet and was shaking his head hard, trying to regain some clarity.

Quinn's head wound looked severe enough to send a lesser man to his grave, but he seemed not to notice. His hatred of Gibbons sustained him. "You'll die tonight, you whore's son, and it'll be for that boy you butchered back in London. He was my son. You think about that on your way to hell!"

The boxer kicked Gibbons' in the side of the chest with a sickening crack. Gibbons screamed and fell to his hands and knees; I knew Quinn had broken some of the man's ribs. He kicked him again. The hunched figure jerked up off the floor and came down on his hands and knees again with a loud groan. Quinn kicked him a third time, even harder it seemed to me. Gibbons screamed in agony and raised his head to look at Quinn. I expected to see pain and fear in his eyes, but there was only hatred and the fearsome, desperate wildness of a vicious animal.

Even as Quinn lunged at Gibbons, the smaller man leaped up at him like an enraged cat and drove the dagger of his cane deep into the top of Quinn's right arm. Quinn locked his ruined arms around Gibbons in a deadly embrace and butted him with his head. Gibbons retaliated by sinking his teeth into Quinn's ear. The big man shook his head violently as if to throw off his attacker, but the effort twisted him off balance. The two men staggered as one, teetered and fell backward onto the rickety table and the burning oil lamp that rested upon it. The table crumbled, and Quinn and Gibbons fell to the floor atop the lamp. I knew with a sickening sense exactly what was about to happen, but there was nothing I could do to stop it. The glass broke with the force of the men's fall.

The reservoir of oil spilled onto the back of Quinn's coat, and he was set ablaze.

I awake from a sound sleep sometimes, even now, years later, with that horrible scene playing itself out all over again in my mind as vividly as though it were happening for the first time. I can hear Gibbons' terrible screams as the flames licked at his face from around Quinn's head and set his own shirt and hair afire. I can see him trying desperately to extinguish the torment by slapping at it with his hands, all the while locked in Quinn's arms. I can see Holmes tearing off his own coat, trying to throw it over the two men. And through it all, Quinn did not utter a sound. I watched in horror as the flames swept around the two men, and Quinn actually seemed to be smiling, but it was a garish death's head grin, for the skin had begun to melt from his face. Gibbons' screams were pitiful and ever more shrill. Quinn staggered through the door of the cottage with the wretch still captured in his gruesome embrace.

Outside, the cold wind whipped the fire all around them. I will never know for sure which of the two men died first, but I believe and hope that it was poor Quinn. Gibbons' screams grew louder, and he died an even more agonizing death enveloped in that bright orange shroud, locked forever in his enemy's arms. Then there was only the wind and the charred, smoldering remains of the two men.

We stared in silence. Holmes threw his oilskin over the bodies and turned to me.

"We have to find the woman, Watson. Is your wound all right?"

I nodded, and we mounted our horses and set off again at a good pace. We rode south toward the cliffs, where Mary McCormick Gibbons had gone.

The night clouds seemed thinner now, and they skittered rapidly before the moon, affording us a broken, eerie light. As we approached the Cliffs of Moher, I looked out across the ocean and could see a rider on a horse silhouetted against the dim sky.

I pointed to it, but the gesture was not necessary; Holmes had seen the rider, too. We urged the horses faster and rode directly toward the figure. We rode to within one hundred feet, when a gunshot kicked up a divot of turf in front of us.

"Stop there," the rider said.

We recognized the voice at once: Mary McCormick Gibbons.

"He's dead, isn't he? My son? Albert is dead?"

Holmes answered. "Yes. We tried . . ."

"And my brother Michael?"

"Dead, too."

There was silence.

"Jamey is alive and well," I shouted.

The woman said nothing, then burst out in anger, "You think you've won, then?"

"We're taking you back," Holmes shouted. "Enough blood has been shed. You will stand trial."

"You fools! I'll not go before any judge. Not ever. And I'll not swing from a British gallows. I die here, where I belong. My home. All I ever wanted. My home."

She was silent again. She looked out over the cliffs and turned back toward us.

"I'm sorry about the boy. The boy in the stable. Albert was . . . sick. Once it started, there was no . . ."

She turned her horse toward the Cliffs of Moher, screamed a piercing cry, slapped the animal on the rump and rode fast toward the sea. The terrified horse tried to stop, but could not. It stumbled and twisted and fell over the edge of the cliff, and even through the howl of the wind we could hear the horse screaming as it plunged to its death with Mary McCormick Gibbons.

Holmes shook himself as if to awaken from a horrific nightmare, and he pointed northward. We turned our horses and set off.

Chapter 36

I wasn't sure why we were riding back to the cottage, but I knew Holmes had to have something in mind. With the exception of a broad scorch mark on the broken table, there was no sign of the fire that had consumed Patrick Day Quinn and Albert Gibbons. Nor, for that matter, was there any sign of the two men. Their remains were gone, as was the oilskin that Holmes had thrown over them.

"Holmes, someone else has been here."

"Obviously, Watson. From these wagon marks, I would guess it was William O'Reilly."

The detective stood to one side of the open door and surveyed the room.

"What are you looking for?" I asked.

"Money," Holmes said.

"Really?"

"Yes. I cannot believe that Gibbons and her son turned everything over to the Irish Republican Brotherhood," Holmes said. "It does not fit with what we know of them. At the very least the two of them would have needed money for travel. And I suspect Mary McCormick Gibbons also would have held back a substantial sum just for the sake of security.

"Consider the poverty she knew as a child, and then the fact that she spent many years in what amounted to an indenture to her husband. I think anyone whose experience fits such a description would have a warped sense of money's importance. When she finally got her hands on a lot of it, some of it must have stuck."

Holmes was right, of course. In a large tin under a loose board in the old worn floor of the cottage, he found a cache that we quickly estimated to total £10,000.

"This should be more than enough to afford us all safe passage home and then provide for Jamey Gibbons' care," Holmes said.

We closed the cottage door behind us, and quickly rode up to O'Brien's Tower.

Outside, we recognized William O'Reilly's light wagon. He and his son Gavin were seated beside Mrs. Masterson on a bench against a far wall.

She looked up at us and smiled, but it was O'Reilly who spoke. "Well," he said, "you two are looking pretty worn. Mrs. Masterson and I have been catching up on old times, you might say."

Holmes smiled. "It's good to see you again," he said. "We are indebted to you for your timely help, and for seeing to Abigail."

O'Reilly nodded in acknowledgment.

"We got to wondering what became of you, and I got to thinking that even Michael McCormick shouldn't be allowed to stand in the way when it's members of the O'Reilly family that are tryin' to look out for each other."

Holmes nodded. "Speaking of McCormick," Holmes said, looking about him, "his body seems to have been moved, and that of Quinn, too."

"'And what bodies would those be, Mr. Holmes?" O'Reilly asked, his face a broad intentional blank.

"Why, the bodies that . . . Oh, I see," Holmes said.

"If it's the remains of that patriot Michael McCormick who hails from these parts o' County Clare that yer talkin' about, why he'll be quietly waked tomorrow with his friend, Ian Donovan. The two of 'em had traveled to Lahinch on some unknown personal business, ya see, and they had a raucous falling out.

"They shot each other dead, they did. Terr'ble thing. Terr'ble. Gavin here saw it all."

"Aye," Gavin said. "I've already told me story to the authorities."

"And when did this, uhm, tragedy occur?" Holmes asked.

"Why, just tonight, on the road between Liscannor and Lahinch. Gavin heard the shots and then found 'em with their guns still warm in their hands."

"I see," Holmes said. "I presume Donovan had been alone, standing lookout for McCormick, before the, uh, falling out occurred?"

"That's reasonable," Gavin said with the merest hint of a smile.

"Too bad about Quinn," said William O'Reilly.

"Indeed," Holmes said. "A good man. At least his son is avenged. He did for Donovan, too?"

"Aye," the O'Reillys said as one.

"Well," said the older man, "are you ready to travel, then? Best we not linger in these parts, you know."

Abigail Masterson kissed her cousin on the cheek and whispered a quiet thank you. He patted her on the hand.

"The missus will put you up," O'Reilly said. "By now, she'll have cooked up a fine breakfast for us. You'll sleep for the rest of the day, and when Gavin and me are done at the shop, we'll get you back on the road.

"In a couple of days, we'll have you in Carrickfergus. Best you stay out of Dublin, just in case, you know? You can take a boat from Carrickfergus back to Liverpool easy."

"If ever you need help, Mr. O'Reilly . . ." Holmes said.

"Well, that's right fine to know, Mr. Holmes, and I thank you, I do. Let's be off, then. It must be half four by now. Cock'll be crowin' 'fore you know it, and I'd as soon we were gone by then."

Not surprisingly, O'Reilly was as good as his word. We made our way to Carrickfergus without event, said our good-byes, and thirty-six hours later Holmes, Abigail and I set our feet on the docks in Liverpool. A long train ride to London and then a jaunt in a hansom cab, and we alighted outside 221B Baker Street.

Holmes had been unusually glum for the entire journey. As we approached the door to our rooms, I broke the silence. "I imagine that you are as tired as I am, Holmes," I ventured, "but I would think you'd be in better spirits. This entire mess is over, and solved rather permanently I would say."

"Not quite over, Watson, though I do wish that were the case," he said. "I most sincerely do."

Mrs. Masterson wore a puzzled expression, and I was about to question the detective when I was startled by the sight of Mycroft Holmes taking up most of the settee in our parlor. I was even more startled by the fact that the detective acted as though he had been expecting his brother.

"Good to see that the three of you are well," Mycroft said.

"Your timing is impeccable, Mycroft," Holmes said with what seemed to me to be a sigh of resignation. "You've not been here five minutes."

Expectancy lay in the silence.

"Well," Holmes said, "the pile on Mrs. Hudson's new hall carpet was still somewhat ruffled by the corner of the door, and the red clay on your boots hasn't quite dried yet. I take that as an indication that the repair work is still under way in Portman Square?"

"Quite," Mycroft said with a smile.

"None of which suitably explains how it is that you knew we were back in London, Mycroft."

"You forget that I have my own sources."

"Right," Holmes said. "Tell me, Mycroft, how does William O'Reilly of Ennistymon correspond with you?"

"You always surprise me, Sherlock," Mycroft said. "You really are quite good at this, you know."

Mycroft may have been surprised at this implied ·

revelation, but Mrs. Masterson was stunned, and so was I.

"Do you mean to say that my cousin, William O'Reilly, is an agent of the Crown?" she stammered. "I don't believe it."

"He is, yes," Mycroft said, "and he's turned out to be a very good one, never once slipping in his portrayal."

"For how long has this been the case," Holmes asked his brother.

"Six months, about," Mycroft said. "Shortly after his sister and her two daughters were blown to bits by a bomb planted in Dublin by the Brotherhood."

"The incident you mentioned when you visited on the eve of our departure for Ireland, was it not?"

"Yes," Mycroft said, "that is correct."

"And you are certain that McCormick was responsible?" Holmes asked.

"And his henchman, Ian Donovan," Mycroft said.

"Then, O'Reilly has evened the score," Holmes said, "with our help."

"It is just the way it worked out," Mycroft said, rather unconvincingly I thought. "It was sheer coincidence that by virtue of Mrs. Masterson's bloodlines, you found yourself in Ennistymon looking for her cousin's help."

"Mycroft, if you were not my brother, I would blacken both of your eyes. Damn you!" Holmes exclaimed. "Damn you to hell!"

"Don't be naive, little brother," Mycroft said, "and spare me your histrionics, please. What put you on to O'Reilly?"

"You know that I do not believe in coincidence, Mycroft. When Watson and I returned to the cottage and I saw the imprint of O'Reilly's wagon, my suspicions were aroused.

"When I saw how efficiently he and his son had disposed of the bodies—and added Ian Donovan's to the lot—*and* covered their tracks, figuratively speaking, I pretty much knew the entire story."

Mycroft Holmes nodded pensively. "Very good, Sherlock. Very good, indeed.

"Ah, It's good to have the three of you back safely, and I say that with all sincerity. Well, I still have work to do today, so I'd best leave."

"Not so fast, Mycroft," Holmes said. He struck a wooden match on the heel of his boot and stared balefully at his brother through the plume of white smoke that began rising from his briar pipe.

"Are you going back to the office alone?"

"I had planned to, Sherlock, yes," Mycroft said.

"Shouldn't the lovely Mrs. Abigail O'Reilly Masterson go with you?"

"Sherlock," Abigail said, her lovely face suddenly contorted. "What are you . . ."

"Don't make it worse than it already is, Mrs. Masterson," Holmes said. "I think it's time for the truth, don't you?"

The detective spoke softly, but his voice was thin and strained. "This charade is over. How did Mycroft and his loyal accomplices in Whitehall turn you? How?"

I was dumbstruck. I could not read Mycroft's expression. Abigail hung her head in a long and most uncomfortable silence.

"The fault is not hers," Mycroft said. "I recruited her, Sherlock. Just as I had recruited her brother. At the same time, actually."

"Yes, yes," Holmes interjected. "Enter Peter O'Reilly of Dublin, late agent of the Crown. The connection was not difficult to make. And some part of you wanted me to make it, Mycroft. You even used his name when you told us about Michael McCormick. I suspect some part of you would rather not deal in grays and dark shadows, Mycroft."

Mycroft snapped at his brother. "It was a slip of the tongue, Sherlock. Don't make more of it than it was."

The detective countered quickly. "You do not make 'slips of the tongue,' Mycroft, and well you know it. In your line of work they are a luxury you can ill afford."

"Stop it, both of you," Mrs. Masterson said. "Michael McCormick and his henchmen killed my sister, Katie; she was five years my senior, the same age as my brother Peter, and the same parade bomb also killed Katie in Dublin." Mrs. Masterson burst into tears. "Her . . . her body wasn't even recognizable. If not for her ring, they wouldn't even have known who she was."

"Do you feel better now that you have taken your revenge, Abigail?"

"Oh, don't," Mrs. Masterson said. "Don't stand there and pontificate. Did you feel better after Sidney Gibbons died? You set him up perfectly, and you know it! You might as well have slain the man yourself. At least I didn't set out to kill Michael McCormick. I wanted revenge, for certain, but I underwent training with the pistol in order to better defend myself. I had always entertained hopes that I might find a way to help bring McCormick to justice without bloodshed. I wonder now if I wasn't hopelessly naive in that regard."

"But you were not, were you, Mycroft?" the detective asked.

"Probably not," Mycroft Holmes said. "If this little drama had played itself out on British soil, the outcome might have been different. But under the circumstances, I regret to say that yes, Michael McCormick's death probably was inevitable."

"Or mine," Abigail interjected sharply. "I am left feeling the fool, and callously used, Mr. Mycroft Holmes. And what of your brother and Dr. Watson? Would their deaths also have been 'inevitable,' as you put it?"

Mycroft cast his eyes downward, almost as if he were ashamed. He said nothing for a moment, and when he uneasily returned Mrs. Masterson's gaze, his face was flushed. "I had every confidence that Sherlock and Dr. Watson would prevail," Mycroft said. "Every confidence. They are experienced, most resourceful and very quick-witted, as you well know. I was sorry to learn about Quinn. I mean that."

"But I was more easily manipulated, wasn't I, sir?"

"I will confess that as you seemed to grow more, um, attached to my brother, my job became easier; but I assure you, my good woman, that I never had malicious intent. I never meant to compromise your relationship with my brother."

"But you did not hesitate to use it to your own advantage, did you?" Abigail replied.

"I suppose not," Mycroft said, rather sheepishly. "You have my apologies for that."

But then his countenance brightened. The change was as quick and visible as his darkening under Abigail Masterson's withering scrutiny had been only an instant ago. It was too fast, too like a chameleon.

"So, Sherlock," Mycroft said, "tell me: How long have you suspected Abigail's involvement?"

"For quite some time, actually," the detective said, his voice flat and listless. "It took me longer than it should have to make the connection to the business in Ireland. The British press never reported the names of the Irish who were killed in the parade bombing. So I had to turn to the Irish newspapers. When I spotted the name O'Reilly among the victims, well . . . Here is a beautiful woman who seems taken with me rather suddenly. What other little elements have we? Let me see.

"It happens that she is independent-minded, at least ostensibly, very intelligent, quick-witted and, oh, yes, did I mention that she carries a gun and is an excellent shot but that she somehow managed to be easily kidnapped to her homeland by murderers we have been chasing for weeks. It was all too neat, really.

"I didn't want to believe she was anybody's agent but her own, but when I saw the way she dispatched

Michael McCormick, I had to believe that my instincts were on the mark.

"She had said that she was a good shot. But I know very few men who could have fired a small-caliber bullet into a man's head at some thirty feet without flinching—and with a derringer no less. Under such duress, most men would be hard-pressed to do the job at half the distance with a larger bore.

"She had to have been trained," Holmes said, "and by a marksman. The overwhelming lot of small-arms marksmen in this country are military men. Hence the government's role, which brought me to you, my brother."

"In fact, she was a student of special attaché Charles Webber," Mycroft said. "I recruited Mrs. Masterson, Sherlock, so you should blame me for the charade, as you put it. For the sake of the Crown, of course, I also solicited Dr. Peacham's cooperation. There had to be considerable rapport between you and Abigail, or you might never have followed her when she allowed herself to be kidnapped by the Gibbonses; I knew that once they were back in Ireland, Mary McCormick Gibbons would make contact with her brother, and it seems I was right.

"Well, there we have it," Mycroft said with an air of finality that was altogether too jovial. "I regret my little ploy," he said, "but the truth is out, and after all, this business is over, isn't it. I suggest that we bury our hard feelings and let it go at that. All's well that ends well, eh?"

I could take no more. I took two quick steps toward Mycroft, fully intending to break his jaw if I could, but no sooner had I clenched my right fist than Holmes had braced his cane firmly against my forearm.

"Watson!" the detective shouted.

Mycroft took a white handkerchief from the pocket of his suit coat and mopped his broad forehead.

"I rather expected something like that from my

brother," Mycroft said, "but not from you, Dr. Watson."

"How could you use us like this?" I blustered. "We were almost killed, the three of us. Would that have mattered to you!? How do you justify manipulating people who have always trusted and respected you, and a brother who loves you!? God save the Queen? Is that it? The well-being of the Empire? All for the good of the Crown, what? You sicken me, Mycroft Holmes! You sicken me, you and everyone like you. You act as though all of the world is just a bloody damned chessboard set up for your amusement. We're all your pawns, is that it?"

Mycroft glared at me. "You are naive, Dr. Watson," Mycroft said. "I am not always proud of what I do, but it must be done or we would have anarchy. Can you understand that? Can you appreciate how perilously close to riot and ruin London is on any given day? No, I suspect not. Where would your noble and safe morality be then, Doctor, hmmm?"

"You had best leave," I told him. He dabbed at his forehead again, turned without a further word to any of us and left our quarters.

"Mrs. Masterson," I said, still angry, "how . . ."

Holmes interrupted. "That's enough, Watson. Please."

"Very well," I said.

I looked at the woman and knew Holmes was right; her forlorn countenance only made me sad. I shook my head in frustration and picked up my overcoat, took my hat from the rack against the wall and closed the door behind me.

Chapter 37

When Abigail O'Reilly Masterson was finally alone with Holmes, she fell into the nearest chair and wept inconsolably. He said nothing. He did not go to her side. He offered no words of solace and understanding. When at last she looked at him, he was staring out the window with his back to her, almost as though she were no longer in the room, as though she were no longer even a small part of his life.

He walked to the sideboard, poured two small brandies and handed her one, his gray eyes flat and expressionless.

"You'll feel better," he said.

She tossed the brandy down as though it were water, and then sat quietly for a moment feeling its warmth and regaining her composure.

"You must know, Sherlock, that my feelings for you exist quite apart from all of this. You must know that."

He said nothing for a moment. He sipped his brandy and sat down beside her.

"And what are these feelings, exactly?" he asked.

"I . . . I thought you knew," she said.

"Knew what? Please. I am not trying to be difficult, but you refer to feelings for me, and I ask you simply, and respectfully, what are those feelings?"

"I am . . . very fond of you," she said.

"I am fond of you, too, Abigail. I truly am."

"I would have hoped that we could explore those feelings," she said, "and let whatever happens happen."

"I am not ready to say no to that outright, but you have hurt me, Abigail, however inadvertently. You saved my life twice, but you have hurt me by being deceitful. It was you who said you would never tolerate a lie, and you were lying all of the time."

"No," she said, "not entirely, and not all of the time. My duplicity lay in what I did not say. The point may be moot now, but the fact is, I never told you a lie. Never. I could not. Not about me or my past, and certainly not where any implication of feelings for you were concerned. I never intended to hurt you in any way."

"But you see, Abigail, what you omitted, what you neglected to tell me, had all of the effect of a lie, and while you most assuredly did not try to hurt me, you did not try very hard to *not* hurt me with this duplicity.

"I am not scolding you. Nor am I so delicate a flower as to wilt from abuse. I am hardly perfect myself, and while I have not had many relationships with women, I am well enough traveled to know that a bit of rough going is normal, especially between two people who might be somewhat charitably described as willful.'

"It's just that this entire Marylebone affair has tested me to such a horrible extent that I must relegate all memory of it completely to the past if I am to continue my work. I cannot afford to let it exact a greater toll by continuing to play on my consciousness."

"And I must be relegated to the past with it?" she asked.

"At least for now," he said. "For a while. My work requires all of my faculties at all times, and usually to the absolute exclusion of all else. As you have seen, much depends on that ability sometimes."

"I have lost you?"

"Perhaps you have merely misplaced me," the detective said with a quick smile.

She snuffled and nodded and tried to return the

smile. "I suppose I will have to settle for that. But what of Dr. Watson and Mrs. Hudson?"

"They are good people," Holmes said. "They will understand."

Mrs. Masterson nodded, stood up and stepped close to him. He did not move. He did not smile. He did not blink. She kissed him softly, and he kissed her back, more softly, and then she left without another word.

She closed the door to 221B behind her and walked down the short flight of stairs to the sidewalk. She turned to find me behind her.

"Do not think ill of me, Dr. Watson."

"I could not," I said.

The sound of Holmes' violin floated down to the street. I turned my head up toward our window and listened for a moment. It was a soft and melancholy piece that I did not recognize.

"I say, do you know that . . ."

But when I turned, Abigail O'Reilly Masterson was gone. That was several months ago. I have not seen her since.

Don't miss the next installment in

the unpublished journals of Dr. Watson

Coming from Signet in 2000.